W9-ARI-395

Praise for

ONE PAST
MIDNIGHT

"By developing a rich and nuanced mythology of Sabine's experience, Shirvington invites readers to consider what it means to struggle with the social pressures of being a teenager. . . . The story is fresh and focused. . . . A complex and compelling tale." —*School Library Journal*

"The intriguing paranormal twist keeps pages turning." —*Kirkus Reviews*

"This psychological mystery will hook readers with its compelling protagonist and philosophical questions. . . . Perfect for readers who like to ponder life's deeper questions, and the romance adds a nice spark." —*Booklist*

"This book is a page-turner from the start. Once word gets out about this riveting story, the book will seldom be on the library shelf." —*VOYA*

"Will engage young adult readers who enjoy romance, teen angst, and the unexplainable and mysterious." —*LMC*

ONE PAST MIDNIGHT

JESSICA SHIRVINGTON

BLOOMSBURY
NEW YORK   LONDON   OXFORD   NEW DELHI   SYDNEY

Copyright © 2013 by Jessica Shirvington
All rights reserved. No part of this book may be reproduced or transmitted in any form
or by any means, electronic or mechanical, including photocopying, recording, or by any
information storage and retrieval system, without permission in writing from the publisher.

First published in Australia in 2013 by HarperCollins*Publishers* Australia Pty Limited
Published in the United States of America in July 2014
by Bloomsbury Children's Books
Paperback edition published in August 2015
www.bloomsbury.com

Bloomsbury is a registered trademark of Bloomsbury Publishing Plc

For information about permission to reproduce selections from this book, write to
Permissions, Bloomsbury Children's Books, 1385 Broadway, New York, New York 10018
Bloomsbury books may be purchased for business or promotional use. For information on bulk
purchases please contact Macmillan Corporate and Premium Sales Department at
specialmarkets@macmillan.com

The Library of Congress has cataloged the hardcover edition as follows:
Shirvington, Jessica.
One past midnight / Jessica Shirvington.
pages   cm
Summary: Each night, eighteen-year-old Sabine transitions between a life of privilege
and security but no intimacy to one of economic struggle but loving relationships, and the
difficulty of this strange situation causes her to consider suicide, at least in one physical reality.
ISBN 978-0-8027-3702-1 (hardcover) • ISBN 978-0-8027-3703-8 (e-book)
[1. Supernatural—Fiction. 2. Identity—Fiction. 3. Love—Fiction.
4. Family life—Fiction. 5. Science fiction.] I. Title.
PZ7.S55845One 2014   [Fic]—dc23   2013046828

ISBN 978-0-8027-3707-6 (paperback)

Printed and bound in the U.S.A. by Thomson-Shore Inc., Dexter, Michigan
2 4 6 8 10 9 7 5 3 1

All papers used by Bloomsbury Publishing, Inc., are natural, recyclable products
made from wood grown in well-managed forests. The manufacturing processes
conform to the environmental regulations of the country of origin.

12/19

For Haz:
I am so lucky to have such
an incredible friend

PREFACE

I am a liar.

Not compulsive.

Simply required.

I am two people. Neither better than the other, no superpowers, no mystical destinies, no two-places-at-one-time mechanism—but two people. My physical attributes, my memory, and my name follow me. For the past eighteen years, everything else, *everything*, about me is different. Twenty-four hours as the first version of me. And in the blink of an eye, twenty-four hours as the second. Every day, without fail, it goes on . . .

I've never told anyone. By the time I was old enough to figure out no one else had two lives—by the time *that* little shock settled in—I didn't know where to begin. *How* to begin. And society, both of them, didn't want to know.

When I was a child, I didn't realize I was different from

1

everyone else. But I'm pretty sure I've always been this way—this two-lives way—which means I was probably born twice, was a baby twice. No surprise I'm glad I can't remember that. Being torn from one set of arms and thrust into another every twenty-four hours? Well, it doesn't matter how much they love you . . . Can anyone say, issues?

Practice makes perfect though, and I like to think of myself as a pro. I've ironed out the kinks; identified the major pitfalls and how to avoid them. I manage. I know who I need to be in each of my lives, and I try not to confuse my brain with the "infinity questions" anymore.

I've learned to accept that in one life I love strawberries, while in the other my taste buds cringe at the flavor. I know that in one life I can speak fluent French, but, even though the memory of the language comes with me, in my other life I must not. Then there are easier things to remember, like Maddie, my gorgeous little sister in one life, and my not-so-great big brothers in my other.

Above all else—though I try not to think about it—I know which life I prefer. And every night when I Cinderella myself from one life to the next, a very small but definite piece of me dies. The hardest part is that nothing about my situation has ever changed—the only thing I can be certain of is that my body clock is different from everyone else's. There is no loophole.

Until now, that is.

CHAPTER ONE

Roxbury, Friday

I broke my wrist today.

Capri and I were heading for the subway. I had a soda can at my feet, soccering it along the pavement, flashing sweet and mostly sour smiles to the suits who gave us "hooligan" looks as we passed. We attracted that kind of attention. Funny how clothes and generous use of eyeliner can do that. In my other life, no one would dare give me that kind of look. But there was something satisfying about it. My faded black mini and lace-up Doc Martens helped give me what I needed.

My identity.

Capri skipped ahead, her black hair bobbing, halfway between dreads and undecided. "I bet the guys are already there," she said over her shoulder, speeding up.

I suppressed a groan, hoisted the soda can onto the tip of my toe, kicked it into my hand, and picked up the pace. At the top of the stairs I paused to toss the can in the trash, and then . . . un-paused. I don't know if it would've happened anyway. But right at that moment, one foot in the air about to step down onto the first of fifty-odd steps, I saw him.

Well, I think I saw him.

A round-bellied, middle-aged man. Dressed in a dated taupe suit and scuffed red-brown shoes. He was thinning badly up top and sweating either because of excess fabric or body weight. He looked different than usual, but in that moment I was certain. *Fruit-stand guy*, my mind whispered.

It was a glitch.

They happened every now and then, and they always threw me.

My foot never found sure landing. Instead, it missed the step and caught the edge. I fell forward, propelled toward the bottom, making a fool of myself the entire way. Legs over ass, I flashed a good few dozen people on the way down, showing them pretty much all I had to offer.

Capri, great friend that she is, was laughing before I even came to a stop. And not just a private little chuckle behind her hand before she could pull herself together. No, she all but wet herself, sliding down beside me as I tried to cradle my wrist and an arm that felt like it could, at any second, fall off my shoulder.

Eventually, and mostly because of commuters grunting about having to go around us, I pulled myself to my feet.

Capri was still laughing, pausing every now and then before obviously replaying the moment in her mind and cracking up yet again.

Jesus. I wished I was in my other life at that moment. This was not the type of thing to let happen in this one.

"I think I'll need to go to the medical center," I told Capri, who was only just beginning to realize I'd genuinely hurt myself.

"Oh, shit. Sorry, Sabine. I thought you were okay."

I shrugged, instantly regretting it when a searing pain shot up my arm. "Probably just a sprain."

Luckily the medical center wasn't far and we could walk. The idea of being crammed into a train with a funky arm didn't work for me at all. Capri sent Angus, her sort-of boyfriend, a text to let him know we wouldn't be meeting up at our usual after-school caffeine haunt. If it weren't for the throbbing pain in my arm, I'd almost have been relieved. Capri and Angus had been trying to set me up with Davis for the past month. Nice guy, no spark.

"It *was* pretty funny, though," Capri said as we walked, still slipping into bouts of memory giggles. She could be a bitch sometimes, but ever since we were thrown together in junior high by our similar "freak" labels—thanks to Capri's in-your-face individuality and my attempts at the time to simply ignore one of my two lives and everything in it—that particular trait had mostly worked in my favor. And she was the only friend in this life I'd managed to keep hold of, mostly because she didn't care that I seemed . . . well, to put it in her words, *like I was somewhere else half the time.*

I flashed her a smile. "Lucky I was wearing hot underwear!"

Which I hadn't been, of course. And thanks to my ass-in-the-sky display, she and more than a handful of Boston commuters knew it.

Capri laughed so hard she snorted. "Yeah. Floral print is making a comeback."

And then my arm hurt, because I was laughing too. Even while dreading that some bastard with an iPhone might have already uploaded footage of my floral booty to YouTube.

Broken.

At least it was only my wrist. But I'd be plastered up like a disaster zone for the next six weeks. Capri had already drawn some weird, screwed-up bat image on it. She was currently into Goth. On top of the half dreadlocks, she'd dyed her beautiful blond hair black and persisted with floor-length skirts even on the hottest days.

I was happy sticking with my streetwise look. I wasn't as fanatical about it as Capri; I just made sure I perfected the don't-mess-with-me part. It was important, especially around

Roxbury—which was still categorized as one of Boston's "due for gentrification" areas. And although Mom and Dad would have preferred an extra five inches on my skirts, my look didn't send them into complete freak-out mode.

By the time I got home it was after 9:00 p.m. As soon as I opened the front door, I could hear Maddie bounding from her room toward the stairs. The door was barely closed behind me when she came barreling down the steps three at a time.

"Binie! Binie!" She was just about to launch herself from the bottom step into my arms—one of her signature moves—when she saw the sling covering my arm.

"What happened?" she asked, coming to an abrupt halt.

To Maddie, I was invincible. Probably because half the time when I was sick I pretended not to be, always worried about unintentionally overdosing if I took medication in both worlds. It wasn't easy when I had tonsillitis, but I couldn't very well have *that* operation twice. And I'd certainly never broken anything before. "It's okay, Mads. I just broke my wrist when I fell over."

She looked worried, the corners of her mouth trembling. Having a six-year-old kid who worships me look so grave caused me the worst pain of the day.

I smiled one of my goofy numbers for her. "Hey, kiddo, check it out!" I pulled my arm out of the sling, revealing the cast and Capri's bat drawing. I twisted my arm to show her an untouched expanse of white. "I saved this whole area for you. You think you can draw something on it tomorrow for me?"

Her eyes lit up. She took hold of her long strawberry-blond braid hanging over her shoulder and swayed. "Really? Me? You wouldn't mind?"

"Hey, you're the best rabbit drawer I know. You think you can draw one of those bouncy ones you showed me the other day?"

She nodded vigorously. I could already see her picturing it in her head.

"Cool. I'll make sure no one else draws on this section and tomorrow afternoon it's all yours. But you better go back to bed before Mom catches you!" Of course I could already see Mom out of the corner of my eye in the kitchen doorway, but experience had taught us all that it was easier if I got Maddie to sneak back to bed by herself. I gave the top of her head a ruffle and she flung her arms around my waist, carefully avoiding my bad side.

"Love you, Binie." Her squeeze tore at my insides. Getting through days without her was one of the hardest things. I squeezed back.

"See you in the morning," I said lightly.

They were the same words I'd said to her so many times. And every time I finished the sentence in the silence of my mind: *the day after tomorrow.*

• • •

Mom had her back to me when I came into the kitchen. "Tea?"

"Yeah," I said with a sigh, slumping into one of the tarnished wooden chairs at our chipped kitchen table. Our less-than-perfect kitchen fitted in well with our coming-apart-at-the-seams house.

Mom filled up the kettle using a massive plastic gallon bottle. It was the same one we'd been using in the kitchen for the past two weeks. The problem wasn't that the pipe was clogged; the problem was that, after one too many drinks, Dad had tried to fix it. Big mistake.

Mom searched through the mugs, pulling out her favorite rose one followed by my preferred Daffy Duck mug.

"What happened?" she asked, barely taking her attention away from her task. Even at this time of night, it wasn't a surprise to see her still dressed in her work clothes, her graying hair pulled back in a tight knot, her heavily starched shirt tucked in at her slender waist. Mom and Dad were all about appearances. Mom, in particular, needed her family functional and firing on all cylinders.

"Subway stairs," I answered.

With her shoulders set, she finished making the tea and sat across the table from me. "You should've called."

I adjusted my sling, glad that I would only have to wear it for a few days—the cast wrapped around my thumb and covering half my forearm was bad enough. "You would've just wanted to come and help." *And take over*, I thought. "There was no point dragging Maddie out of bed just to sit in the stupid waiting room at the medical center. Anyway, Capri was with me."

Mom pursed her lips as she passed me my mug. "Such a comfort. Don't suppose she's discovered the many uses of a hairbrush yet?"

I shrugged and blew on my tea. "She has a look going, Mom. She's happy with it, so what's the problem?"

Mom stared at me as if the answer to that question was oh-so-obvious. She'd prefer I hung with a different crowd. Sometimes I wished I could tell her that I did. I stared into my mug as once again I considered that, given the choice, Mom would probably want my other life for me rather than this one. But that kind of thinking was never worthwhile.

"Dad still at work?" I asked.

Mom nodded.

Dad worked long hours. He kept the drugstore open late Tuesday through Saturday, which meant he was rarely home before midnight. The drugstore would be a good business if they actually owned it, but instead they'd signed into a lengthy—and unprofitable—management contract. Even with extra staff, Mom and Dad split a heavy workload. They saw little of us and even less of one another. But they were relentless, determined to send Maddie and me to a good college.

At least that was one thing I could do for them. Going through school twice does help in the smarts department. Last year I'd pulled out the brain gene in Roxbury—much to Capri's disgust—and even cashed in last month with a partial undergrad scholarship to Boston University.

The thing is, I'm not even excited by the whole college thing. School twice is bad enough: *college* twice will suck—and God knows I won't be able to avoid it in my other life, so I'd been hoping to skip it in this one. But when it came down to it, I just couldn't do it to Mom and Dad. Or face the wrath that would follow.

Pleasing everyone in my two lives has left me feeling raw at times. And frustrated. And exhausted. And . . . well, a lot of things I tried hard not to admit. There was no point.

"If you're hungry, there's leftover cake in the fridge."

I shook my head. For the past week, we'd been working our way through the gigantic chocolate cake Mom had made/massacred for my eighteenth birthday.

"I grabbed something earlier," I mumbled, looking away.

"I could've called Dr. Meadows," she said, still hurt I hadn't contacted her.

"Mom, don't worry. Everything's okay now." I flashed her my arm and an I'm-just-fine smile. "Wrist broken, forearm in a cast. There's nothing else anyone could do. In a few weeks it will all be back to normal."

And that's when it dawned on me.

"Shit!" I barked, catching a mouthful of tea in my good hand. I'd been so thrown by the glitch, by seeing fruit-stand guy, I hadn't even considered the real problem.

"Sabine!" Mom snapped.

That was one thing my moms had in common: the no-swearing rule. But right then I didn't care. Mom was lucky I hadn't let the F-word fly.

"Sorry, Mom. I just . . . I remembered my final history essay is due on Monday and I haven't finished it." I straightened my back to strengthen the lie. The days of feeling guilty about lying to my parents were long gone.

Mom looked at me skeptically. "Since when do you do homework on a Friday night?" She gestured to my arm. "And I'm sure your teacher will cut you some slack."

"No, it's fine. I'm almost done." I wiped my tea-wet hand on a dishcloth and grabbed my mug. "I'll go finish it now so I won't have to worry about it all weekend."

I wove through the kitchen and up the stairs, my mind scrambling to figure out exactly how I was going to handle this one.

Broken wrist.

Two lives.

This had never happened before.

It was close to 10:00 p.m.

Shit.

Only two hours to figure out a plan.

I wouldn't be sleeping tonight. In either life.

I hated problems that flowed over—it meant I wouldn't be able to sleep before the Shift. I could already feel my palms getting clammy. It always scared me, being awake at midnight.

I tiptoed past Maddie's room. Right then, I couldn't cope with her; I didn't have a brave face at the ready.

After loading up the pillows on my bed, I sat down, resting my arm on top of the pile.

"I am the master of my own world," I chanted to myself. "I manage what happens to me. I can do this." But my words were false and quickly fell away as the truth slammed into me and held on with an iron grip.

I've broken my wrist.

I. HAVE. BROKEN. MY. WRIST.

"Idiot!" My stomach tightened with fear and I tried unsuccessfully to slow my breathing.

Usually I have a built-in radar for this type of stuff. The cans and can'ts. How it all works. It's pretty simple really. My body, and anything inherent to my body—my mind, my memories—goes through the Shift. But that's it. Material things—clothes, jewelry, even nail polish—get left behind. The only other thing that stays with me is my name. For reasons I can't explain, both sets of parents called me Sabine.

Bottom line, if I cut my hair in one life, it will be changed in the other. I dyed a hidden section of hair pink once, and although the dye didn't travel, the pigment of my hair was affected enough to look different in my other life—I've never dared to experiment further. If I'm sick in one life, then I'm sick in both. If I get a tattoo in one world—not that I plan to, much to Capri's disappointment—I'm almost certain it would only be visible in that life. Ink won't travel, though the healing pains would be felt in both. If I had my nose pierced, the hole would exist in both lives, but the ring would stay in only one.

I pressed my fingers to my temples. I hated thinking about this stuff. Most of it was just weird and made me feel . . . wrong. Like *I'm* wrong. To avoid mistakes, I was careful *all* the time—trimming my hair only when I needed to, keeping it long and its natural boring brown, never giving it the kind of style either of my worlds would really approve of. Hovering somewhere in between. Safe. That's where I stayed, all the time. Safe. Prepared. Alone.

I have two lives and yet I'm a ghost.

In less than two hours I'd be in my other life and I'd have three *very* big problems. One, I'm not supposed to have a broken wrist there and have no reason to have broken it. Two, the cast won't come with me; it's a material object. And three, it's my belated eighteenth birthday party tomorrow night, and a broken wrist will not go with my dress. At. All.

I lay back, stared at the paint peeling off the ceiling, and tried to figure out a solution. The only one that made any sense was going to hurt. A lot. But throwing myself down the stairs when I woke up was the only way I could be sure to convincingly fake the same injury.

About half an hour before the Shift I changed out of my clothes, shimmying my fitted mini off with one hand and wriggling into my oversized T-shirt nightie. I ditched the sling; it was more hindrance than help. I left my black Doc Martens for last, wincing as I gave a one-handed pull to loosen the laces before using my feet to kick them off.

I relied on rituals. Found comfort in the patterns I'd developed over the years. I settled into bed, ignoring the sheen of sweat on my forehead and the sick feeling in my gut as I arranged myself against the pillows as usual, making sure there would be nothing out of the ordinary to return to tomorrow night.

I almost made it too.

But with only minutes to go, my mouth started its telltale watering. I had to bolt to the bathroom to throw up before hurrying back to bed before midnight struck.

The last thoughts that slipped into my mind marked the beginning of the change in my worlds. *How could this have happened? How has nothing like this happened to me before?*

CHAPTER TWO

Wellesley, Friday

I knew the Shift had happened.

I'd been asleep in this life, so it took me a while to rouse my body, despite my live-wire mind. It's an awful, drugged feeling, willing your eyes to open.

The second lucidity took hold, I sat bolt upright in bed and felt the panic flood my chest. I should have known better. Eighteen years of going through the Shift, I shouldn't have been so frightened . . . but I was. Every. Single. Time. It petrified me.

I concentrated on taking slow, deep breaths. My good hand slid out over warm silk sheets that exposed no signs I'd been somewhere else for the past twenty-four hours. Nothing about this world was aware I'd been cheating on it, living another life. Without looking, I knew it was the exact same time it had been when I left.

My eternal enemy . . . midnight.

I'd done all sorts of things to prove it, to document the truth. When I was fifteen, I filmed myself through the midnight minutes. Not so much as a *Blair Witch* moment. One second I was there, the next I had a confused look on my face. *I* could tell something about me was different in that blink of an eye, but there was nothing that would prove it to anyone else.

Then there was the time I lit a match a couple of seconds before midnight to see what would happen. That was not a good idea. My bed—with me in it—almost went up in smoke. I just wasn't quick enough to pull myself together after the Shift and blow it out before it touched my fingers. *Hey, you live and learn.*

I slipped out of bed and made my way to the bathroom to wash my face. But with still-sleepy legs my judgment was off and klutz mode set in. I staggered into the door frame, my bad arm taking the brunt of the impact.

I froze, dreading the shooting pain that would follow. But after a few stunned seconds I was still waiting for the agony to set in.

"No way," I gasped, slowly letting my not-so-broken— actually not-hurt-at-all—arm straighten and move about. I fisted my fingers over and over.

"No. Way."

• • •

I wanted to spiral.

I wanted to press all internal panic buttons and scream for help.

I wanted to understand for once.

No, that wasn't it. What I wanted . . . it was the same thing I'd always wanted, just in different packaging.

I wanted this not to be my life.

I wanted *this*—whatever it was that made me this two-lives person—not to be the definition of who I am.

I squeezed my eyes shut. "And you can't do anything about that," I scolded myself, letting out a resigned breath.

I stumbled into my squash-court-sized bathroom, where I threw up again, then went straight back to bed and tried in vain to get a few hours' sleep.

It was useless.

Thoughts raced through my mind. I had to force myself not to jump up and start pacing. This changed nothing, I reminded myself. *This* was just one more thing that fitted into the overflowing basket of weird that was my life.

I focused on the upside; for once I had been given a get-out-of-jail-free card. It was a welcome relief that I wasn't going to have to throw myself down the stairs in a few hours.

Take it! Be happy. At least the dress will look pretty tonight.

At 7:00 a.m., I gave up on sleep and had a long hot shower. By the time I emerged, I felt more like myself again. Well, *this* me anyway—the one I needed to be in this world. But just to be sure, I moved slowly. Allowed myself a little extra time. Normally I wouldn't stand for it—*pathetic lingering*—but today I took in my surroundings. My huge four-poster bed, with its pink silk bedding and pillows piled high. I walked past it, my toes sinking into the plush cream carpet, letting my hand glide over the heavily lacquered walnut frame on my way to the large French doors. I pulled back the cream curtains, carefully tying them with the sash bow at the wall, and opened the doors to my small Georgian balcony.

Home. Everything just as it should be.

I took a deep breath, letting in the suburban Wellesley air. It was one of the best things about this place, the clean air. It was different in every way from Roxbury—thinner, sharper, and the smell: newly cut grass under the sun. I loved the smell. Today would be a typical June Massachusetts day—hot, and probably a thunderstorm in the afternoon.

I'd just closed my eyes to soak it in, when a high-pitched car horn made me almost jump out of my skin.

I looked down to the driveway. My oldest brother, Ryan, was standing by his retro convertible Porsche, one foot in, one foot out.

"If you want a lift, hurry up. I've got to get back to school," he said, looking up at me like he wished he could just get in the car and go. But at Thursday night dinner with Ryan and my other brother, Lucas, Dad had ordered Ryan to drive me to school this morning, since my little Audi was at the garage getting new tires. As far as Ryan was concerned, he paid his family dues by turning up at the house a few days a month. That, and that alone, apparently entitled him to the more-than-generous allowance he pissed away at Harvard while half-assing his way through business school.

"Hello! Earth to Sabine! You're not even dressed," he said, exasperated.

I gave him a delicate middle finger and a blatantly fake smile. "Guess you'll just have to wait, Ry. I'll be down as fast as I can manage." As soon as I spun my back to him, my smile faded. I was being a bitch. I'm not sure exactly when it was that Ryan and I slipped into this type of role-play, but at some point it had become the norm. All part of living up to Wellesley expectations.

I got dressed and did my hair. When I was finished I surveyed myself in the full-length mirror approvingly. Simple yet chic. A high-waisted plaid skirt in shades of blue, finishing just above the knee, paired with a cap-sleeved white silk top and gray wedges. After a quick brush and a touch of lip gloss, I grabbed my Balenciaga bag and headed down the marble stairs to the foyer where my mother was waiting.

She watched me take the last few steps, and then waited while I finished reading a text from Miriam that had me smirking. When I gave her my full attention, she smiled. "Make sure you remind your friends that there will be no drinking tonight at the party." She was in a cream suit and caramel flats, every detail purposely chosen: the natural, flattering makeup, the hair in a casual updo, and the delicate showering of accessories.

"Yes, Mom. Everyone knows how you feel about underage drinking." *Which is why everyone who is drinking will be hanging out at the pool house just in case someone comes snooping.*

She smiled and took a step forward, eyeing my outfit. "That's a pretty skirt, darling. Plaid really has made a comeback this season." She brushed away nonexistent lint from my shoulder and looked me up and down again thoughtfully.

"But . . . ?"

"Oh, nothing, darling. It's very sweet. You know me, I just love you in green—it brings out your eyes."

"Mom, I'm wearing green tonight. I don't want to overdo it." I smiled to reassure her and didn't take it to heart. Mom was the most insecure person I knew. It wasn't just me; she was toughest on herself. I was sure she changed at least a dozen times each morning before she settled on an outfit, and she was rarely in the same one by the time I arrived home from school. She's always been like that, but it's been even worse since Dad left.

She nodded, looking contrite. "You're right. You look beautiful. Like always. I'll see you tonight. Everything will be ready and perfect."

I fiddled with my bag strap. "Ah . . . Mom, you know how we discussed . . ."

She looked at me for a moment, not getting it, but then she blinked, catching on. "Oh, darling. I know, I know . . . you're eighteen now and I promised I'd give you some privacy. I'll be going out with your aunt Lyndal. She's sworn to keep me away from the house. I just want to be here to see you in your dress and make sure everything is—"

"Perfect," I finished for her.

"Yes."

I reached over and gave her a kiss on the cheek. "See you after school. I better get going."

Mom watched me walk out the door. I closed it behind me so she wouldn't see the next scene unfold. Just as I walked down the steps and Ryan sneered at me for having been made to wait so long, a white SUV came screaming up the gravel drive. Miriam, my best friend in this world, was behind the wheel. Perfect timing.

Ryan watched the SUV until it pulled to a halt and then looked back at me, eyes narrowed.

I smiled the special smile I reserved for him. "Oh." I batted my eyelashes. "Sorry, Ry, did I forget to tell you that Miriam was giving me a lift to school?"

He returned the finger I'd delivered to him earlier and took off in his car, leaving a spray of gravel in his wake.

For a moment I felt bad. But then I reminded myself—this

is me. This is who I am here. I'd tried other ways, but I'd soon learned that if I wanted to function in each of my worlds, then I had to really embrace them and accept my place. The Sabine in this world had to deal with a twenty-two-year-old jerk of a brother called Ryan—a guy who, when I was eleven, once locked me in the garage for five hours while he had a bunch of friends over—and *that* was the only way to do it.

I slid into the passenger seat beside Miriam.

"Your brother is hot," Miriam said, her eyes fixed on the dust storm Ryan's car had left behind.

"Yeah, well you see hot, I see pain in my ass. He's just—" A frustrated noise escaped my lips. "He's so *selfish*. He never helps Mom out, never . . . anything. All he has to do is turn up at the house for a few days each month. Get this, he can't stand to be without his drinking buddies for more than a day, so next month he's bringing one of them with him."

"Ooh, is he cute?" Miriam asked, her face lighting up at the thought of more potential eye candy.

I shrugged. "Don't know, don't care. All I know is that next month I'll have to deal with two of them."

As we drove through the village center, my mind suddenly flashed back to yesterday—well, my version of yesterday. "Hey, can you stop? I . . . I want to grab some fruit."

Miriam didn't slow down. "You can get fruit at school."

Already my subconscious was niggling uncomfortably, but before I'd thought it through, my mouth was open again.

"Yeah, but I want *this* fruit. Just stop. There. Just outside the fruit stand."

Miriam looked at me like I was crazy. I gave myself a mental check and yep . . . it *was* crazy. This was exactly the type of thing I worked obsessively every day to avoid, and here I was slipping right into the kind of behavior that earned me crazy stares.

Shit.

I was about to tell Miriam to forget it when she swerved into a parking spot in front of the stand.

"If you're going on a fruit diet, there's no *way* you're doing it without me."

"Oh." I opened my mouth to explain that wasn't what I was doing and then realized I'd been thrown a safety net. I stopped fidgeting and raised an eyebrow. "Party season *is* upon us, Miriam," I said, with a tone that told her she should have already been prepared.

She nodded solemnly. "I'll have whatever you're having."

I took my chance and jumped out of her SUV.

Inside the stand, everything was demoralizingly normal. No sign that anything was any different from how it had always been. Then, through the multicolored plastic strips hanging from the internal doorway, came fruit-stand guy. Chubby, balding, wearing oversize jeans, and flashing an unwelcome glimpse of his butt crack when he bent over a stack of apples. The same guy who'd owned the stand for as long as I could remember.

"Can I get you something, missy?" he asked, casting me a quick glance before returning to his apple pyramid.

"Oh, um, yeah. Just, um, just some apples and strawberries, please."

He grabbed a paper bag. "How many of each?"

I felt sick. "Two apples and two pints of strawberries. Thanks."

He had them bagged within a few seconds and was at the register.

As I paid him, I cleared my throat. "I'm . . . I think I saw you yesterday. Coming out of the subway . . . in Boston."

He glanced at me briefly. A crazy stare. "Not me, missy."

"Um, oh, well, it looked like you and I was just wondering if you saw me too. You were, um, you were in a light-brown suit coming up the stairs. You, um, you walked right by me."

Fruit-stand guy passed me the bag and gave me another crazy stare on the house. "Not me. I don't even own a suit and I haven't been in the city for, oh . . ." He thought about it. "At least a month since my last visit. Must've been someone else."

I nodded vigorously. "Yeah, yeah. I was probably . . . It was getting dark and I couldn't see clearly."

"Young girl like you shouldn't be in the city late like that. You should be careful."

I nodded again, backing away from the stand.

Shit.

I never should've gone there.

"Yeah." I held up the brown bag. "Thanks, I better get to school."

My heart pounded in my ears; the dry bitter taste in my mouth was the familiar flavor of disappointment.

Whomever I'd seen, whether it had been him or not, he had no idea. He wasn't like me.

No one was.

CHAPTER THREE

Wellesley, Friday

One more week and freedom is ours!" Miriam proclaimed as we walked down the hall. We'd been counting down for the past twelve weeks. For me, it had been twice as long, so there were smiles all around.

"I, for one, intend to make the most of the break," I said with a sly bite of my lip.

"You and Dex?" Miriam asked, raising a well-manicured eyebrow. Miriam had long blond hair, which she'd worked into a stylishly messy updo. She had a thing for clips and today she was sporting at least a dozen embedded in her hair, all varying pastel shades. Combined with her pale complexion, ice-blue eyes, and today's outfit of a soft-pink pencil skirt and a cream off-the-shoulder T-shirt, she looked like a fashion goddess.

I shrugged. Miriam had already traveled the "first-time" road with her boyfriend, Brett, and I'd been trying to pull her out of the backseat of his BMW at every party since.

"I think he's waited long enough. It would be an appropriate graduation marker," I bluffed, holding my smirk and not letting my dry mouth give me away. It's not that Dex wasn't perfect on paper. And it's not as if perfect on paper wasn't exactly what I wanted in this life. It worked for me, made it easier to be who I was. It was just . . . when he kissed me I could feel . . . everything. And not in a good way. The shape of his lips, which didn't quite melt into mine the way I'd dreamed about, the rough grating of his stubble against my skin, the way he leaned in so close I couldn't breathe, and held me behind my head so there was no escape. It wasn't that he was a bad kisser technique-wise, it just wasn't the way I'd imagined it would be with someone I really . . . We were just a beat off. And then there was the way his hands . . .

I closed my eyes and shrunk away from the thought. Dex was gorgeous, and we fitted in the ways that mattered. No couple was perfect.

Okay, so Dex wasn't going to rock my world. But I'd been waiting to make this decision for twice as long as every other eighteen-year-old, and had already held off a lot longer than most people with one life. I refused to keep going on as a twice-lived virgin. And if something better were available to me, something earth-rockingly good, *surely* I would've spotted it by now.

In either world.

"So . . . ," Miriam started, her sly tone cutting into my thoughts. "Tonight?"

"No," I said, casually flicking my hair while my mind screamed—*NO!* I was *not* going to be sex ready by tonight. "I'm thinking graduation night. We'll go to the dinner and I'll have everything arranged. It'll be perfect. And besides, tonight is about a different kind of fun. How are preparations?" I asked, redirecting her focus just as the third of our powerhouse trio joined us.

"Morning, ladies," Lucy said, a notebook in hand and cunning smile on display. "Did I hear someone ask how preparations were going for this evening's blowout?"

I smiled back, relaxing for the first time all morning. Lucy always helped with that. She didn't bother with annoying questions. She stuck to the fun.

"You sure did. How are we looking?"

"Done, done, and done. The boys have drink arrangements in hand. I have the music and decorations taken care of. Invites and RSVPs are all confirmed. The juniors who applied have been assessed and selected for serving." She ticked off her list, then squealed. "Tonight is going to be legendary!"

"So how many people?" I asked.

"Oh . . . you know," Lucy said vaguely, looking around the hall.

I stopped mid-step. "Lucy, how many?"

Miriam was standing behind me, but I could feel her cringe.

Lucy bit her lip sheepishly. "Well, most of the senior class, and there might have been a few invites to some of their friends outside of school. You know, I mean, word got out and I didn't want to say no."

I just stared and put my hands on my hips.

"Eighty to a hundred."

I kept staring.

"Okay, a hundred and fifty, max!" she said quickly.

My immediate reaction was to freak out. I'd told Mom no more than fifty people! But then I remembered that both Lucas and Ryan had had parties after graduation. Those bashes weren't even combined with their birthdays, and they were both huge—police at the door—affairs. Mom survived those. So instead of losing it, I regrouped and rolled my eyes. "I hope you've arranged for security."

Lucy nodded, relieved. She tossed back her tight brown curls and smiled brightly, strawberry-glossed lips framing super-white teeth. "Sure have. The boys know they are on duty."

By "the boys" she meant our respective boyfriends. More specifically Miriam's and mine—Lucy was still flying solo and in a permanent lust-crush with Noah.

We weren't with the football guys or the basketball boys.

Our school, thank God, operated on a more even hierarchy. If you could keep up and you looked good in whatever group you were hanging out with, you could stay. It wasn't a perfect system—if you were a geek who couldn't socialize or work a look, then you were a geek and that was it. But it was better than most high schools.

And actually it was people like Dex who'd made it possible.

He was smart, studious, athletic, and hot—in whatever he wore. Everyone wanted to either be him or date him, and he was nice to everyone. A few years back he'd started having parties, inviting the whole class—not only the cool group—and everyone just started being friends. And then . . . he picked me. We'd been together for the last two years and it made total sense. Our social statuses complemented one another seamlessly.

When the three of us walked into English class, I saw Dex right away, sitting in his usual seat right in the middle back. I immediately smiled and took my place beside him.

"Hey, Sabine," he said, leaning in to talk close to my ear.

"Hey, Dex."

He really was a beautiful guy—six-pack, sandy-blond hair, and a dazzling smile that he delivered with such confidence, it made the whole package even more attractive. Only problem . . . when I looked at him I just didn't feel *it*. Whatever *it* was.

Part of it I'd never be able to fix. The fact was, Dex was only eighteen. His life so far had been a smooth ride and the rest of it was turning out to be just as blessed. And I . . . well, if there was only one of me, that would have been fine, but I was eighteen *twice*, and my life was . . . complicated. The bottom line was that even though I was never going to, would never dream of . . . But if there *were* someone I might one day consider telling about my whacked-out existence, it wouldn't be Dex.

"What's up? Your face is all twisted," Dex whispered, giving me a curious look.

I forced my forehead to relax and pushed the thoughts aside. Normally I was better at keeping them at bay. "It's nothing. I just remembered that I need to pick up my new shoes from town before tonight." Lie, lie, lie.

Dex smiled, buying it too easily. For some reason, it made me mad. I turned my attention away from him and pretended to concentrate on the lesson to avoid having to talk to him again.

Giving myself all that staring-into-space time wasn't helpful. My mind was on a mission and I found myself prodding at my not-broken wrist. And the questions began . . .

Have the rules changed?

No. This must be a one-off. Was this a one-off?

Will my wrist be broken when I go back to my other life?

Was this a glitch and will it only last for a day?

Maybe my wrist will be broken when I go back and then stay that way when I return so that this day never really happened?

But . . . if the rules *are* changing, what does that mean? Was there a way . . . ? But I won't let myself finish that long-forbidden thought.

My head started to hurt. I tried to distract myself by thinking about the party tonight.

Then I felt sick.

I didn't stay up past midnight often—and never around other people. But everyone had insisted. I was the only one who hadn't had a party this year, and this was my last opportunity. I wasn't going to risk my reputation by not following through, so when a birthday-graduation bash at my place was suggested, I'd smiled brightly and said, "Absolutely!"

I knew I'd have to be awake for the Shift. But after being awake for last night's, I was now dreading tonight's Shift even more. I hadn't been awake for two consecutive Shifts in years. Not to mention how it was ratcheting up my string of awake hours.

Just as I tried to formulate a plan to get myself somewhere private at midnight, the bell rang and Dex was at my side.

"You do realize all the exams are over?" he teased in his deep voice—the one that said he needed me to acknowledge him. He was pretty easy to read sometimes.

I followed him out into the hall, slipped an arm around

his waist, and kissed his cheek. "I know, but with only one week left, I plan to finish on a good note."

He quirked an eyebrow. "You've already received your acceptance to Harvard; what better note could you finish on?"

I shrugged. Truth be told, I was dreading going to Harvard and having to be around Ryan constantly. But when it came time to apply, I just couldn't bring myself to pick colleges farther away from Mom. If I wasn't around to help her, she'd go to pieces.

Out of nowhere, Dex pushed me up against the lockers. I gasped, but let him do it, hoping to feel something . . . more. His hips were dangerously close to mine. "The smart thing really does something for me," he said huskily.

I smiled and let him kiss me.

I felt like I could've pulled out a notepad and started documenting. At Second Two, he made a movement with his upper lip. At Second Four, his hand tightened around my waist. At Second Seven, he made that sound he does. And at Second Nine, my damn skin crawled and I had to pull away.

"Will I see you at lunch?" I asked, looking hopeful even though I knew the answer.

"No," he said, staying close to my ear. "I've got track. You could come watch."

Hmm . . . let me think . . .

"I would, but I have party planning to finalize."

"Yes. I guess you do." He kissed me again, this time

finishing at Second Four's hand tightening before releasing me. "I'll see you later."

I nodded and watched him leave so that when he looked over his shoulder he saw me.

Lucy, who had obviously been waiting for me, rushed to my side, and we walked to calculus together. "You know he is, like, stupidly in love with you, right?"

I laughed, feeling bad that my main feeling was relief he'd only gone as far as the fourth second on the last kiss.

God. How was I going to get through sex? How many seconds would he actually last?

"And so he should be," I answered teasingly before quickly moving on. "Back to party issues. Can you come over and get ready at my place tonight? I need your help to get Mom out the door."

Lucy beamed, in her element. She wanted to be an event planner, and viewed all of our parties as valuable work experience. "No problem, leave your mom to me."

CHAPTER FOUR

Wellesley, Friday

I stared at myself in the mirror as Miriam styled my hair. Thankfully the rest of the day had gone by in its usual predictable way, helping me get on top of things again. Now everything was perfectly on schedule. Even the afternoon thunderstorm had come, thundered, and gone away with barely a trace.

"Honestly, Sabine, if you would just let us put a color through it. I swear your hair would look amazing platinum blond."

The worst part is, I agreed. I'd love to go either way—to Miriam's beautiful blond or Lucy's gorgeous rich brown. But I just shook my head.

"I like it the way it is," I said confidently.

"Yes, but a change is as good as a vacation and you could use a serious break!" Miriam persisted.

"No, I really couldn't," I mumbled. Change was not my friend.

"What?" Miriam asked, pausing with the brush mid-stroke.

"Nothing. You're right. Maybe after graduation or something," I lied. But at least it stopped the conversation.

When she'd finished, I slipped into my dress and strappy high heels and almost laughed at what the *other me* would think of herself looking like this. I smoothed down the beautiful green silk on the understated but sexy halter-neck dress, which showed off my figure and said to the world: *I'm not a schoolgirl anymore*. Finally. I felt myself smile, knowing that although it had taken twice as long as it had for everyone else, I was at last reaching a landmark moment in my life.

Things would become easier for me as an adult. I wouldn't have to hide as much. Dumb it down. Not have an opinion on issues I shouldn't be concerned with. Things would get better. They had to.

And then I swallowed hard, knowing that out of everyone, I was best at lying to myself.

"Okay," I said, pulling myself together. "Mission Mother."

Lucy and Miriam followed me downstairs. Miriam looked amazing in a knee-length cream dress that fit snug to her body and kicked out at the bottom. The intricate beading that snaked its way from the low-cut back, tapering off toward the bottom hem, set off the fabric perfectly. Lucy had gone for the fresh look with a spaghetti-strap peach dress. Also stunning. Together we were kind of rocking it.

We posed for some photos to satisfy Mom—then a few more after Lyndal, Mom's sister and best friend, arrived. Finally we managed to get them into the car, promising we would behave. In return they promised they would stay away until 2:00 a.m. It was the time we'd settled on over the last three weeks. Mom's midnight suggestion was never really an option if my social standing was to be upheld, and my 4:00 a.m. opening offer was only on the table so we could meet in the middle. Two o'clock was respectable, and it was all I could be bothered with anyway.

When I walked out to the pool area where everyone would gather in the next half hour, I was stunned.

"Oh my God," I gasped, for once not faking it.

Lucy was jumping up and down. "Legendary. I told you." She beamed.

"Lucy. Did you . . . ? How . . . ? How did you . . . ?"

"Actually most of it was your mom. She asked me the other day how all the preparations were going, and when I told her some of my grand vision, she offered to help."

Miriam glided up to one of the three clear plastic Perspex walkways that hovered over our long pool—lit from beneath with sunken balls of light—and lifted her hand to catch a stray bubble floating out from one of the many discreetly placed bubble machines.

"My *mother* did this?"

"Most of it." Lucy nodded.

"Wow," I said, taking in the hundreds—no, thousands—of tiny fairy lights scattered all through the gardens: in the tall maple trees and down in the garden beds, lighting pathways and wrapping around the hedges along the pool. The entire backyard was alive with a beautiful, fairylike glow. "It's breathtaking."

By ten, I was drunk.

The boys had delivered in the drinks department, arriving right on time with two vans full of alcohol. God knows how they managed to get hold of everything, but they had—and they were, as always, manly proud of their efforts. I was surprised they refrained from beating their chests as they unloaded the loot. Champagne, kegs, and vodka punch were set up on the makeshift bar in the pool house. Before long, the entire backyard was flooded with laughing, drinking, dancing eighteen-year-olds. And every time I turned around, Dex was there, looking handsome, with a full glass in hand to exchange for my empty one.

I knew what he was doing. He'd been waiting a long time, and I hadn't made it altogether easy. But I wasn't going to sleep with him tonight, so I took the drinks and let him kiss me up to Second Ten on a number of occasions. The effects of the drinks even helped me relax enough to let him go up to Second Eighteen a few times. But then I discovered that other things happened to Dex's body after Second Fifteen . . .

I went back to calling it quits at ten seconds shortly after.

It was a mystery how many people actually turned up. At least the 150 Lucy had predicted. At some point there might have been more, but just my luck, Lucas turned up some time before midnight. He offered to keep an eye on things and help pull the plug on the party at 2:00 a.m., before Mom turned up.

"Did Mom tell you to come?" I was a little offended I hadn't been trusted.

Lucas shoved his hands in his pockets. It was his standard uninviting pose, the one that always made me feel as though he thought I was beneath him or something. "No. Just thought you might need some help if things got out of hand."

"Oh." I eyed him suspiciously, knowing it wouldn't be out of character for Mom to have sent him. But Lucas generally told the truth, so I let it go. "Do you want a drink?"

"No. Not really my crowd." It was a dig. Lucas approved of very little when it came to me. He thought I was a spoiled brat who got everything she wanted.

If only he knew.

Then again, it wasn't like any crowd was *his* type. Lucas, with his broody-yet-clean-cut look, was as much of a loner as anyone in this town could get away with. I think that's why he chose to go live with Dad. It meant he could avoid having to deal with more than one other person on a continuous basis.

"I'll just go hang out in the front room. If you need me, come get me." With that, he walked stiffly past me, leaving space between us as if we were strangers instead of brother and sister.

"Thanks, Luc," I said to his back, which earned me a shrug in return.

Lucas and I didn't often see eye to eye, but I tended to trust him unlike Ryan. Even if he didn't particularly get me, he was honest and I knew he'd do as he promised. It was hard to remember sometimes that there were only two years between us. Part of me wished he'd just grab a drink and talk with me, loosen up. But simply making an appearance was about as friendly as Lucas could manage, so I let him hide away in the front room, knowing that at least with him there I could relax and enjoy the party.

At 11:30, I was itching for an out. It had always been part of my plan—to just slip away for a while so I could go through the Shift in private. But when I started searching for rooms, there was someone, or *someones*, in all of them. I barged into my own room only to bolt back out when I got an eyeful of Brett and Miriam—which was no doubt now permanently seared into my memory.

"Shit," I said to myself over and over. It was 11:50 p.m., and I was still desperately pushing through hordes of people trying to find a private space to shift worlds. But there was nowhere; even the bathrooms had lines of people waiting.

"Shit, shit, shit."

I picked up the pace, heart racing. Only one option left. I headed for the basement door through the kitchen, passing an almost topless chick I did not, thank God, recognize surrounded by three guys I *did* recognize trying to talk her into letting them do shots off her. I threw them a disgusted look before I pushed through the door and stumbled down the stairs in the dark. I just needed to find somewhere quiet. Midnight was only a few minutes away, and I needed to at least be sitting down. I felt around in the dark, my arm jerking away when it caught on something sharp. I gasped, feeling the sting, and grabbed at my arm, trying to see how bad it was.

The door at the top of the stairs opened, spearing just enough light into the room to glimpse the blood beading from the cut on my forearm. I looked up in time to see the light disappear behind someone who had let the door close behind him.

"Sabine?"

Shit. It was Dex. I considered not answering, holding my breath and pretending no one was home. But he'd obviously seen me come in. Hell, he could probably hear my pounding heart from where he was. Could things get any more out of control?

"Down here. I'm just . . . I'm . . ." *Just hiding in the basement in the pitch-dark so I can shift between my two lives in private.*

"Needed a minute?" he suggested.

I considered telling him about my arm to distract him, but I quickly ruled it out. He'd just insist on taking me up to the kitchen to clean it. The Shift was so close I was going to be sick. "Yeah. I'm just . . . you know. I'll be back up in a minute." But then I half-jumped, because he'd followed my voice and was right in front of me. His arms slid around my waist. "Ah, Dex . . ."

"*Shh*. I know you don't want to tonight. But that doesn't mean we can't do other . . . things." His hand slid up my side, grazing the edge of my breast. I fought back the urge to swat his arm away.

"Dex, I just . . . I think I'm drunk," I said, which was true and not helping at all at that moment. I knew I only had about a minute left to get out of the situation, but my stupid mind wouldn't work. My airway felt like it was closing up on me.

I wriggled a bit, but since Dex chose that instant to move closer, he interpreted it in the *very* wrong way.

His voice deepened. "I'm good to wait until you're ready, but just so you know . . . I'm ready whenever you are."

Evidently.

I opened my mouth to tell him I needed to be alone, but I

was too slow. His mouth was on mine and suddenly I was up against something uncomfortable.

Oh no. No, no, no. This isn't happening.

But it was.

On Second Four, his hand tightened on my waist . . . and I shifted.

CHAPTER FIVE

Roxbury, Saturday

I gasped for air, kicking my feet out as if trying to escape from invisible restraints.

As I thrashed around, something that felt like a lead pipe smacked me on the forehead, forcing me to finally take stock of my surroundings.

"Shit, shit, shit!" I'd just shifted with Dex's *tongue* down my throat. I was going to be sick. In some bizarre screwed-up way, for the next twenty-four hours Dex was going to have his tongue lodged in my mouth until I shifted back and threw him the hell off me.

"Shit," I said again, swallowing back the urge to throw up and concentrating on slowing my breathing. I had to get a grip.

The "lead pipe" that had hit me in the head was in fact the cast on my arm. I wiggled my fingers and could feel the familiar pain flare up. Still broken. Interesting.

What was going on? I pulled my right arm out from under the covers and felt my stomach slide to an all-bad place.

The cut I'd just gotten in the basement—the cut I'd just been looking at—was gone. Not so much as a scratch. And though I'd never really experimented with alcohol and the Shift before, I was no longer drunk. In fact, I felt horribly sober. Something had definitely changed.

It was a dangerous thought, but it was there nonetheless.

The physical wasn't crossing over.

I slipped out of bed and walked out into the hall. The house was silent; everyone was asleep.

"Shit," I whispered, lost for any other words, frozen in no-man's-land. I don't know how long I stood there, mouth agape, but eventually I about-faced and shuffled back to my room to try—somewhat pathetically—to go to sleep.

But in those dazed and confused moments . . . the seed of a thought was watered and had begun to grow. I tried to stop myself. Tried to block it out.

I failed.

When 7:00 a.m. rolled around, I got up and headed for the kitchen.

I could hear Mom humming away in the shower. Since we all shared the one downstairs bathroom, I decided to start on breakfast while I waited for my turn. Today was Saturday, so at least I didn't have school. Four-day weekends were not the worst parts about my lives.

Partly for Maddie—and partly to block out the mental image of Dex and me before the Shift—I started whipping up some pancake mix. Before long, Mom was in the kitchen with me, frying up some bacon and helping me hold the bowl while I tried to whisk with my good arm.

By the time Maddie's feet shuffled into the kitchen, Mom and I were sitting down to our pancakes with Maddie's waiting on the warm stovetop. I'd let Mom take over while I showered and dressed, opting for a deep-purple stretch mini and gray tank top to avoid buttons. I still had to ask Mom to lace up my boots. She suggested I might like to borrow a pair of her slip-ons. I asked her if she was high. She gave me her Mom smirk, then laced up my boots.

We always sat in the kitchen for meals. We did have a dining room, but Mom and Dad had it stacked to the ceiling with stock for the drugstore. They insisted on buying in bulk for better pricing from their suppliers—if that meant we filled the best room in the house with toilet paper and diapers, so be it.

I didn't mind. It seemed homier, even if the kitchen was our most run-down room. If I had it my way, Mom and Dad would use my college money to fix up the house a bit. But they weren't about to listen to my suggestions. Mom would see it as me being disrespectful, and Dad would just accuse me of not living up to my potential. He was big on always telling Maddie and me that we could be more. I never missed the subtext, the one that translated to *you're not enough.*

Mom put Maddie's plate in front of her and poured her an apple juice. Without a word, Maddie smiled and started eating. She wasn't a morning person. Mostly because she spent half the night snooping around. It would take her a couple of hours to hit her stride, so Mom and I kept the conversation going.

"Do you need help today?" I offered, already knowing the answer. Usually I hated helping out at the drugstore; it was bang-your-head-against-the-wall kind of work, and there are only so many seventy-plus ladies you can show to the hair-coloring section. But today I had ulterior motives for helping.

Mom nodded. "A few hours this morning. Maddie is going over to Mrs. Jefferies's house to play with Sara, and I was hoping Dad could take a day off."

I mopped up the last of my maple syrup with my pancake and nodded. "No problem. Capri and I were going to meet up at the mall before she starts work, so I can head in by nine."

Mom stood up and started to clear our dishes away, both of us ignoring Maddie as she quietly worked away on her own breakfast. Mom took a deep breath. "Sometimes I don't know what I'd do without you," she said softly. Then she sniffed and added with her usual pragmatism, "Try not to get sidetracked with Capri."

I smiled uncomfortably as I grabbed my backpack and headed for the door. "See you there." On my way past Maddie, I mussed up her hair. "Don't make Sara climb too high in the tree this time, kiddo." Last time it had taken forty-five minutes for Mrs. Jefferies to climb up and get Sara down.

Maddie gave her standard 8:00 a.m. grunt and shoveled a piece of bacon into her mouth, but when I reached the front door she called out, "Can I still draw on your cast when I get home?"

It wasn't great timing given everything I had planned for the day, but it was Maddie. "You know it!" I yelled back, and headed out, knowing I'd left her smiling at the kitchen table.

Capri worked weekends at the secondhand music store, Thrifty Tunes. There was double incentive for her: she needed a job plus she got to hang out with Angus, her most-of-the-time boyfriend, who worked weekends there too.

Even if Capri wasn't ready to admit it, they were perfect for each other: both into the Goth look, both into music, both opinionated, strong-minded people. And when they were together . . . well, even unfortunate bystanders could tell they were into one another in all the right ways. But part of that meant they also drove each other crazy and fought like maniacs. Last fight they'd had, Capri had given him the silent treatment for two weeks.

"You wanna meet up later, go catch a movie or something?" Capri offered as we meandered toward Thrifty Tunes, each with a Mocha Frappuccino in hand.

"Can't. Gotta hang out with Maddie this afternoon," I said between sips, somewhat satisfied that my lie actually held a grain of truth.

"Davis is planning to stop by." She said it as if it were an incentive.

"I've already told you, Davis and I are just friends. That's it."

Capri threw her empty bottle in the recycling bin and popped a few pieces of gum in her mouth before reapplying her black-currant lip gloss, all while still on the move.

"That's not what he thinks. I can see his smaller version thinking other things when you're around," she said teasingly.

I smacked her on the arm. "Please don't go there." *Please!* It was bad enough knowing how close I currently was to Dex. "Davis is cool. As a friend."

"Come on, Sabs, what's the deal? You holding out for Mr. Sweep-you-off-your-feet or something? Or are you holding out for me? Cause you know . . ."

I smacked her again, but I was laughing. "You wish."

She was still looking at me, wanting an answer. I groaned. "I don't know, Cap, I just don't like anyone like that at the moment." I gave her a stern look to emphasize my point, since I was pretty sure Capri was happy to swing either way. "But when I *do*, it will be a guy."

We stopped outside the music store and she shrugged, satisfied that I wasn't lurking in any kind of closet. "Just want you to get some. You know, before you're fifty."

Part of me, a fairly big part, totally agreed. But I glared anyway. "You're a bitch, you know that?"

"I might've been told once or twice before," she called out as I walked away.

I stopped by an office-supply store and bought a lined black notebook. I would need it as part of the plan. With shaking fingers I also dialed a number on my phone and made an appointment for later.

At the drugstore, I said hello to Mom and the pharmacist Denise, then I wriggled awkwardly—thanks to my cast—into one of the white jackets that were supposed to make us look more "medically informed." When Mom and Denise weren't looking, I slid my notebook onto the counter. I kept a magazine resting on top of it, so when customers came in they wouldn't see the list.

1. *Test blood theory—exterior physical reaction*
2. *Test hair—pigment and removal*
3. *Test laxatives—internal physical response*

4. Test poison—loss of consciousness and organ failure.
If points one through four achieve a successful outcome,
proceed to next point

My hand trembled as I wrote number five.

5. Choose

I chewed on a fingernail, staring at what I'd just written. Could it really be that simple? I didn't know, but even so . . . I crossed out the last point. It was too early for that. Points one through four first. Then I'd worry about what would happen next.

Giddy from the rush of thinking such forbidden thoughts, I did what I'd really come here for: I stocked up on everything I was going to need, waiting until Denise went on her break to grab some items from behind her counter. By the time I returned to the register, someone was waiting and looked like he'd been there for a while.

"Sorry for the wait. What can I get you?" I was sure I was flushed from guilt. I hoped he hadn't seen me shoplifting from my own family's store.

The guy, who'd had his back to me, spun around and glared. I let out a little gasp before I could stop myself. He was probably in his early twenties—and his presence packed a punch. Trouble and attitude radiated from him. And there was something . . . more. In his eyes. They were startling: dark blue and intense, with a depth you didn't normally see. Eyes that could too easily see through someone.

I set my shoulders and got ready to deny any accusations. But he just gave me an up-and-down look I couldn't read—other than to know it wasn't flattering—and shoved a handful of crumpled prescriptions toward me.

"How long?" he asked, his full lips set in a straight line.

I gave him a tight smile as I sifted through over a dozen prescriptions, more than a few for heavy-duty medications. That explained the aggressive, defensive attitude: drug dealer.

"These are going to take a while," I told him. "Since there are so many and they're not all in one name." *Hint: I know what you're doing.* "The pharmacist will need to see ID and get an authorization." *After which we'll call the police.*

I kept a firm hold of the prescriptions, expecting him to snatch them and make a run for it. But he simply shrugged, leaned against the counter, and folded his arms.

"Just call Roxbury Hospital and give them the prescription codes and my ID details. They'll verify." He slipped a driver's license out of his wallet and tossed it on the counter before narrowing his eyes at me. "How long?"

This guy was an ass. And thankfully I wasn't in Wellesley today; I didn't have to behave. I sucked in a breath and was about to tell him to take a hike when Denise came back from her break.

"Ethan!" she said, looking delighted. "What are you doing here?"

Drug guy shrugged, sending me a sly look. "Being interrogated."

Denise looked at me, the wad of scripts in one hand, phone barely balancing in my other, and smiled. "It's okay, Sabine. Ethan works at the hospital. They have weekly prescriptions, but usually not till Monday." She turned to Ethan, closing the distance in a few steps. "I haven't seen you around in a while. How are you?" She squeezed his arm tenderly.

"Amazing." His voice dripped with sarcasm.

Denise just nodded as if he wasn't being a total jerk and took the scripts from my hand. "I'll take care of them, Sabine."

I shot a look at Ethan, who now seemed to be enjoying himself, just as Mom emerged from her pigeonhole office and called out, "Sabine, can you do the dry-cleaning and coffee run?"

"Yeah, 'cause I can really carry all that," I answered. But Mom had already closed the door, forgetting my broken wrist. End-of-month accounts can do that.

Denise looked up from typing prescription details into the computer. "Ethan, why don't you give Sabine a hand? You don't mind, do you? I'll get these processed while you're out."

Ethan frowned, looking annoyed that I'd suddenly become his problem.

My jaw clicked to the side in anger. I picked up my note-book, intending to stuff it in my backpack, but instead I accidentally knocked the bag off the opposite side of the counter with my cast. The unzipped backpack and all its contents—including my notebook—landed right at Ethan's feet.

"Shit!" I exclaimed as Ethan bent down to pick up my things. I scrambled to get around the counter, but by the time I got to him he was already straightening up, my backback in one hand, my open notebook in the other.

He passed the bag over, face blank.

"Thanks," I said, putting out my other hand for the notebook. I was sure he must have seen the list, and I wanted to kick myself for using a black marker.

He handed it over calmly. I shoved it back in my bag while he bent down again to pick up something from under the counter. My heart pounded in my ears. It was a box of pills.

He looked at me curiously. "Yours?"

At least I'd had enough foresight to put the pills in a generic white box. He couldn't know what they were—if he asked, I'd shut him down by saying they were for period pain. But the fact that there was no label or prescription sticker had him looking over the box suspiciously.

I snatched it from his hand and quickly shoved it in my bag. "Thanks," I mumbled.

Now who looked like the drug dealer?

"Not a problem." He raised an eyebrow, and I was again

struck by how dark his eyes were. A deep ocean blue. My gaze traveled down to his mouth and somehow became stuck there. I stared at the arc of his full bottom lip just as his teeth slid smoothly over it as if he were contemplating something important. He cleared his throat and I blushed, caught mid-gawk. "We should get going then." He gestured toward the door.

"Oh no. You don't have to . . . I'll make two trips. It's fine." Then, finding some backbone, I narrowed my eyes and added firmly, "Really."

He shrugged and half-smiled, enjoying my discomfort. "I've got nothing better to do."

Oh, the flattery.

"Whatever," I said. If he wanted to play help-the-invalid, that was his issue. And I did *not* stare at his ass after I took off my white coat and followed him out of the store. It was more of a fleeting glance.

CHAPTER SIX

Roxbury, Saturday

If Ethan had been frosty to me in the drugstore, he was positively arctic after we left. I let him suffer the awkward silence I had no intention of fixing. It was clear he didn't want to be doing this any more than I did.

"You in college?" he asked finally.

"Graduating high school," I answered, avoiding eye contact. I didn't want to encourage small talk with this guy.

"Graduation, huh? Big plans for the future?"

I rolled my eyes. Like he cared. "I suppose. I'm looking forward to finishing school and some new possibilities."

"Oh?" He raised his eyebrows. "And what are those?"

I shrugged, confused by his interest. "I'm not exactly sure yet, but I like the idea of a future I can take one day at a time and, I don't know, live each day to the fullest, I guess."

He nodded, his gaze moving down to my cast. "So what'd you do?"

I cringed, shaking my head at myself. "Tripped on the subway steps."

"It happens."

"Not to me it doesn't," I said without thinking.

He gave me an odd look.

"I mean, I just . . . I've never broken anything before."

He was still staring at me curiously, but thank God we hit the dry cleaner's and he stopped asking questions. He didn't speak again until we were back out of the shop, when he insisted on carrying the white coats wrapped in plastic.

"Thanks," I said, trying to stop my gaze from traveling below his rolled-up shirt sleeves, where his forearms flexed as he gripped the hangers. He wasn't super built or anything—if anything he was lean—but everything was just . . . annoyingly nice to look at.

I cleared my throat. "So you work at the hospital then? You a doctor or something?"

He didn't look like the doctor type—dark jeans, black shirt, and overgrown dark hair curling at the ends—but you never knew.

"Or something," he said wryly, shooting me a look as if he knew exactly where I'd pegged him. "Your mom owns the drugstore?"

We went into Starbucks—thankfully no line—and I ordered Mom and Denise their usual caramel lattes. "Nope. She just manages it."

"Surprised I've never seen you before. I used to go there every week."

I remembered what Denise had said about the Monday prescriptions. "I'm at school on Mondays. For one more week anyway."

Ethan nodded. After I'd paid for the coffees I turned and caught him staring at me with the same odd look on his face before he quickly glanced away.

"Here, I'll carry one," he offered.

I loaded one on top of the other and lifted them easily in my good hand. "I've got it," I said, heading for the door.

As we neared the drugstore I tried not to pick up the pace. I knew that if he was going to say something it would be now. But we made it all the way inside without so much as a: "I read your notebook. That's some messed-up stuff in there." And once the coffees had been handed out and dry cleaning hung on the rack, Ethan collected his pile of drugs, loaded them in his bag, and left with barely a nod in my direction.

I busied myself restocking shelves and made a point of *not* thinking about Ethan—every single time his curvy lips and muscly forearms crept their way into my mind.

Mom let me go just before two, which was perfect timing to make my appointment. I headed straight for the hairdressers, forbidden excitement bubbling up inside almost as much as the fear that I was about to make a very big mistake. And pay for it . . . in another world.

"What do you want to do?" the hairdresser asked, chewing on gum and holding out my long dreary hair.

I swallowed, watching in the mirror as her fingers combed through my hair. "Can you just make it look good? You can cut off as much as you want, and color it too. Darker."

She looked at me like I was an unwrapped Christmas present. "I can do anything?"

I hesitated. "As long as you didn't know me and hate me in a past life, yeah. I . . . I've never colored my hair and it's always been really long. I want a change and I figure you know what you're doing, right? Just . . ." I looked at myself in the mirror, taking in my miniskirt, fraying tank top, and boots. "Make me look good."

She smiled. "I've got you covered, hon. Sit back and relax."

So I did.

Mrs. Jefferies delivered Maddie home right at 6:00 p.m. When I opened the front door, Maddie's eyes lit up and she started jumping up and down on the spot.

I couldn't help the goofy grin on my face.

"Binie, you look so cool!" she wailed, hugging me tight.

"Thanks, Mads," I said, wriggling out of her hold. I was usually happy to have her attached to me, but today, with all the thoughts I'd been pretending *not* to think, her affection left me feeling ashamed.

I waved to Mrs. Jefferies, who was still in her car, and took Maddie inside. She continued to ooh and ahh over my shaggy, almost-black styled cut, which gave me more edge than I'd ever dreamed possible.

I'd stopped by Thrifty Tunes on the way home and Capri almost fell over herself before teasing that Davis would now never leave me alone. I'd just laughed and soaked it in. I'd never had a makeover before, and I'd be lying if I didn't admit I was loving it.

With Maddie pawing over my hair, in between drawing on my cast and telling me my hair was so, so pretty, it made it easier to keep up the act. Helped me not consider just how much of a problem I'd have on my hands if, come midnight, I shifted to Wellesley—and back into Dex's arms—with short, shaggy black hair.

By the time Maddie had finished drawing a family of bunnies, I started making us dinner, figuring Mom would work late. As for Dad, the moment he walked in the door it was clear that he had not had a good day, something that was increasingly frequent. He'd taken one look at my hair and I guess it was the final straw, since he'd simply picked up his keys and said he'd be back later.

I hadn't been surprised he didn't like it. Of course, that didn't mean some part of me hadn't held out hope—and wasn't hurt to, once again, be a disappointment. At least silence was better than launching into one of his "we don't do all this work for you to go around looking like a tramp" lectures. And gone were the days when he could drag me back to the hairdresser and demand she fix it. So instead he would drink. It was what he had started to do after a particularly bad day at work, or when he felt one of us was not "being our best" at home. It wasn't like it happened every night, but still it was enough. And completely hypocritical.

After our macaroni and cheese, Dad stumbled in right on cue, went straight into his and Mom's room, and shut the door, leaving behind a waft of bourbon. I distracted Maddie until the banging around stopped. Despite my parents' flaws, they never took anything out on Maddie. She was the sun. For us all.

By the time Mom got home I'd read *Alice in Wonderland* cover to cover, twice, and just managed to convince Maddie to stay in her bed and go to sleep. Mom looked at my hair and sighed.

"Well, it's definitely different."

Her way of saying she didn't like it. She sighed again, looking toward her closed bedroom door.

"I take it your father has seen you?"

I nodded, looking at my feet. "He's crashed for the night."

Mother's intuition finally kicked in and her look

softened. "It's such a big change, Sabine. I'm just not used to it." She smiled weakly. "But the cut is already growing on me." Translation: *the color isn't.*

"It's fine. Not everyone has to like it, just me, right?" I said, not waiting for her response. "There's leftovers in the fridge if you're hungry."

Mom shook her head, her exhaustion obvious. "No, thanks. Straight to bed for me tonight."

It was the reply I'd been hoping for. "Me too."

As soon as Mom was in her room, I slipped into the bathroom and closed the door. I took my time organizing everything, needing it to be just right. Maybe delaying a little too. I couldn't decide what kind of blade to use, so I grabbed a pair of scissors and a shaver and wrapped them up in a towel along with everything else. It took a few trips, but when I was finally back in my room I wedged a textbook under the door. The last thing I needed was for Maddie to barge in on me.

I placed most of the items on my bed, then took the roll of toilet paper and put it, along with a bowl of warm water, on my bedside table. I stopped a number of times to remind myself to breathe, but once I had everything arranged and was sitting on the towel there was no reason left to delay.

First thing—I ran a lighter flame over the blades.

It was slow going to start. Scissors weren't a good idea. I'd misjudged just how hard it would be. Forcing myself to make the cut was bad enough—using almost-blunt scissors was impossible. By the time I'd hacked away at my thigh for a while, sucking in sharp breaths each time I tried to make a quick cut, I had to accept the scissors weren't creating enough impact.

But I couldn't give up. I needed to be sure.

The rules had changed. At least, that's what I was starting to believe. Ever since I'd woken up in Wellesley minus one broken wrist, I'd been thinking. Reminiscing over all the times I'd imagined what it would be like if the physical didn't cross over. I remembered how Casey Tulin slit her wrists in junior year, and while everyone else was mourning, I was daydreaming. *If the physical didn't cross over . . . maybe I could . . .*

I didn't agree with Casey's decision, but my situation was entirely different. I've always felt deep down that by having two lives they somehow canceled each other out. That maybe the end of one life could mean the start of my first *real* one.

That's all I'd ever dreamed of.

I'd cried myself to sleep for so many years. Confused, distraught, not knowing why I was different from everyone else. Not knowing why I wasn't enough in either one of my worlds. Not knowing who I am . . .

If there was a chance . . . If I could make it so there was only one of me . . .

I growled in frustration and dropped the scissors. They weren't doing anything substantial.

I moved on to the razor blade, warm tears slipping down my cheeks. I started with my right thigh again, selecting the same area. My hands trembled, but I managed to get a few clean swipes of the blade across my skin. The result wasn't exactly what I'd planned. Using a disposable razor only allowed for a surface cut: three in my case—triple blade. What it *did* do was cause a lot of blood. It seemed like as soon as I wadded the toilet paper and covered the cut, it was already drenched.

More tears flowed. I wanted to stop, to figure out another way. But I knew there wasn't one. I needed to know if the blood theory worked; if what happened to my body in this world was *only* going to affect this body and not my other. Knowing this might be the key to a future I actually wanted.

I took a few deep breaths and waited for the bleeding on my leg to slow. Then I covered the cuts with Band-Aids and slipped into a pair of sweatpants.

I opened my bedroom door a crack. No light. The house was silent. I let the door swing just wide enough for me to slip out without it creaking. My heart thumped in my chest as I made my way downstairs. I felt like every step, every breath, was so loud that at any second Mom or Dad would come rushing out of their room and catch me in the act.

In the end, it took a while to find what I was looking for.

Someone had put it away in the wrong drawer. By the time I'd placed it carefully under the side elastic of my underwear and shuffled back to my room, I'd built up a light sweat of pure panic. It was twenty minutes before my hands stopped shaking and the churning in my gut settled down.

Once I'd steadied myself, I concentrated my efforts on the base of my ribs, hoping it was the right choice. I figured it was one of the safest, most discreet areas. Until I knew more, I didn't want to go making a terrible mistake.

You see . . . I didn't want to die.

It was the exact opposite.

I *wanted* to live.

I used the lighter to burn off the edge of the filleting knife I'd just lifted from the kitchen. It wasn't the biggest—but oh, it was the sharpest.

To my surprise, it made everything a lot easier. After a couple of false starts I managed to talk my hand into holding the knife with enough pressure to make a decent cut.

"Shit," I said over and over as I tried to clean up. I used the warm water and toilet paper. Kept up the pressure until the bleeding slowed and then applied the antiseptic cream I'd five-fingered from the drugstore before putting on a few big Band-Aids. Afterward, I paced around my room, which meant four small steps in each direction. It wasn't much of a workout, but it gave me time to think.

"Shit."

I sat back down on the towel, pulled off my T-shirt, and picked up the knife again. Today wasn't the day to be half-assed.

"One more," I whispered, goading myself on as I placed the blade on the back of my upper arm. I tried to swipe the knife across in one quick movement, but I chickened out mid-slice, releasing the pressure, and barely scratched the surface.

"Shit." I shook out my trembling hand before repositioning the knife for another go. Once the blade was in the right spot I closed my eyes, took a deep breath, and pulled it across my arm with no intention of going back for a third try.

I didn't need to.

It took a while for the bleeding to slow down. Half an hour after I'd bandaged it up, I needed to start the dressing process again. I suspected this one could have used a few stitches, but that was definitely not going to happen.

Eventually the bleeding settled and I put everything away, hiding it in the bottom of my closet. I got into bed to count down the minutes.

There was no way to stop the panic. I had to run down to the bathroom twice to throw up. Partly over knowing what I'd just done to myself, partly the same sickness I always felt this close to midnight—and in *very* large part because I had not, for one moment, forgotten what would be waiting for me the second I went through the Shift.

But there was still one more thing to do.

At twenty minutes to midnight, I swallowed five laxatives.

CHAPTER SEVEN

Wellesley, Saturday

Reflexes took over before I could stop myself.

I knew what—*who*—it was suffocating me. I'd been waiting for the Shift and trying to prepare myself, but the second I slipped back into my other self, back into my green dress, back into the basement and Dex's arms, his warm face and wet lips slapped up against mine, I snapped.

Sometimes our own strength can be a real surprise. Mine sure as shit surprised Dex when—somewhere around what must've been Second Seven or Eight of his kiss—I launched him clear across the pitch-black basement. He fell into something that tumbled with him to the ground, making a loud clanking sound.

Too preoccupied with trying to breathe and hold off another bout of nausea, I barely even heard his response. Something about "what" and "hell."

I felt the same way.

He clattered around, getting to his feet. I opened my mouth to start a long-winded apology, hoping I wouldn't throw up on him in the process, when the door flew open at the top of the stairs.

"Whoever is down there, get up here. Now!"

It was Lucas. Come to the rescue a little late.

"Luc, it's me," I said, bracing myself with my hands on my knees.

His tone changed from heated to hesitant. "You okay? Who's down there with you?"

Oh, great. Inquisition.

I swallowed, still trying to pull myself together and stop the shakes. It didn't help that the effects of the alcohol in my system had hit me like a freight train. The light from the stairwell gave a dim glow to the room. Dex was moving toward me, hands out cautiously.

"It's just me and Dex," I called back. "Luc, can you hold the door? We'll be up in a minute."

He grunted in reply.

Dex stopped in front of me as I struggled for words. I had no idea how I was going to fix this. "I'm so sorry, Dex. I . . . I just . . . You caught me by surprise. I think I've had more to drink than I—"

"Sabine," he said carefully, hands still out like he was approaching a wild animal. "Are you okay?"

"Yes, I'm so sorry . . ."

I was mid-headshake when he cut me off again. "Sabine, you're bleeding."

My whole body froze.

It hadn't worked.

My mind flew into overdrive. What was I going to say? How was I going to explain this? Oh, shit—my hair!

"I . . . I can explain—"

"Here." He passed me a scrunched-up cocktail napkin from his pocket. "You must've caught it on something."

Stunned, I looked to where he was gesturing with the napkin.

The scratch on my right arm. The *scratch*!

I grabbed at my left shoulder frantically, patting it down, followed by my ribs. And then I went to Crazy Town and yanked up my dress to look at my thigh.

Nothing.

I ran my hands through my hair. Long. Normal.

"Ah, Sabine? You okay?"

"Oh, yeah. I, um, I bumped into a few things when I came down here. I was just checking I didn't have any other scratches. You know, I, er . . . didn't want to damage the dress."

Dex nodded as if this sounded reasonable enough.

"Sabine! Are you coming up?" Lucas called out.

We started walking up the stairs. Dex was rubbing his elbow.

"I'm really sorry, Dex."

"Hey, don't worry about it. I'm sure I can think of a way you can make it up to me," he said slyly.

I looked at him and smiled. It seemed to satisfy him and I was glad—I couldn't think of a single thing to say.

Lucas eyed me disapprovingly as I passed by. "I suggest staying out of the basement in the future if you can manage it. It's never easy to throw off a basement-girl reputation— even for you, Sabine," he said quietly.

In the kitchen Dex insisted on fussing over me, honorably tossing almost-topless girl her blouse and telling her and the guys to get lost while he cleaned my arm.

"It's just a scratch," I said, uncomfortable with the attention.

"So you keep saying," he said. I stared at him blankly. I hadn't realized I'd said anything since leaving the basement.

I needed to regroup. This was my party, and if I didn't get it together it would be a disaster. And in this life I simply couldn't afford the social downfall. Not after all the work I'd done to secure my reputation.

"Dex, I'm . . . ," I started, straining for something to reassure him after what I did downstairs. "I . . . I've made some plans for graduation night."

Dex kept working on my arm, but his eyes came up to meet mine. "Plans?"

"Yeah, you know . . . *you* and *me* plans."

His eyes widened. "Oh! I see. *Plans.*"

I nodded, blushing.

The corners of his mouth went up. "Plans sound good." He went back to his doctoring, putting a Band-Aid on my arm. "You should probably get a tetanus shot. You don't know what you might have cut yourself on down there."

I nodded just as Miriam came gliding into the kitchen.

"Whoa. You okay, Sabine?" She paused in the doorway. Miriam doesn't do blood.

"I am now, thanks to Dex." I hopped off the counter and planted a kiss on Dex's cheek, making a quick getaway before I had to divulge any more about the "plans."

I slipped an arm through Miriam's on my way out of the kitchen to cover my shaking hands. As we headed to the pool she proceeded to tell me in graphic, and unwanted, detail about her last thirty minutes with Brett. In my bedroom.

Some things are best left unshared.

Someone passed me a drink, and despite my still feeling sick and light-headed I sipped on it, claiming a lounge chair at the head of the pool. The next two hours passed by in a welcome blur.

At last Lucas shut off the music.

No one seemed to mind, and I couldn't have been happier to hear the pounding stop. Lucas launched into adult mode: patrolling, telling kids to get lost, checking that the drinkers weren't driving. Then he simply up and left. That was Lucas.

I figured he didn't want to stay behind and explain any of the night to Mom, who walked in about five minutes after he left, took one look at me, and ordered me upstairs to bed.

I guess it was obvious I was drunk.

Her parting words informed me we'd be having a more in-depth discussion in the morning. I nodded and told her tipsily I was looking forward to the follow-up.

By some miracle, I managed to get out of my dress and into my pajamas before I collapsed, face-first, onto my bed.

When I woke up, it took no time at all for everything to come flooding back. It felt like reality reached out and walloped me across the face. Hard.

I was out of bed and in front of my mirror in an instant, staring at the same image of myself I always saw in this world—if a little puffy around the eyes. My long brown hair was stuck to one side of my face and hung down to just above my waist. I lifted my top to show a very normal bare expanse of skin over my ribs and belly, and both my legs and arms were unmarked, except for the relatively small scratch I'd received in the basement.

I grabbed my watch off the nightstand. It was just after midday, which meant the laxatives had had plenty of time to work their way into my system.

I went to the bathroom. No sign of the package-promised results. But while I was in there I did throw up. Due, I'm fairly sure, to my vodka-punch consumption over the course of the night more than anything else. I mentally chastised myself and resolved never to get drunk again.

Having no idea what to do with all this newfound information, I opted for routine. I took a shower, changed into a cute sundress, and put on my favorite red kitten heels. I couldn't decide whether to laugh or cry, so I plastered a smile on my face and went downstairs—only to endure a forty-five-minute lecture from Mom.

After the tenth time she said, "I just want what's best for you," I zoned out, studying the walnut grain of the dining-room table. Her heart wasn't in it anyway. And when she huffed and pushed a sandwich in front of me, saying, "You look like you're fading away," I knew the lecture was over.

The smart thing would've been to go back to bed. I needed more sleep. I'd lost count of how many hours I'd been awake—in both lives—before finally passing out in the early hours of the morning. But with my swirling thoughts sleep wasn't really an option. And besides, there was something even more pressing that I *absolutely* had to do.

• • •

"Cut it. Not too much, and shape it around the sides, leaving the length at the back. Color needs to be much lighter, but with tones. Make sure you keep some warmth in there. But definitely blond."

The stylist forced a smile, looking at me like she was having second thoughts about her career choice. I sympathized, but held my ground. I wasn't going to let the hairdresser have free rein in this life. It was essential that my new hair be Wellesley appropriate.

While she shampooed and conditioned my hair with organic products, I finally let my mind slide into murky waters. The thing was, now that I was in this new situation, I couldn't imagine a way back. Not knowing what I now knew.

All my life, there'd been no choice. I lived two lives and that was it. Never just one or the other—broken in two and all alone. But now . . . now there was a chance. Hope. The possibility of a *normal* existence.

If the physical parts of me were not connected . . . If what I did in one life in no way affected the other . . . If I could bleed in one and not the other, cut off parts of myself, dye them different colors . . . If I could take laxatives and get drunk and have none of those things cause any reaction in my other body, then to some degree—a very *relevant* degree—I was two *separate* bodies. And if I was two separate bodies—and one of me was to stop existing—the other should continue.

And I'd have just the one life.

But . . .

There was still one more test to carry out before things could go any further.

CHAPTER EIGHT

Wellesley, Saturday/
Roxbury, Sunday

My new blond hair, styled the way it had been crying out to be for so long in this world, did not disappoint.

When Mom saw me, she was so delighted she forgot all about being unhappy with me and shooed me away when I offered to help with the cleaning up.

A multilevel victory.

It would have been the perfect opportunity to visit Miriam and Lucy for a gloat session. Or better yet, Dex. I was certain he would forgive my strange behavior last night when he saw the new me. But I was dead on my feet after the three-hour makeover and still had a hangover. Bed was the only option.

Lying back on my silk sheets in the early evening, confidence on high, I decided on my next move.

It was a risk.

But if I could get through this final test, I would have

options I'd never thought possible. I considered setting an alarm to wake me up before the Shift, but I was so tired I couldn't be bothered. Waking up groggy in this world or the next, it made little difference right now, and at least I wouldn't have to go through the pre-Shift jitters.

The transition turned out to be the smoothest in days. I'd been fast asleep in my Wellesley world when I shifted back to Roxbury. Normally the conflict of a sleeping mind being thrust into an alert physical body was disorienting to the extreme. But I was so exhausted, I was almost numb to the change. Post-Shift I simply registered my still-broken wrist, the cuts aching on my leg, belly, and arm, and then rode the adjustment period, dropping off to sleep soon after in my gray flannel sheets.

I'm sure I could've slept for hours, but instead my sleep was seriously interrupted as, several frantic times, I paid for my experiment.

The laxatives had kicked in.

By the time I had no fluid left in my body, I crawled back into bed with every intention of spending the entire day sleeping it off. Maddie, however, had other ideas.

By mid-morning she was bouncing persistently on the end of my bed. At first I mumbled for her to go away and buried my head under the blankets, but then I remembered that today was . . . well, *today*.

I had things to do.

"Binie, come on, get up! Mom says you have to come down and see her before she goes to work."

I groaned, rubbing my eyes and sitting up. Everything hurt.

"I didn't think she was working today," I muttered.

Maddie just shrugged and took one final jump on the bed, landing on her butt beside me. "Said she's going in with Dad to do something."

"Oh," I said, still sifting through my thoughts. "What are you up to today, kiddo?" I tried to keep my voice light, but I couldn't look after her today.

Maddie slumped. "Mrs. Jefferies is picking me up."

I gave the top of her head a rub and kissed it. "You'll be okay. You always have fun in the end."

She squirmed. "Yeah, but I want to stay here with you."

"I'd love that too, but I have to go out today and do some stuff. We can hang out tomorrow after school if you like. Maybe go to the park?"

Maddie never missed a beat. "What stuff do you have to do today? Are you going to be home tonight?"

"Not sure, kiddo. I might be staying out."

She slid off the bed and trudged toward the door.

"Love you, Maddie," I said lightly.

She couldn't help but turn and give me a little smile. "Love you *too*, Binie." Then she leaped into my arms and gave me a Maddie specialty death squeeze before she was gone, her feet bounding loudly down the stairs.

I dropped my face into my good hand and sighed.

"What are you doing, Sabine?" I whispered, but just as quickly I rubbed my hand up and down, as if I could scrub the thought from my mind.

I *had* to know.

After an awkward, arm-wrapped-in-plastic-bag shower, I reapplied Band-Aids to last night's handiwork, dressed in a black cotton skirt, longer than usual at just above my knee, and a fitted burgundy T-shirt with long sleeves. It took twice as long to get ready with my banged-up wrist, but I managed to work out most things—even my standard heavy-handed application of eyeliner and mascara, which worked well with my new black shaggy cut.

I sat down on my bed to start grappling with my boots, but instead I picked up my bag and found myself holding the plain white box of pills that would be my final test. I cringed when I remembered dropping my bag and how badly things could've gone when Ethan found the pills.

I couldn't risk something like that happening again.

Without another thought I started popping out the pills and placing them on my bedside table. One by one, I used the base of my water glass to crush them, reminding myself not to crush too many, but just enough.

Digoxin was the perfect drug. I'd seen people come into the drugstore after taking an incorrect dose. As a heart medication, mistakes resulted in an array of side effects, including blurred vision, heart palpitations, nausea—it was quite a long list. It was the ideal way to test an internal physical response to a toxin. Best of all, there was an antidote—Digibind—so if things went completely out of control, something could be done about it.

"A responsible risk," I murmured while I searched around my room. "Aha!"

I pulled the necklace out from a pile of junk on my dresser and started to twist the top off the silver butterfly pendant. Capri and I had both bought pendant necklaces at the flea market last year. Hers had a silver skull, but I'd preferred the butterfly, and we'd both liked that they had secret chambers. At the time, we'd joked that they'd come in handy when we were smuggling drugs.

Carefully I swept the powdered digoxin onto a piece of paper and funneled it into the bullet-shaped body of the butterfly before securing the head back in place.

If only Capri could see me now.

I cleaned away the evidence, taking the rest of the digoxin and packing it, along with my slice-and-dice tools, into my backpack. I'd keep it with me and dump it at some stage during the day. I didn't want stuff like this lying around, especially the pills, where Maddie could stumble across them. I slipped on the pendant, grabbed my backpack, and headed down to the kitchen just as the front door closed.

"Maddie?" I asked Mom and Dad, who were sitting at the kitchen table rifling through paperwork.

Mom glanced up briefly, her glasses resting halfway down her nose, making her look older than she was. "Just left with Mrs. Jefferies."

I nodded, poured some water into the kettle, and began making toast. I also doled out a couple of painkillers the doctor had prescribed for my wrist. It wasn't actually causing me much trouble, but I figured the pain relief might help with my still-throbbing cuts.

When I sat at the table, no one was talking. Mom stared at Dad like she was waiting for something, but Dad ignored her and readjusted his pale-blue tie. He insisted on wearing one every day. As if the tie alone could make him, make *us*, better somehow.

The silence became uncomfortable.

"What's wrong?" I asked between mouthfuls of toast. Dad continued staring at the same piece of paper he'd been focused on since I'd walked into the room. Mom squirmed in her chair.

"It's probably just a misunderstanding, sweetie." She gave me a reassuring nod that didn't match the concerned look in her eyes.

"What is?" I put down my slice of toast, my cast clanking on the edge of my plate.

Dad looked up at me from behind the sheet of paper. Something in his eyes—the way they looked at me, but didn't *focus* on me—set off my internal alarms. "Denise called this morning. She did a random stock check before she closed up last night. On the prescription meds." His glare intensified. "Is there something you want to tell us?"

Oh.

Shit.

I thought I'd covered all bases. Normally inventory happened midweek, which would have given me a few days between working at the store and other casual staff taking shifts. It should've been impossible for the missing drugs to be traced back to me.

Why the hell did Denise decide to . . . ?

Then I remembered how I'd been too nervous to look around when Ethan handed me back the box of pills. Denise must have seen enough to be suspicious.

I wasn't ready for this.

"Sabine?" Dad snapped.

I grabbed hold of my pendant, sliding the butterfly up and down the dainty silver chain, thinking fast.

"I don't know what you want me to say."

"You could start with the truth," Dad replied.

I looked at Mom, holding her gaze as if I had nothing to hide. "About what?"

Think, think, think!

My mouth was so dry, my words were starting to stick.

"About the box of heart medication that walked out of the store yesterday. They were only delivered in the morning and were gone by the afternoon. Apart from Denise, you and your mother were the only ones in the store with access." Dad's neck was getting red patches. He was starting to lose it, glaring at Mom like she should be doing something.

Mom jumped in. "Sabine, I don't know what you . . . Maybe you could explain—"

But it wasn't good enough for Dad and he cut her off. "It's heart medication, Sabine!" He stood up, scraping the chair roughly across the floor. "What were you thinking? If you think you can get high on that stuff, you're sorely mistaken! You would've had better luck in the cough medicine aisle!" He started pacing around the table.

Eyes wide, I couldn't think, couldn't focus. Mom was reaching across the table to hold my hand, as if pleading for an explanation, something that could stop this runaway train. Problem was, my mind was drawing a blank.

"I didn't—"

"Don't even go there! We know it was you. Even *Denise* knows it was you! How do you think that makes us look?

Having staff who know that our own daughter would steal from us? Did you even think about what people would say?"

Dad's foot snagged one of the straps of my bag and he stumbled, almost taking a nose-dive. It was the final straw. After regaining his balance, he grabbed my backpack and upended it on the table.

I leaped up to stop him, but Mom's previously comforting hand suddenly morphed into a viselike grip.

It felt as if everything happened in slow motion. The contents of my bag spilled onto the table. Amid the stash of blood-soaked bandages sat a half-emptied box of pills and a box of extra-strength laxatives.

And just to complete the parental nightmare—the kitchen filleting knife landed with a dull thump.

Mom gasped and Dad looked at me as if every terrible thought he'd ever had about me had been leading to this moment of ultimate disappointment. Before I could think, my mouth was open.

"I can explain! Let me explain."

Mom nodded, squeezing my hand and then releasing some of the pressure. Dad raised his eyebrows at me.

"Go on then, Sabine," he said. "Explain." His tone was flat and dubious.

I took a deep breath, tried to start and failed. Heart pounding, I took another breath and mentally counted to ten. And then, my life of hidden truths, of divided worlds, my secrets, my *wrongness* . . . The walls I'd worked so hard for so long to construct tumbled down around me. I didn't know if it was because I'd been caught thanks to the change in the rules or the result of some dire need to defend myself and shock my quick-to-judge parents, but when I searched in the bottomless barrel of lies that never seemed to fail me . . . Nothing. Not one little excuse sprung to mind.

"I have two lives," I blurted.

Mom looked perplexed. Of all the things she'd expected me to say in my defense, this was certainly not one of them. But then, as her mind ticked over the possible explanations for that one comment, the color drained from her face and her expression changed to horrified.

I took another breath. "I've been this way ever since I was born—living every day twice. I wake up in the morning here, in my bed with you as my family, and I live my day. But every night, at midnight, I go through this kind of *Shift*— that's what I call it. One second I'm here in this life. The next, I'm in another life, and for the next twenty-four hours until midnight I'm in that life, with my family there. When I get back here, it's as if no time has passed."

Tears slipped down my face as I looked at my parents, desperately willing them to see past the craziness of my words to the truth in my eyes. "I know this is weird. It's why I've never told anyone—I never thought there was anything I could do to change it. But . . . but lately something *has* changed. Before, if something happened to my body it would affect me in my other world—like when I got tonsillitis in this world, I had it there too. Now, for some reason things aren't crossing over. So I've been . . . trying to figure it out." I swallowed.

"You live in two *worlds*?" Dad said very softly.

"Dad, please believe me."

"You have two different families?" Mom said, equally stunned, eyes welling.

"Look, I know this sounds crazy. But I can explain it all so you understand. I just need you to know why I have the pills"—I glanced at my bag's incriminating contents—"and the other stuff."

Finally Dad nodded and turned to face me. "Well, make it clear to us, Sabine."

"Okay," I said, blowing out a breath, relieved he seemed to be at least willing to hear more. "I don't know when the change happened, maybe since I turned eighteen, but when I broke my wrist, that was the first sign. When I shifted the other night, my wrist wasn't broken in my other world."

Mom was silent, but Dad nodded me on and I couldn't help but feel a rush at finally being able to tell them all of this. My deepest fears of him yelling "liar" and throwing me out of the house weren't coming true.

I sat up in my chair. "After that, I decided I needed to know for sure. I mean, the physical parts of me have always been connected, but now . . . Well, if they aren't, everything is different. So I started conducting tests. First my hair."

"And how did that go?" Dad asked.

I felt myself nodding. "Great. I mean, for the first time I was able to cut my hair and not have it change in my other world." I couldn't help the hesitant smile. Dad made a feeble attempt to return one. I took it as another encouraging sign. "When I went back there I had my hair dyed blond, and it didn't change anything here either. And then . . ." I stalled.

"It's okay, Sabine, you can tell us. We can see you've been . . . trying out some other theories," Dad said, sounding surprisingly calm as he glanced at the bloodied bandages heaped in the center of the table.

For the first time in my life, I considered that maybe they'd always known, had figured it out somehow. I felt a surge of relief as I continued to explain. Maybe they could help me work this out. Maybe I wasn't as alone as I'd always assumed.

"Well, I wanted to test everything. So after my hair, I tested my skin and . . ." Rather than trying to tell them I'd been hacking at myself, I pulled up the sleeve of my top to expose the bandage and grimaced. "I know it was stupid, but I was really careful and the thing is, it worked. When I shifted last night, none of the wounds came with me!"

Dad nodded and pressed his lips together. Mom was sobbing at the table. I decided to keep my focus on Dad. He seemed to be taking it better.

"How many areas have you tested?" he asked.

"Just my arm, leg, and belly," I said, wincing a little as Mom gasped. "But I was careful and none of them are deep, I swear!"

"It's okay, Sabine. It's just a lot to . . . take in for your mother and me. We've always known that you've been . . . dealing with some things that other people weren't. It's good to get it all out in the open, and we're grateful you've confided in us." He scratched at his neck. He always did that when he was nervous.

Or lying.

Instinctively I recoiled and turned to Mom. She was still crying, barely looking at me.

"Mom? You believe me, right?" I said, suddenly fearing I'd made a horrible mistake. Mom couldn't stop sobbing, but Dad came around and put a hand on my shoulder.

"Of course we do, Sabine. It's just going to take some time for us to absorb. How about you give your mother and me a few minutes to process everything and then we can have another chat? I'd like to know more about your other life."

Still feeling uneasy, my eyes darted between them. "Okay. Well, I was going to head out for a bit anyway." I stood up. Exit was a good plan. Dad seemed to be trying to understand, but Mom wasn't coping. Plus, those alarm bells were ringing louder in my mind.

"Actually, would you mind staying around here? I think it's important we talk this through. Could you wait in your room?" Dad looked at me and then glanced pointedly at Mom, as if imploring me for a chance to calm her down before I left.

I thought it through. I would never have expected Dad to take all of this so well, but he seemed genuinely interested in what was going on with me. I still felt a gnawing unease, but if I took off now, it would only look bad. Make them think that I was lying. And he would never, *ever* trust me again. No. I needed to stand up to this, make them understand. So I clung to the hope that it would all be for the best, nodded to Dad gratefully, and went to my room.

CHAPTER NINE

Roxbury, Sunday

I wedged myself up against my door, straining to hear what Mom and Dad were saying. Besides a few loud sobs from Mom and the occasional stern use of her name by Dad, they spoke in hushed tones. The phone rang a few times, but even then all I could hear was Dad's muffled voice, which sounded relaxed and formal. Must be work related.

I waited.

When it was clear I wasn't going to overhear anything, I collapsed on my bed and started to rehearse all the things I was going to tell them, carefully selecting the examples I'd use to help them understand. It wasn't going to be easy. I'd had my whole life, twice over, to come to terms with this existence, and I still didn't fully understand it. Plus, I'd seen Mom's face when I told them I had another family . . . That was *not* going to be a pleasant conversation. I decided to keep the details as vague as possible for now. There was also the money issue; Dad wouldn't like that. But I couldn't help the small bubble of excited anticipation. I was *finally* telling someone.

I waited.

Dad would come and get me. I hoped that when he did, we'd get a few minutes alone together and he'd bring me up to speed on how Mom was taking it all.

I waited.

It seemed like the whole day passed, several hours at least.

It was quiet. I'd run out of theories and practice speeches and had started to wonder if they were still even out there. I was about to go looking for them when I heard a knock downstairs at the front door.

A stern knock. Three life-changing thuds.

I wasn't sure exactly why, but my stomach flipped and I started instinctively backing away from my bedroom door.

I hadn't even made it to the window when Dad opened the door and held it there for the man and woman who walked in. Our family doctor followed, standing beside Dad.

The bed was between them and me—and since my bedroom basically only *fit* the bed, the situation became instantly defensive. I could see the man and woman calculating how they were going to close the distance.

These people were not my friends.

These people were my worst nightmare.

"Sabine," my father—no longer Dad—said in a low commanding voice. "Sabine, we are trying to help you. These nurses are here to help."

They held their hands in front of them—reminding me of the way Dex had approached me the night before—like I was a wild animal. In that moment, that's exactly what I felt like.

Trapped.

My eyes darted from the door to the bed to the people trying to entrap me, then to my window. But I was cornered. My father and I both knew it.

"It's okay," he told the man and woman. They were dressed in white slacks and jackets, not unlike the drugstore uniforms.

The air left my lungs. I knew what was coming next.

"The window is jammed shut," he said.

Bastard.

I glared at my father, overcome with fury. "How could you do this to me? Oh, I get it. This isn't about me at all—you just want the problem to go away!" I screamed.

"Sabine," the woman said in a deliberately calming tone. Her mousy-brown hair was tightly braided, highlighting her overly blushed cheeks. She gave me a fake smile, as if the two of us had friend potential. I stared back at her with a "don't fake a faker, bitch" look. She looked away first. A small victory, but it wasn't going to last long. I was boxed in.

"You're not well, Sabine," my father said. "Your mother

is petrified with worry. She needs you to get help. Dr. Meadows has come here as a special favor—he has a doctor he would like you to see at the hospital. He's going to fit you in immediately. They're going to make you better. Please, don't make a scene." His look added the line he didn't say aloud: *They're taking you either way.*

The man and woman took another sly step in my direction, the tall man with the buzz cut leading the way around the base of the bed. I was up against the wall, nowhere to go.

I couldn't stop shaking my head. I felt so betrayed. "Did you ever consider it? Even for a second as you nodded me on earlier? Did you even *listen* to what I said?"

"Oh, I listened, Sabine. That's why I've been forced to get you help. You're suffering from delusions. You are clearly a danger to yourself, and possibly others. If you're asking whether *I*, at any moment, considered it possible that my daughter is living an alternate life, then the answer is no."

They took another step.

My heart was racing, my pulse thumping in my neck.

"So you're just going to lock me up?"

My father sighed, impatient with me. "If that's what I have to do until you are well, yes."

"You can't! I'm eighteen!" I didn't add that if you took my other life into account, I was almost as old as he was.

"You are a threat to yourself," my father said, his

95

words snappy with a combination of embarrassment and disappointment. "You've been placed on a forty-eight-hour hold pending your evaluation. After that . . ." He looked beyond me, no longer meeting my eyes. "We've appealed that the state be awarded control of your health until you are well again."

All those phone calls.

Desperate, I leaped onto the bed, thinking that if I could get to the other side I might have a chance at pushing past my father and Dr. Meadows.

But the male nurse had anticipated the move. He was on me mid-jump, slamming me onto the bed, keeping me down as I struggled.

Dr. Meadows moved farther into the room. "Sabine. We're here to help. Please, let us help," he said.

The woman dashed around to the side of the bed and went for my arms. But as she grappled with my cast, I leveraged against the mattress, bucked my body, and kicked the guy in the face.

He stumbled back, and the woman's grip loosened as her attention focused on him. I used the advantage, ripping my arms from her hold and pushing her back a few steps. I bounded off the bed, past Dr. Meadows, who didn't try to stop me, and straight into my father, who instantly grabbed my upper arms, his right hand squeezing hard on the cut he knew was there. I couldn't hold back the cry of pain. He ignored me and simply maneuvered me into a reverse bear hug, pinning my arms to my sides.

It hurt in so many ways. I sagged in his arms.

Nurse guy staggered back to his feet, blood dripping down his face. I'd smashed my foot right into his nose. The woman had righted herself too. She was no longer bothering with the "we can be friends" look. She'd moved on to a big-ass syringe and a look that said: *I'm gonna enjoy this.*

"I warned you she might be violent," my father said, ignoring my attempts to struggle against his tight hold.

"Yes," nurse guy replied flatly. "I suggest we sedate her now."

"But Dr. Levi was going to see her immediately," my father argued.

Nurse guy used the edge of his white jacket to wipe the blood off his face and stared at Dr. Meadows, who took his cue and turned to my father. "I think it would be best for all involved if we could get her safely to the hospital. It's a fast-working sedative, but it won't last too long." He waited for my father's approval.

"Mom!" I screamed.

"Sedate her," my father said quickly.

"Mom!" I screamed again.

She came into the hall, but stayed at the far end, leaning against the wall as if she needed the support. She was crying, covering her face with her hands.

"Why didn't you tell us you were so unhappy?" she said in a broken tone. "How long, Sabine? How long have you been having these thoughts?"

"Mom, I swear to you, I'm not crazy. Make them stop. I'll explain. I'll . . . I can prove it to you!"

"Hurry up," my father insisted. I twisted my head and shot him a look of pure hate. Nurse guy moved in to help hold me still. I'd endured being a kid for so much longer than any normal person—endured the rules, curfews, judgment—but this . . . this was totally demoralizing.

"You need to listen to me! God, just for once stop thinking about yourselves and listen!"

I could hear Mom's gasp from the other end of the hall, but she said nothing and made no move to help me.

I shook my head. It was hopeless. "I never should've told you," I said brokenly.

I jolted one last time against my father, trying more to hurt him than free myself and then glared at my mother.

"I should've just done it!"

No one missed the meaning. It even surprised me.

"Would you get on with it!" my father snapped at the woman. To me he simply said, "You'll thank us for this one day."

The woman moved toward me. Some of the earlier hate in her eyes had gone and was replaced by something much worse. Sympathy.

"Don't feel left out," I sneered at her. "I promise to give your face the same makeover as his." I glanced at her colleague who was still dabbing at the blood coming from his nose.

Her eyes narrowed, her compassion quickly dissolving. The needle went into my arm and in seconds everything began to blur.

It was a bitter realization: the confirmation that for all these years, living my lives in secret and solitude, I'd been right not to trust them with the truth. But that wasn't the only thought that catapulted into my mind as consciousness began to fade.

What have I done?

The last plea that fell from my lips was heavy and slurred. "Don't . . . tell . . . Maddie."

CHAPTER TEN

Roxbury, Sunday

My eyes felt glued together. At first I thought I must have shifted, but then I managed to haul my eyes open. And along with the memories the room slowly came into focus.

I was still in my Roxbury life. Lying on a bed in a room whose only light came from the small fluorescent bulb in the high ceiling. Apart from the bed and nightstand, there was an empty doorless cupboard, a well-worn armchair, a small barred window—which told me it was dark outside—and a door, closed and no doubt locked. Not that it mattered anyway. My wrists, even over the top of my cast, and ankles were restrained in leather bindings.

And as if that wasn't bad enough . . . they'd taken my watch.

I wanted to be sick. I barely had room to move. If I threw up now, it'd go all over me.

I swallowed repeatedly, trying to force my stomach

100

to settle. It didn't help, and when my eyes glanced at the window again, I almost lost it.

Shit.

What time was it?

I couldn't go through the Shift like this. The thought of being tied down, of leaving myself like this in one world for a full twenty-four hours . . . it increased my panic until I was on the verge of screaming.

How could they have done this to me?

There was no clock. No way to know what time it was. I could shift at any moment. I wasn't even sure *where* I was.

I yanked my arms, testing the restraints. Yeah, not a chance.

I considered calling out, desperate enough to plead for the bathroom or something, *anything*, to free myself. But before I could open my mouth I heard footsteps. One set first, then another.

I wriggled around as much as I could and realized that under the blanket I wasn't in my normal clothes. I was in a hospital gown. For some reason that tipped me over the edge and hot tears started pouring down my face. For someone constantly striving to remain in control, the idea that other people had been controlling me—my movements, my clothing—felt like a total violation.

This just couldn't be happening.

My breakdown threatened to get vocal, but I kept my

mouth shut and gritted my teeth against the sobs. Then I heard talking outside my room.

"One new admission in there. Everything fairly standard and on the charts."

"Sounds easy enough," said a slightly familiar voice.

"Careful with her. They have her on SW until further notice. She'll be due for meds in the next hour, which should keep her sedated for the night. Doc's already dosed it out and left it at the front desk."

The other guy paused before he asked, "He wants her kept under all night?"

I didn't hear an answer.

The other guy spoke again. "Okay, then. She do that to you?"

"She's stronger than she looks."

A chuckle. "What about the restraints?"

"Doc says she won't be going anywhere after her next round of meds, so you can undo them if you want. Your call." He said it in a way that suggested if it were his call, he'd keep her restrained.

"Okay, Mitch. See you tomorrow."

Mitch was obviously the guy who'd come to my house. The one I'd kicked in the face. Can't say I was feeling anything that resembled remorse.

There was a slapping sound, like some annoying "dude" handshake.

"Don't know how you do it, man. Working nights like you do. It doesn't seem right," Mitch said.

"Gotta pay the bills," the other guy replied. "And it beats doing nothing." I could almost hear the shrug.

Footsteps started up again. Just one set. I waited, barely breathing, tears still slipping down my cheeks. When my door finally clicked open, I quickly closed my eyes and pretended to be asleep.

The guy walked in, messed around with something at the end of my bed, and then came closer. I could feel his presence moving in on me, then a broken gasp I wasn't expecting.

"Oh God," he whispered. "Sabine?"

My eyes shot open.

Ethan.

I couldn't respond. Seeing him somehow made everything more real, more painful. Tears kept streaming down, rolling around to the back of my neck.

I expected him to start speaking. Say something consoling, or nice, or even patronizing. But as I watched, his expression changed from shocked to severe, as if he'd just decided something hateful about me. I became instantly defensive.

"What time is it?" I blurted.

When he didn't respond, I grew more desperate. "Please, you have to tell me! The time?"

He blinked, looking shocked at my behavior, but glanced at his watch.

"Eight p.m." His brow furrowed. "Why?"

Relief washed over me, and the terror of an uncontrollable Shift subsided with a flush of fresh tears. I still had four hours.

"Sabine, what happened? They said you were on SW?"

I sniffed. "What's SW?"

He looked at me strangely. "Suicide watch."

Oh.

Then, without waiting for my answer, he went back to the end of my bed and picked up a folder. He flipped through the pages, reading quickly, ignoring me. Pausing at one section before coming back over to my side.

"It says you hurt yourself. Did you?" His voice carried the bite of accusation.

I shook my head. "It's not like that."

"It says they think you may have broken your own wrist." He looked ill at the suggestion.

I shook my head again. "No. No, I didn't. I . . . I fell—"

He cut me off. "Down the subway steps." He pulled down my blanket and I flinched, helpless to stop him.

"Wait. What are you doing?" Unfortunately I knew exactly what he was doing.

He glanced at me, determination in his eyes. And anger. But why? What did it matter to him what I did? We barely knew one another. He lifted the sleeve of my hospital gown, revealing my makeshift bandages. "And these happened, how?" he growled.

"I don't have to tell you anything," I said sharply.

He ignored me and started unwrapping the bandage until he got down to the Band-Aids. He was shaking his head, not looking at me.

I tried to squirm away. "Don't touch me."

'Trust me, I'd prefer I didn't have to, but these need to be cleaned properly. Did you even bother to wash them, or were you hoping you'd die from an infection?" His eyes darted from my arm to my face, daring me to argue. Carefully he began removing the Band-Aids.

I bit the inside of my cheek and refused to show any reaction when the last one, which had dried to the wound, was eased off. Ethan was breathing heavily through his nose, shaking his head every few minutes. I felt like a two-year-old.

He disappeared and came back with a tray of ointments and fresh bandages.

"I don't need this from you," I said, after one too many headshakes.

He paused, mouth half open like he was about to say something, but then he just went back to tending my arm. I don't think I'd ever met anyone so frustratingly obnoxious.

I felt my face heat up. "If you just undo these straps, I can do it myself."

"That's not going to happen."

Now it was my turn to shake my head. "You don't know me. You don't know the first thing about me."

"Let me guess. There's more than one of these *harmless* little cuts on your body?"

I didn't answer.

He gave a grim smile. "Thought so. I guess I know something about you then. Where are they?"

I didn't answer again.

He grabbed a handful of my blanket. "I'll pull it off if I have to."

"And I'll scream bloody murder! Who the hell do you think you are?" I snapped.

He didn't let go of the blanket. "I'm the guy who has to come in here and clean you up. So when you're done feeling sorry for yourself, *if* that's possible, would you mind telling me where the rest are so I can get this done and get on with something else." His tone was even, but the words cut.

I considered a long list of ways I could tell him to go screw himself. But there was something . . . It wasn't like with Mom and Dad. He was angry at me, which he had little right to be, since he didn't even know me, but there was an urgency to it. To *fix* me. Not my head, but my body.

I sighed. "I'll tell you if you promise me one thing."

That earned me another headshake. "Whatever you're going to ask for, I can't do it. Can't get you out, can't get you drugs, can't smuggle you food, can't get you a phone, can't take you for a joyride, can't even bring you a toothbrush."

"You can do this much, I know you can." I'd heard Mitch tell him.

He clenched his jaw. "What?"

I took a deep breath. "Promise me that before midnight . . . Swear that you'll release me from the restraints. I need to know that at midnight I won't be tied down."

His confusion showed. "Why?"

"Does it matter? I'm here and can't go anywhere. It's just . . . It's important to me. Please."

He paused, watching me curiously. "What's going on with you, Sabine?"

"That's . . . It's complicated, Ethan, and we don't have time." And then our eyes locked, and without thinking the mouth that had already landed me in so much trouble today opened again. "But if you truly want to know, I'll tell you. Another time."

He kept watching me. "And why would you do that?"

I shrugged. "Well, I'm already tied up. Things can't get much worse."

Ethan gave a small nod. "Famous last words," he muttered. "Where are they, Sabine?"

"Promise me."

For a moment I thought he was going to say no, but then he sighed. "You won't be restrained at midnight. You have my word."

"And I can trust your word?" I asked, watching him carefully.

He half-smiled. "With your life."

It was a dig, but somehow I knew it was also the truth.

"My right thigh and stomach. And I didn't break my own wrist."

His look softened momentarily before he got back to work, moving the blanket up from the bottom of the bed to reveal one leg, folding back my hospital gown until he found the bandages.

As he peeled back the Band-Aids, I tried not to cringe.

"That one isn't as bad," I said.

There was a sharp intake of breath when he got the last of the bandages off. "Jesus. What did you do this with, a butter knife?"

"Scissors and a razor. The scissors were a bad idea."

"You think?" he deadpanned, then went back to shaking his head. "Does your life mean so little to you?"

"No. Having a life is exactly why I'm doing this. And you can stop shaking your head like it matters to you. You don't even know me, or care."

After he'd finished re-dressing my thigh, he lifted my gown to just below my chest without looking, and then replaced the blanket at my waist. It was gentlemanly. Even if his other actions weren't. The rest of him radiated anger.

"I don't know you. What *I* care about is being made an accessory to suicide."

"*What?*"

Ignoring me, he pulled the Band-Aid off the cut beneath my ribs and studied it. "So you started on your thigh, moved to this, and then your arm?"

I blinked. "How . . . ? How do you . . . ?"

He shook his head again and it made me want to scream. They get progressively neater and deeper. I saw your bag yesterday at the store. You were planning, weren't you?"

I looked away.

"Knew it. And that book? All planning, wasn't it?"

"Yes, but not for what you think. I mean, take a look, Ethan. Do you think I'm really that stupid? Do you think I would cut myself on my thigh, my stomach, and my upper arm if I wanted to die? My parents own a drugstore. Do you think I don't know the long list of how and how not to kill yourself?"

He crossed his arms as I went on the attack. Somehow it made me even more annoyed.

"Do you think I *want* this? To have everyone call me crazy? Think I would put myself in this position willingly for a failed attempt at death-by-small-cut-to-the-thigh? Yes, okay, I did it, but I have my reasons. And if you saw that stuff in my bag and thought I might be doing something with it, why didn't you just say something?"

Ethan stared at me. Time stretched. I was out of words and simply exhausted. Just when I thought he wasn't going to respond, he began to speak. "You were . . ." He clenched his jaw. This time he seemed unhappy with himself rather than me. "I saw that stuff in your bag, so I went with you on your errands. I looked for signs." He glanced down at his hands. "I thought . . . You didn't fit the mold. You talked about your future, seemed so full of life."

After that, he left the room. I panicked that he wouldn't come back. That he would leave me tied up as some kind of punishment. But a few minutes later he returned. With a syringe.

I tried to back away, but the restraints stopped me and my broken wrist ached at the pressure.

"Ethan, I . . ."

Shit.

He was going to put me under. I'd dealt with the issue of the restraints, but not this.

"Is there anything I can do to convince you not to drug me until after midnight?"

"No." He didn't even look at me.

"Ethan, I'm sorry, okay. I was angry. You try being tied to a bed and drugged. It's not a happy time."

He paused. "What is it with you and midnight?"

I wanted to cry. "Please. Please don't do this. It will . . . It hurts . . . It . . ."

"You're shaking," he said, now watching me intently.

"It frightens me. Please." I looked at him, trying to hold his gaze while he watched me. "I'll do anything."

He reached forward and moved a strand of my dark hair out of my eyes, his own eyes shadowed with sadness. "That's just the problem, Sabine. You could do anything." His hand dropped away quickly.

The syringe stung.

Tears streamed even as I tried to blink them away. The drug kicked in fast.

"I'm so alone," I stammered, feeling empty and cold as everything went black around the edges.

"You're not alone, Sabine," he whispered. "You're lost."

The last thing I felt before I lost consciousness was the release of the restraints from my wrists. I'd be free of them when I shifted at midnight.

Ethan had made sure I'd know.

CHAPTER ELEVEN

Wellesley, Sunday

I stretched out like a cat, silk sheets gliding beneath my hands. The morning birds were out in full force, probably nesting in the tree outside my room.

As lucidity wormed its way into me, the memory of the last twenty-four hours descended like a heavy blanket. My parents. Being hauled away. The hospital. Ethan.

Ethan. Drugging me, putting me under.

Ethan releasing the restraints, shaking his head at me, dressing my wounds, and that small gesture: brushing the hair from my eyes.

I'd been locked up. Medicated.

I'd been put on SW!

I bolted upright in bed. Everything had turned to shit.

My hands bunched up my silk sheets, gripping hard. The morning birds kept chirping. I'd slept right through the Shift and I was grateful for the small reprieve. Mom called out from downstairs. She was leaving, but she'd left waffles in the kitchen. Sunday ritual.

I glanced around my same-as-always Wellesley bedroom. Everything had gone wrong.

"But not here," I whispered to myself. "Everything's still okay—*here*."

After staring into thin air for a while, routine kicked in. I got out of bed, showered, and dressed.

I was downstairs, lost in thought and nibbling on cold waffles, when the sound of the doorbell almost made me fall off my kitchen stool.

Both hands on the front door, I peered around the small crack to find Dex wearing an eager smile on the other side.

"You okay? You look like you expect someone to jump out of the bushes and attack?" he joked.

He didn't realize how right he was. With everything that had happened in my other life, it was exactly what part of me had expected. I tried to relax my stance and let the door drift open.

His eyes widened. "Whoa! I mean, *whoa*. Your hair! You look . . ." He fumbled, something Dex, athletic god loved by all, did not do very often. "Hot."

The corners of my mouth curled into a smile as I patted my newly blond hair. "Thanks."

"No, I don't think I'm being clear here. I mean, you look . . ." And then his eyes traveled down my body and up again, and I knew exactly what he was thinking.

"You're being plenty clear, Dex," I said.

His gaze flicked back to mine sheepishly. "I really can't wait until graduation. You and me, we're so right together." He pulled me into his arms hungrily. "Everyone envies what we have."

Something about what he said touched a nerve, and I felt uncomfortable in his arms. And unsure why. In many ways it was true—Dex and I *were* a golden couple. Our friends all spoke about us as if we were perfect for each other. Even Dex's controlling parents had given me the big vote of approval. Essentially we were a great fit, but it being so important to Dex that everyone knew it unsettled me.

But I didn't want to upset anything in this world right now, so I planted a quick kiss on his lips before moving casually out of his hold.

"I can't wait for graduation either," I said with a small smile.

He closed the distance again. "You know, we don't exactly *have* to. By the looks of it, your mom's not home." He raised his eyebrows suggestively.

In some ways, I agreed. I would have preferred less buildup around our "first time"—just getting it over with seemed an easier option. But at the same time . . . I found myself smiling back at him and saying, "I've planned the whole night, Dex. It's only days away. Patience."

He bit his lower lip. I could see he wanted to argue, but the gentleman in him won out and he nodded. "I can be patient when I know what's waiting at the end." A devilish smile played on his lips. "And anyway . . ."—he stepped back, putting a little space between us, for which I was grateful— "I came to see if you wanted to see a movie in the city."

My knees almost gave out under me. "The city . . . Boston?"

He rolled his eyes. "Yes, Sabine. The city. I know you don't love going into Boston, but they have the best movie theaters, and I thought it would be nice to get out of Wellesley for the day. What do you say?"

I usually avoided city outings like the plague, trying to stay off the streets of my other life. It felt wrong. On so many levels. One time curiosity had led me to the address of my other home, only to discover that while the house was still there, it wasn't the same. Just like everything in my two worlds, it was similar and yet just slightly "off." To start with, another family lived there, and they—or the previous owners—had attempted to build an addition. Since then, being anywhere near Roxbury unnerved me. I preferred to keep my two lives completely separate.

Dex watched me with a hopeful glint in his eyes. He would only pester me and ask questions if I refused, and

I hadn't been quick enough to blurt out an excuse. And besides all of that, I needed to do something that was normal. So I painted on a smile and said, "Sure. A movie sounds great."

Dex had planned the whole day, parking in a garage and then walking us toward a French bistro, where he'd already made a reservation. I tried not to let that irritate me and instead to embrace the sweetness of the gesture, but for some reason I failed to gush very convincingly.

The bistro was named *Le Bon Goût*—Good Taste—and it was one of the most expensive lunch spots in Boston. Dex was out to impress.

We talked about our plans for the year ahead. About Harvard. Dex slipped in the idea of us getting a place together after freshman year. I tried to hide my frozen reaction—after all, it was the natural progression. Just not usually so soon. It was even one that I wanted. At least . . . I thought I wanted.

Lunch was delicious, both of us feasting on fish and sharing a crème brûlée for dessert. I smiled, even laughed, and desperately tried to ignore the thoughts that threatened to dominate my mind: the downfall of my other life, the sadness of knowing my parents hadn't believed me, had not even given me the chance to explain.

I'd been locked away. And now I was polishing off crème brûlée.

The waiter came over and started to clear our plates.

"Bonne?" he asked.

I smiled. *"Oui, merci. Tout était délicieux!"* I replied, the words rolling off my tongue.

The waiter's eyes sparkled. *"Votre accent est presque parfait,"* he said, complimenting my French.

My smile widened. *"J'aime la langue. J'ai été l'apprentissage toute ma vie,"* I replied, telling the waiter that I loved the language and had been learning it my whole life.

He beamed in response. *"Oui. Pas assez de gens réalisent les avantages de parler une autre langue. Vous pouvez prendre la compétence partout avec vous."* He gave me a small bow even as I sat there, stunned by what he'd said.

The waiter turned to Dex. "Please excuse me. Your friend is very lovely and so few of our customers speak French so well."

Dex didn't look impressed. "Yeah. She's amazing." His expression grew sour and even a touch threatening as he added, "And she's my *girl*friend." He passed the waiter money for the check.

The waiter smiled, unperturbed. "Of course." He glanced at me again and left the table.

"What did he say?" Dex asked, trying to hide his irritation at not knowing. But I couldn't be bothered placating him.

"He said it was such an advantage to know another language. That a person could take the skill anywhere once they had it." I stared into space.

The waiter was right. Languages could go anywhere.

For the life of me, I couldn't say what movie Dex and I saw. I can't remember watching any of it—I was too busy trying to stay afloat in my flooded mind. Dex didn't seem to notice. Or perhaps he did and didn't know what was wrong. Either way, he drove me home afterward and I did my best to keep up with the small talk. By the time he pulled up in front of my house it was starting to get dark, and I felt guilty that I hadn't given him the kind of day, or attention, he'd obviously envisaged.

He walked beside me, unusually silent, to the front door.

When I stopped and turned to him, he tilted his head. "Are you okay, Sabine?"

I nodded. "I'm fine. I just think I'm still a little tired after the party on Friday night and . . . I don't know, nervous about graduation and finishing school."

He exhaled. "Yeah. Change can be daunting. But there's no point holding on to things just because it's scary to take the leap and move on. Once people do, I figure they rarely look back. You just have to know when the time is right."

The thing was, I totally agreed with what Dex was saying. I just didn't know what that meant for me—or my lives.

I leaned in toward him and he responded, closing the distance and giving me a kiss. It lasted eight seconds before I morphed it into a hug.

"On the other hand," Dex said cheekily, "sometimes it's important to hold on to the good things. And you're my good thing, Sabine. I'm never going to let you go. I'm looking forward to moving on . . . to *our* future. There are some things I'll be more than happy for us *both* to say good-bye to."

I was glad we were hugging so he couldn't see me cringe. I knew he was talking about our ever-nearing graduation night; that this was his way of telling me he hadn't done "it" before. I'd generally figured that out for myself. We'd been together for two years and Dex wasn't the type to cheat. He'd been understanding and patient and I wanted to give him all of me, but thoughts of us fumbling through our first time flashed into my mind and I felt my brow furrow. Then, out of nowhere, the image in my mind changed—the *person* in the image changed—surprising me.

I pushed the thought aside. *That* was not what I wanted. I don't know how Ethan had wormed his way into my head, but he wasn't going to stay there. He was *not* part of my plan—of any plan. Now, more than ever, I had to stay the course.

And that meant I had to finish the tests. There was no other option.

I pulled back from the embrace and looked into Dex's

eyes. "Me too," I said, because it was time to start saying good-bye to some things.

And that's when I decided that graduation night and being with Dex was exactly the right time to start the rest of my life. Because if the final test went the way I was starting to believe it would, then the day after in Roxbury . . . everything was going to change.

Mom was setting the table for dinner. Just two places, which was a relief. I didn't think I was up to seeing Ryan or Lucas tonight.

Mom was a great cook, but she preferred desserts. So we snacked on grilled cheese sandwiches followed by one of her famous peach tarts. Baking was one of the only things that really soothed Mom, so I always made sure I ate every last crumb and told her how delicious it was. If I could manage it, I'd even dig in for a second helping just to see the twinkle in her eye.

"So you and Dex are spending a lot of time together lately," Mom hinted.

I shoveled a large spoonful of tart into my mouth and nodded.

She rolled her eyes. "Fine, fine, you don't have to tell me about your boyfriend. I just want you to know that I think he's a lovely boy. The two of you are a good match." She lifted her glass to salute her approval.

I shoveled another spoon into my already full mouth and nodded between chews.

Mom smiled. "Okay, I get the picture. Anyway, I just wanted you to know I'm very . . ." She straightened in her seat. Mom never did these conversations well. You know, the ones with "feelings." She cleared her throat. "I'm glad you'll be going to Harvard. I would have missed you if you'd gone to a college far away." And with that she stood and cleared the plates.

"Love you too, Mom," I mumbled through a mouthful of tart as she walked to the kitchen.

Before I had a chance to swallow, my cell phone rang.

"Hello," I said, my voice barely audible.

"Sabine? Hello? Are you alive?"

Miriam.

"Maybe she's with Dex," Lucy snickered.

"Or under him," Miriam added.

It was time for our Sunday night conference call.

I rolled my eyes and swallowed as much tart as I could manage. "Peach tart, you tarts!"

They both laughed.

"Well, did he or did he not take you to some fancy restaurant in the city today and then to the back row at the movies?" Miriam demanded.

I sighed, thinking of the not-so-successful date.

"So . . . ," Lucy prodded, her voice sounding a little breathless. I could just imagine her sitting on her bed, bouncing up and down eagerly.

I considered telling them that it hadn't gone so well. But that would only get back to Dex one way or another, so instead I did what I did best.

I lied.

"It was great. Dex pulled out all the stops and took me to *Le Bon Goût* for lunch. You guys know how much I've wanted to go to that place. Best of all, even though I was still a bit tired from the party, Dex was just a sweetheart. He talked about Harvard, about our future . . ."

"About graduation night," Lucy chimed in.

I laughed. "He might've mentioned it. All in all, it was pretty perfect."

"Well, that's Dex for you; he *is* the perfect guy," Lucy said.

"So true," I agreed.

In theory.

"Aw, you two are so made for each other," Miriam said, boarding the we-all-love-Dex express. "You know that of everyone, you two are the ones who'll make it. I can just see it now—Mr. and Mrs. Dex Holdsworth."

"Ah," I stammered. "One step at a time."

"That's right, Miriam. At least give them a chance to have a test drive first," Lucy teased. I didn't respond to that. I didn't need to—they were too busy laughing.

I really didn't want to be having this conversation, but I kept my tone light and willing, and Lucy and Miriam maintained most of the banter. Eventually I fell into old habits and found myself giggling along with them—gossiping about potential scandals and what everyone else would be doing after school. If nothing else, my friends had given me back *me*—the Wellesley me—for a time at least. An hour later, exhausted from laughter and allegations, we hung up.

As I called out good night to Mom and headed to my room, I glanced at my watch and shuddered. Two hours until the Shift—and all I had left to do was think about what was waiting for me on the other side.

CHAPTER TWELVE

Wellesley, Sunday/
Roxbury, Monday

After I'd had a shower, flipped through the Harvard course guide, and even cleaned my room, I still had an hour to go and my hands were trembling. I'd never shifted knowing that I was going back to a drugged version of myself. The idea terrified me, and once again I had to run to the bathroom and throw my head over the toilet. Peach tart is disturbingly self-preserving.

I don't know how many times I was sick, only that it was a new record. As the minutes ticked by, my level of anxiety built. I had absolutely no way to prepare for what was to come, and no way of controlling it after the Shift.

At the best of times, I hated shifting from one life to the next. I'd worked hard over the years to perfect the routines that meant I had to face as little of this panic as possible. This time, even more so than shifting with Dex's tongue down my throat, that one small element of myself I usually had control over had been stolen from me.

I threw up again.

Finally, determined not to shift back to Wellesley tomorrow night to find myself hunched over the toilet mid-vomit, I forced myself to my feet and shuffled back to bed. I slid between the sheets just in time to take a series of shaky breaths before midnight struck and I shifted.

As soon as I was back in my Roxbury body I felt the dead weight. It was like being paralyzed while sinking in water. I couldn't move.

I. Couldn't. Move.

My eyes were shut and I couldn't access the muscles in my body that would open them. I wanted to thrash around, shake myself, slap myself. I wanted to scream. But my mind, completely alert, was imprisoned in an inert, silent chamber of a body. And then, whatever it was that was coursing through my system, the drug that had originally put me under started to catch up with me. No, chase me.

I don't know how long it took from when I shifted. Even though it felt like a lifetime, it was probably only seconds before the drug with its cotton-wool-like suffocation stole my conscious mind, melting it back into a sedated state.

Just before my mind slipped into oblivion, I thought I felt a pressure on my hand, as if . . . as if someone was *holding* it, squeezing tight.

A noise woke me. First my eyes fluttered, then my fingers twitched lethargically. I heard the noise again and realized it was voices. Slowly my mind cleared. I was in Roxbury, in the hospital. My parents had had me admitted. I'd been sedated. By Ethan.

I opened my eyes to a slit. Everything was blurry, but I could recognize my parents. As my vision sharpened I saw they were talking to two men: Dr. Meadows and a man I didn't know. Then I saw another figure beyond them, leaning against the door frame. I almost started when I realized it was Ethan. Slumped against the door jamb in his dark jeans and long-sleeved T-shirt, his hair as unruly as ever, he didn't look like he belonged.

"It's up to you, John," Dr. Meadows said, addressing my father. "If you want her transferred to another facility that's better equipped for this type of thing, I totally understand. Otherwise, she can stay here. Dr. Levi has offered his services and he's one of the best. He stops by on a daily basis to tend to some of the other patients, and he's offered to add Sabine to his rounds," he explained.

I stayed silent; I knew if they realized I was awake

they would take this discussion elsewhere and I needed to hear it.

"Dr. Levi, what do you think we're dealing with here?" my father said, as if asking a mechanic about a broken-down car.

"I'll need to spend some time with her to make any formal diagnosis. She's obviously experienced some kind of mental breakdown. She could be suffering from a number of things: hallucinations, substance abuse, compulsive lying, a personality disorder—"

"Schizophrenia?" my father interrupted.

"It's possible. We've sent her blood for testing. The easiest thing to identify or rule out is a drug problem. We'll start there."

"Christ."

"I assure you we'll take good care of her. The main thing at the moment is to ensure that she doesn't make another attempt on her life."

Someone cleared his throat. I opened my eyes a fraction again just as Ethan pushed off the wall. "Ah, Dr. Levi, I . . . I'm not so sure that's what she was doing. She appears to know full well the injuries inflicted were not life threatening. I dressed the wounds myself. They're nasty, but for someone who is currently on SW, she was incredibly careful to avoid major arteries."

"She broke her own wrist!" my father roared.

Ethan didn't seem bothered, which almost made me

smile. "She told me how it happened and I'm sure there were a number of witnesses that saw her fall."

I wanted to applaud Ethan and give my father the finger.

Dr. Levi chose this moment to intervene. "Do you have a suggestion for what we should be looking for, Ethan? Clearly you've managed to draw some information from her."

Ethan was silent for a moment and then he sighed. "I don't know. Like you said, she's clearly going through some kind of psychological trauma. She was petrified about being restrained last night, with a particular fear of midnight."

Something inside me sank to hear him analyzing me in such a detached way.

"What I want to know is when she became so disturbed that she created an entirely different world." Mom spoke up for the first time. She wasn't crying today. No, Mom had pulled herself together the way she always did, and now she was on a mission.

"Different *world*? Sorry?" Ethan said.

Mom straightened. "My daughter believes she lives in an alternate reality. She says she goes there every night. To another *life!*" she hissed.

"Oh my God," Ethan whispered. I felt the urge to jump up and tell him it wasn't like that, but really . . . it was. They just didn't realize it didn't make me delusional.

"Ethan, you might be of some assistance with this patient," Dr. Levi said.

My father scoffed. "He's a nurse. He's hardly equipped to be dealing with this."

"Actually, along with his nursing qualifications, Ethan has been studying psychiatry. He's one of my star pupils and has a very promising future ahead of—" Dr. Levi stopped mid-sentence before awkwardly starting up again. "Establishing a connection is key in these cases. If Sabine has already formed a bond with Ethan, he may be our best hope of getting her to open up."

"Ah, I don't think . . . I can't . . . No. She needs someone more . . . someone better," Ethan stammered.

"And I will be here," Dr. Levi continued as if Ethan hadn't spoken. "I'll assess her when she wakes up and hold daily sessions with her. But if Dr. Meadows does not object, Ethan will be in charge of her care during the night shift. It's not the most conventional method, but it's possibly the time she might feel the most comfortable opening up."

Ethan started up again. "Dr. Levi, I'm not the one to . . . You know why this is not . . . Please don't—"

"Ethan, what's the problem? You're here anyway. May as well keep busy." Dr. Levi shrugged as if it was all decided.

Before Ethan could object again I rolled over, keeping my eyes closed.

"She's starting to wake up," Dr. Meadows said.

No shit.

"Here are some of her things," Mom said quickly.

"We've checked it all as you requested," my father added.

"Thank you. Would you like to stay and talk to her?" Dr. Meadows asked.

"Er, no. We have to get back to the drugstore. We'll stop by in the next day or so," he said. I heard their footsteps as they walked toward the door.

"Very well. I assure you she is in good hands."

I heard my father stop. When he spoke his voice was low and private. "Dr. Levi, we're sure you understand. We work in this industry. It would not do well for too much of this to get out into the medical community . . . We need to protect our business."

"Discretion is a given, John." It was the right thing to say, but the reply sounded weary.

"Well then, let's keep her here," he said firmly.

"Certainly, John," Dr. Meadows said. "I'll see you out."

I waited until I was sure my parents were gone. They hadn't wanted to talk to me, but the feeling was definitely mutual. I didn't know if I could ever look at them again.

"You can open your eyes now," came Dr. Levi's voice from beside me.

I looked up at him. He was the only one who'd stayed behind. "How did you know?"

He smiled. "Years of experience. So, where should we go from here?"

I turned my head to the side and took a few shaky breaths. "Am I going to be tied down again?"

"I hope not. We don't like to use force to achieve our goals. Hopefully you will soon see that. We have four levels here, though you will be confined to the lower two. The second floor is the eating-disorders unit; drug and alcohol on the third; and the top floor is extended-stay and terminal care."

Wow, fun times.

"And where am I?" I didn't imagine they had a floor for multiple lives.

"This is the first floor; it treats mood disorders and provides intensive care. For now, you will be confined to your room until you earn privileges."

"Privileges?"

He nodded. "Once we start working together and you show a willingness to cooperate, we can add privileges to your daily program. Outside time, personal items, television, phone—those kinds of things."

He checked his watch while I stared at him in horror. Privileges? As in out-frickin'-side time? I was in prison!

There was a knock at the door and Ethan came in.

"I'm off now, but I'll be back tonight, Levi," he said.

"Thank you, Ethan. Leave a report for me in the morning."

With a nod he backed out, barely glancing in my direction before closing the door. I don't know why it upset me, but it did.

Dr. Levi turned back to me. "Right, well, I have rounds to make. We'll meet every day at ten a.m., starting today. The nurse will bring you to my office. Do you have any questions?"

I pressed my lips together to stop from crying. When I had myself under control I ventured, "My parents said they brought some stuff?"

He pointed to the small bag on the floor. "These items have been approved, along with the clothes you were wearing when they brought you in. They've been washed and placed in your closet."

I swallowed. "Is there a bathroom?"

"Yes, but you will be escorted there for now. You've been assigned a day nurse who will assist you."

He saw the tears welling in my eyes and sighed. "Sabine, it will get easier. Things seem at their worst right now, but we are going to help you find the clarity you need."

Clarity? Right. By sedating me, tying me up, and not letting me go to the bathroom on my own? Things really couldn't be clearer.

Instead of arguing, I turned my head toward the wall. He'd never get it, and I had no intention of trying to explain *anything* to him.

CHAPTER THIRTEEN

Roxbury, Monday

I didn't walk into Dr. Levi's office expecting reclining armchairs and mahogany bookshelves, but I definitely hadn't pictured a white-walled room—empty apart from two cheap-looking cane chairs, two cardboard boxes positioned as footstools, and a large dartboard hanging on the far wall.

My day nurse, who'd collected me from my prison cell, was the same woman who'd come to my house the previous day. She was still wearing too much blush and was smaller than I remembered. Perhaps holding a syringe added height. She ushered me into Dr. Levi's office, holding the door open for me.

"The doctor will be here in a moment. I'll be outside when your appointment is over to take you back to your room," she explained.

I gave her a look that wasn't pretty. She ignored it and shut me in the room. I didn't bother checking the door after she left—I knew it would either be locked, or she'd be waiting on the other side. Instead, I pulled one of the rickety cane chairs to the window and took a seat facing into the sun. It was a strategic move. I wasn't about to sit facing Dr. Levi so he could control the appointment, or me. I had attitude in this life and I'd been forgetting that. I needed to remember who I was here. With that in mind, I leaned back, slung my feet up onto the windowsill and closed my eyes.

The sun's heat was just starting to seep into my bones when the door opened and Dr. Levi walked in. I didn't so much as flinch; just kept my face toward the window.

"Hello, Sabine. It's good to see you again," he said, moving through the room.

I shrugged, but otherwise held position. "Budget cuts, huh?"

He gave a small laugh. "I just like it this way. Keeps the focus on the right things."

"What's that? Room echo?"

"Not exactly." I heard the other chair creak as he sat down. "What do you think should be the focus in this room?"

Here we go.

I decided this was as good a cutoff point as any. I folded my arms across my chest.

After a stretch of silence, Dr. Levi sighed. "All right then, Sabine. I take it you're not in the mood to chat today."

It was something he was going to have to get used to.

"Would you like to tell me about your other life, Sabine? I'd like to hear about it. Anything you say in this room will remain between us."

Yeah, right. I could just see it all playing out, where it would end. Me tied to the bed again. Not going to happen.

I had to give Dr. Levi credit—he didn't seem surprised. I heard him get out of his cane chair and then a whooshing sound followed by a thud. I forced myself not to look. Was he seriously going to play darts for the whole hour?

Yep. That's exactly what he did.

And for my part, I stayed in place by the window. It wasn't until the whizzing sounds stopped that I cracked open an eye to glance in his direction.

"Perhaps tomorrow we can talk," he said, throwing the loose darts onto his chair. He smiled. "Or maybe you'd like to try your luck against me at darts."

When I didn't respond, he shrugged. "I'll see you tomorrow, Sabine. Ethan will be stopping by to see you this evening. Do you have any objections to him passing on his notes to me?"

Silence.

Dr. Levi clicked his pen a couple of times. "I'm sorry, Sabine, but this is one question I will need an answer to before you leave the room."

I closed my eyes again, wanting the appointment over with. "I don't care what he tells you," I mumbled.

He scribbled something on the otherwise untouched page of his clipboard and opened the door. "Macie, can you please see Sabine back to her room?"

"Of course, Dr. Levi," Macie responded, walking up to me. "Sabine, let's go."

I drew in one last sun-warmed breath and stood up to follow her.

As we walked down the hall, she watched me carefully, as if half-expecting me to bolt. Honestly—I considered it.

"An early lunch will be delivered to your room. Would you like to use the bathroom before you go back?" she asked in a flat tone.

I sighed, but said, "Sure."

The bathroom reminded me of the one in our gym at school. Open shower stalls and a row of toilets. I headed straight for a toilet stall.

"You'll need to leave the door unlocked," Macie said, positioning herself by the sinks.

I stared at her.

"You can pull the door closed," she explained. "But if I feel the need, I will open it at any time. Until you are off SW, no locks. It's the rules."

I gritted my teeth and went into the stall. It was utterly humiliating to have someone waiting right outside the door who could, at any time, decide to "open sesame." Needless to say, I did my business quickly.

Macie walked me back to my room, returning when my lunch was delivered to watch me eat every mouthful of my sandwich. By the time she had checked the tray to make sure I hadn't palmed the plastic wrap—probably in case I had some grand suffocation plan—I was seething. This should not have been happening to me.

"It gets easier," Macie offered, her expression softening slightly.

I didn't respond.

"Room checks are on the hour during the day and randomly at night," she said as a parting comment.

Great.

Once alone, I sorted through the small bag of belongings my parents had left. I almost laughed at the clothes they'd chosen. Not a single one of my favorite minis. My old stuffed bear was in the mix, my pillow, a ten-dollar bill with a Post-it note that said "vending machine money," and—surprise, surprise—my new notebook.

Stunned, I opened the book, not sure what to expect. It was blank. The pages I'd already written on had been ripped out. Anger reaching overload, I threw the book at the wall.

Nice one, Mom.

There was a quick rap on the door. It opened a fraction and Macie's head popped through the gap. "All okay?"

I collected the book from the floor. "Fine. Do you have a pen?" I asked.

She paused. "No pens, but I can bring you a marker."

I nodded. "Thanks."

When Macie returned with the marker she informed me that dinner would be at 5:30 p.m.

"What? No one eats dinner that early!" I argued. Were they kidding?

Macie just shrugged and left.

For the millionth time, I had to hold back the urge to scream. I sat on the edge of the bed and stared at my notebook, marker in hand. I needed to regroup. But where did I go from here? Being locked up had not been part of the plan.

Hours drifted by, but the page in front of me remained blank and my frustration only intensified.

Eventually I gave up and decided to change out of my hospital gown.

I glanced at the clothes my parents had sent and decided to stick with the outfit I'd been wearing when they brought me in. As I yanked my skirt off the top of the pile, something fell to the floor.

I crouched down and picked up my silver butterfly necklace. Hands shaking, I glanced at the door. It hadn't been that long since the last room check, so I dared to unscrew the top.

Mouth agape, I stared at the ground-up digoxin and almost laughed. Of all the things to allow in this room with me, somehow *this* had slipped through. I replaced the top on the butterfly and dangled it from my hand, trying to figure out why they hadn't confiscated it. Maybe they'd decided the dainty chain was barely strong enough to hold the butterfly, let alone cause any damage. And what could one really do to hurt themselves with a butterfly pendant?

I put the necklace around my neck, tucking it beneath my T-shirt, and finished getting dressed just before Macie came back.

"Are you ready to go to dinner?"

I nodded and followed her to the food hall, my hand going often to the butterfly beneath my shirt. Finally I felt empowered again. Finally I had the chance to follow this through—to find out one way or the other if there was a choice ahead for me.

Dinner was much like lunch, just in a large, empty cafeteria. I now understood why I was eating so early. Apparently I couldn't be trusted in company yet. Macie told me that I would integrate over the next day or so. I could barely wait.

After forcing down a few mouthfuls of rubbery lasagna, I grabbed a banana and a carton of milk. What I really wanted was a soda, but there were only three drink options: water, milk, or orange juice.

On our way out of the cafeteria, I grabbed a bottle of water and gestured to Macie. "Can I take this back to my room?"

She nodded. "That should be fine."

"You sure about that? I mean, I could always try to drown myself in the bottle. You know, get all Alice-in-Wonderland tiny and leap right in," I sniped.

Macie raised an eyebrow. "Would you like me to reconsider?"

"No, I'm just helping you look at all the angles." I smiled. It was probably stupid, since I really did want the bottle of water, but I couldn't help myself. Luckily, Macie took the high road and ignored me.

When we got back to my room, two guys were rummaging through it. One was looking under my bed. The other was actually on a ladder, searching the ceiling cavities. I recognized the one on the ladder as Mitch, the guy I'd kicked in the nose. When he saw me, his eyes narrowed.

"You'll have to sit in the chair until we've finished."

My mouth dropped open as the other guy upended my bag and began spreading out my underwear.

"What? Why? You can't . . ." I shot a look at Macie. "You've basically been with me all day! What do you expect to find?"

Macie's face was expressionless. "Sit in the chair, Sabine. It's protocol."

My hand flew in the air. "You have to be kidding me. He needs a *ladder* to get up there, so how the hell do you think I could've gotten up there to hide things?"

"Sit," she ordered.

I shot daggers at her. Macie simply returned my gaze, as if daring me to say anything else.

I stomped over to the chair, my hand wringing the bottle of water as I watched them rifle through my few measly belongings. They searched every corner, stripped my bed, overturned the mattress then inspected it for any tampering before setting it right and remaking it. Then all eyes turned to me.

"Sabine, you need to stand up now," Mitch said. I eyed his black-and-blue nose. I'd gotten him good and it made me feel a little better. He glanced at Macie. "You'll need to pat her down, Mace." I noticed his tone changed considerably when he spoke to her.

Macie nodded, smiling at him before turning back to me. "It'll only take a second. Stand with your legs apart and arms out."

I stood up and crossed my arms. "And if I don't?"

She shot Mitch a look. She seemed to see past his swollen nose to something more. Can't imagine what; he gave me the creeps. "Then we'll have to sedate you again. It's for your own safety."

Mitch looked smug. His ego was bruised and he was gunning for a second round with me. It was that, along with the fear of being put under again, that finally made me reluctantly move my feet apart, spread my arms wide, and let Macie pat me down.

Nothing.

She didn't even spare a glance for the silver butterfly around my neck. Now I was the one hiding the smug smile. Not my fault if they're sloppy.

Macie stepped back. "Okay, all clear, Sabine. I'll see you tomorrow."

"Can I use a phone?"

"Phone privileges come from Dr. Levi. You can ask him tomorrow."

Of course they did. Even criminals were permitted one phone call.

The male nurses filed out.

"Are you locking me in?"

Macie's sympathetic smile didn't fool me. "No, but it's lights out soon and you're not permitted to leave your room without an escort. Trust me when I say it's not worth breaking the rules. Do you understand?"

"And I thought you said things were going to get easier." I threw her my own false smile.

"They will. You just have to work with us instead of against us. Believe it or not, we're doing what's best for you."

Deflated, I sat on the edge of the bed and gnawed at my lip. "What about a clock? Is there any way to get a clock in my room?"

Macie shrugged and headed out of the room with a casual "We can look into it tomorrow."

"What time is it?" I called out, now panicked.

"Almost seven," she answered, and the door clicked shut.

CHAPTER FOURTEEN

Roxbury, Monday

I changed into the nightshirt my parents had packed, grateful I didn't have to get back into a hospital gown, and lay in bed. Eventually a nurse walked through the hall calling "lights out." Soon after, the main lights switched off and the small fluorescent bulb in the ceiling flickered on. I almost laughed. Could I seriously not be trusted to have complete darkness?

I sobered when I realized that, on this occasion, they were actually right.

As soon as the noises of the ward settled down and I was confident I'd be able to hear approaching footsteps, I slid out of bed. I figured it was about 8:00 p.m. Too early to do anything with the digoxin yet, but judging from last night's shift change, Ethan would arrive soon and I didn't know how much of an opportunity I would get to organize things once he did. I had to have everything ready to go.

First, I opened my bottle of water, fumbling with my infuriating cast, and gulped down half the bottle's contents. Then I pulled off my butterfly necklace and tried to keep my hands steady as I unscrewed it and carefully emptied the powder into the bottle, swirling it to dissolve all of the tiny granules.

It wasn't perfect. The drug was not designed to dissolve, and even after I replaced the lid and gave it a good shake there was still a layer of tiny white grains that settled to the bottom. But it would have to do. I got under the covers and tucked the bottle out of sight.

When I picked up the marker my hands were trembling again.

What was I thinking? Was I really going to do this?

I took a deep breath and ran a hand through my hair as the enormity of what was about to happen washed over me. This was crazy. But like it or not, it was my only shot. The best thing I could do for myself now was ensure I was as ready as possible. I gripped the marker and wrote one word on the strip of white cast that covered the heel of my palm.

I was putting the marker back on the nightstand when I heard footsteps. I considered drinking some of the mixture, but if my calculations were right, it was still too early. I'd have to find a chance later on. I rearranged my blankets, making sure the bottle was still well hidden, and prayed room searches were over for the night.

I could tell the minute Ethan walked in that something

about him was different. Calmer. He was in jeans and a loose black shirt, his dark hair still a mess, but there was a change in the way he held himself. The tension in his shoulders and the lines around his eyes were gone.

"Do you mind if I come in?" he asked, in a way that suggested it was actually a question rather than a token gesture.

"Does it matter?"

"I'd prefer we started on the right foot tonight," he said, and seemed to mean it. But I was stuck in attitude mode and couldn't bother to reply. He clearly took my silence for agreement, because after a moment he walked into the room and sat down in the armchair.

"How are your wounds? Your wrist? Are you in any pain?"

I swallowed, unsure why his husky tone affected me. "No," I managed.

"Would you like me to re-dress them for you?"

"I get a choice this time?" I blurted.

He gave a small smile. "Yes."

"No, then."

He nodded and ran a hand through his messy hair.

The silence stretched and I found it hard to look in his direction. I didn't want those eyes boring into me, trying to search out my secrets. I kept thinking about the moment I'd shifted back into my drugged body. How just before the drugs had claimed my consciousness I'd felt something, *someone*, squeezing my hand. Had I imagined it?

"Thanks," I said, my voice breaking on the word.

He seemed taken aback. "For what?"

"For taking away the restraints last night."

"Oh. How did that go for you? Midnight, I mean," he said, inching toward me in his chair.

I couldn't help it, I laughed. I hated being played. "I know they told you, Ethan. I heard you all in here this morning."

He shrugged. "I wondered if you were awake."

I rolled my eyes. "Whatever. Look, you clearly don't like me and I don't particularly have generous thoughts toward you."

He grinned at that, which only irritated me more.

"Let's just cut to the chase and save ourselves all the drama. There's nothing you can do or say that's going to 'fix' me," I added the air quotes for emphasis, "and I have nothing to say to you that you're going to be able to get your head around. So why don't you just fill in your charts, say whatever it is you need to say to not get in trouble, and go back to your break room or wherever it is that you would rather be."

Ethan watched me, unperturbed. He paused as if contemplating everything I'd just said. I braced for the comeback.

But he just stood up and said, "Okay, then," before heading straight out the door, closing it behind him.

What?

I had so not been expecting that.

Suddenly I was alone again. I couldn't understand why

I felt so terrible. I did *not* care what Ethan thought of me, or about spending time with him. I definitely didn't need to have him know the truth about my life, lives, whatever. And yet . . . I couldn't stop watching the door, waiting to see if he would come back.

Every so often I heard him walking up and down the hall, opening and closing doors. Room checks. After it had been quiet for a while, I gave up expecting a return visit. At what I thought must be close to 11:00 p.m., I decided to drink the first half of my concoction.

I almost spat out the first mouthful. It was offensively bitter—the flavor assaulting my taste buds and making me gag. Somehow, I managed to keep that mouthful and subsequent ones down, wishing the whole time I had something to chase it with to take the edge off.

After drinking half the mixture I waited awhile to make sure it would stay down, then finished off the rest and slipped the empty bottle under my pillow. Just as I settled myself in bed again, Ethan reappeared.

"Not tired?" he asked, walking toward me.

"Waiting," I said without thinking.

"For what?"

I shrugged. "A better life."

He threw me an odd look.

"So what's your deal anyway? I never see you in a uniform. Are you really a nurse, or are you a student?"

He must have seen it as an invitation because he repositioned himself in the chair. "I'm a licensed nurse and med—I was a med student. Now I work nights here."

"To pay the bills," I said, repeating what I'd heard him tell Mitch. He didn't miss it and smiled. I bit down on the return smile that threatened my lips.

I guessed he must have had some big bills to pay if he'd dropped out of med school.

"Something like that." He shrugged. "Anyway, I like it. I'm a night person. How about you?"

I rolled my eyes. "Smooth."

He laughed and the sound filled the room. An easy, liquid sound that moved its way right through me. When he finished, he looked at me closely, tilting his head.

"You said last night that you would tell me, if I truly wanted to know." He leaned forward, elbows on his knees.

"That was then. Things have changed."

"Ah."

"What does that mean?" I replied sharply.

"It sounds like you've given up on the world."

I sat up a little, noticing that the lighting in the room seemed different. I crossed my arms. "Not on the world—on people. And I *get* that that makes me sound insane, but you have no idea what my lives have been like."

"So tell me," he said, not missing a beat.

"Why?" I answered softly. "It doesn't matter anymore."

He raised an eyebrow. "Do you prefer your other life?"

I looked at him, trying to figure out his angle.

"I guess things are pretty good there," he went on.

"No. Actually things are hard there too."

"Do you have a sister there as well? What's your sister's name here?"

I narrowed my eyes. "Maddie," I said, unable to hold off the pang of guilt. She was hands down the best thing about this life. "And no, I have two brothers. Ryan and Lucas."

He watched me, no doubt looking for telltale crazy signs.

I huffed. Something about this guy got under my skin. "Whatever," I said, knowing I was on shaky ground. "All right, Ethan, get out your pen."

He didn't, but I kept talking anyway. I don't know why, but once I opened my mouth I couldn't seem to stop. I told him how the Shift worked. What it was like to have to live every day twice, but have no two days ever the same. To go through every year of school twice, get my period for twice as long each month, know that in some ways I was almost as old as my parents. It all just came out. When the verbal onslaught finished, and he'd had a few moments to get over his shock, he leaned closer to me.

"So no one can ever know for sure? They can't see you 'shift,' as you call it?"

I sighed. That was all that mattered—proof beyond all

reasonable doubt. "You were with me at midnight last night. What do you think?"

His eyes widened. "How do you know I was with you at midnight? You were sedated."

I thought of the hand that had held on to mine, that had seemed to anchor me somehow. "I . . . I don't know. I just . . . I thought I felt someone holding my hand when I shifted back. My mind was awake for a few seconds before the drugs caught up with me. It's hard to explain. I still don't even . . ."

He bit his lower lip. Once again, I found myself mesmerized by the action, staring at the fullness of his mouth, the way his teeth let his lip slowly slide back into place.

"So what did you do yesterday in your other world?" he asked.

"I went to lunch and a movie. I chatted to the French waiter—he liked talking with someone who could speak French—then Dex drove me home. I had dinner with Mom and talked to my friends on the phone. That's pretty much it. Frankly it was just nice not being tied down and knocked out."

He let the dig slide. "You can speak French?"

"Yeah. I learned in my other life. I speak it fluently there."

He nodded slowly. "But not here."

My eyebrows pulled together in frustration. "Of course I can speak it here, but I don't because I've never *learned* it in this life. It would be kind of weird if I just started rambling in French one day."

"Right," he said, disbelief painted on his face.

I'd had just about enough. "My memory comes with me, Ethan." And for the first time in my Roxbury life, I began to speak in another language. *"Si vous voulez que je parle français pour vous le prouver à vous, je peux parler toute la journée. Et pendant que j'y suis, je n'ai aucune idée pourquoi je ne peux pas cesser de regarder vos lèvres!"* My comeback was delivered in perfect French. You can't fake that accent.

Ethan looked stunned. "What . . . What did you say?"

I shrugged. "Just that if you need me to speak in French to prove it to you, I can speak it all day long." I didn't add I might have also said I found it odd that I couldn't stop staring at his lips.

He did the head-tilt thing again, as if trying to work me out. I was suddenly self-conscious, wondering if he knew I hadn't translated everything.

As he paced around the room, I realized the waiter in *Le Bon Goût* had been right. Once you learned a language, you really could take it anywhere.

"So," he said, between paces, "if you can do that, can you get lottery numbers from one world and bring them back in time to win in the other? Or . . . change a disaster, prevent a car crash or something?" His tone was still dubious, as though he was only humoring me, but I was sure I'd heard a hint of something more, a new interest brewing.

I shook my head, noticing how much my vision was

now playing tricks on me. I held out my hand discreetly and saw the tremble. The digoxin was working its way into my system.

"Sabine?" Ethan prompted.

"Oh no. It's not like that. No get-rich-quick perks or superhero opportunities. There are crossovers, but each world is different. The only things you can fully rely on to remain consistent are language, math, materials, chemicals— stuff like that."

"Weather?" he suggested.

"Seasons, but not the daily forecast."

"Places, buildings?"

"Are often similar, but slightly altered. Which makes sense to me, since I guess the people who live or work in them would be different."

Ethan looked at me strangely. "You're slurring, Sabine."

I tensed, but he was right. I was starting to lose my grip on things and I was feeling increasingly nauseated. I closed my eyes and swallowed, willing my stomach to keep the medication down. When I opened them, the light in the room had a yellowish tinge. I glanced up; there was a halo surrounding the small ceiling light.

"Sabine?" Ethan persisted.

"Must be tired," I said, carefully enunciating each word.

"Should I go?"

"Ah . . . maybe not."

He nodded, looking both concerned and relieved.

I noticed each and every time his teeth bit down on his lower lip and internally chastised myself for wondering what those lips would feel like on my own.

"Have you always hated it?" he asked.

"It's never been easy. At first, when I was a kid, I didn't realize it didn't happen to everyone. Then, when I started to understand, I just got . . . scared. I thought I'd done something wrong and didn't want to tell anyone. Eventually I learned there was no way to control it, so I accepted I had to live with it. I learned to be the person I was expected to be in each world and forget who I was in the other."

"Sounds hard."

I nodded. "I got used to it. Didn't think there was any other way. Until now."

"Because now the physical connection isn't traveling between the worlds?" he asked, disbelief shining through again.

My vision was getting worse and I had to close my eyes a few times to regain my focus. "What time is it?"

"About 11:40. You're sweating, Sabine," he said, inching closer.

"Hot," I replied, but my heart was racing and I was starting to feel breathless.

Ethan was watching me, but I couldn't hold his gaze.

"Just let it go, Ethan. Nothing I say is going to convince

you. I can't bring things back magically or foresee the future. All I have is my memories, and me. So unless I can help you there, we're at a stalemate."

He smiled. "How about you come back at midnight in," he looked at his watch, "seventeen minutes and tell me how to say 'My name is Sabine and I live in two worlds and I want Ethan to believe me' in . . ." He thought about it, his smile widening. "Can you only speak French?"

I nodded slowly, not really following. My whole body was going into overdrive.

"Okay, come back and say that in German."

I didn't respond.

"Sabine?"

I could feel my eyes rolling back, my head falling to the pillow. Then a hand on my forehead.

"Sabine?" Ethan's tone had changed. "Why are you so pale?" His hand moved to the back of my neck. "You're wet all over."

Before I could say anything my body took over, rolling to the side and convulsing as I threw up on the floor. Something fell to the ground as I did.

Ethan gasped, holding me up. He righted me on the bed, then bent quickly to grab the object from the floor. "Jesus Christ, Sabine! What was in this bottle?" he yelled.

"Water," I stammered before leaning over the edge to vomit again.

"Tell me what was in it," he said urgently.

But I couldn't answer. My whole body was shaking and the retching wouldn't stop.

Ethan reached over me and pressed a button on the wall. An alarm sounded. He grabbed my right hand and felt for a pulse. The meds were kicking in harder than I'd planned.

Knowing I might not get another chance, I opened my fist, revealing the inside of my cast, and held it out to him.

"Digibind?" he said.

Silence.

Then . . .

"*Digibind!* Jesus, that's an antidote, isn't it? Sabine, what have you done? *What have you done?*"

I couldn't talk. I just stared into his deep-blue eyes and let them be my anchor.

My door crashed open, people rushed in. Hands moved over me, things were wrapped around my arm. Something cold was on my chest.

Ethan shouted even as his eyes stayed locked on mine. "She's OD'd. I think she's taken digoxin. She needs Digibind!"

Someone was pushing him away. I could feel his grip on my hand loosening. With every ounce of will I had, I held on to him.

He stayed. Squeezed back.

Whoever was pushing things over my chest yelled out,

"Her heart's going into failure. Somebody get the Digibind, now!"

Hands were all over me. An oxygen mask was strapped to my face.

But it was too late.

Blinking into Ethan's desperate eyes, I shifted.

CHAPTER FIFTEEN

Wellesley, Monday

My body heaved convulsively as I scrambled off my bed and fell to the floor on all fours. Tears dripped from my eyes as the pressure built and I lurched forward, vomiting nothing but bile.

Oh God. It hadn't worked.

I was in Wellesley.

The test failed.

I was dying here too.

What had I done?

I retched again and slumped onto the ground, panting weakly when there was nothing left.

Is this what it had all come to?

The moment, the choices, over?

Had I fooled myself into this?

I gasped and hiccuped through silent, fear-filled sobs. I would die alone. After all this, I would have no one with me.

My heart was pounding in my chest. But despite my panicked thoughts, I noticed that my breathing had started to slow down. I opened my eyes. My bedroom was mostly dark, but my bedside lamp, still on, appeared normal. I stared into the light—just a normal globe-white glow. No halos surrounding it. No yellow tinge.

I dragged myself into a sitting position with my back resting against the side of my bed. With each breath I was feeling calmer, more . . . myself. I put my hand over my chest and felt my pounding heartbeat, but as time went on, the rhythm seemed to stabilize.

Hands shaking, I stayed where I was and waited.

I don't know how long I sat there, but eventually I had enough confidence to attempt to stand. My knees wobbled and I held on to the side of the bed until I managed to straighten up. But with each passing moment, I felt stronger and my footing was surer.

There was only one explanation.

I'd been suffering from some kind of mental overlap. The effects of the last hour on my mind—its expectations of what *should* have been happening to my body given what had just happened in my other life—had taken over and were causing a physical reaction.

"I'm okay, I'm okay," I whispered, coaxing myself, over and over. "It's just in my mind, all in my mind."

Somewhere, in another world, perhaps currently frozen

in time, I was overdosing on prescription meds. My heart was in major overdrive, my vision yellow, but here . . . my chest beat steadily and, after the initial reaction to the shock, there was nothing to indicate I wasn't all systems go. I took in more deep breaths as I tried to let the knowledge sink in, and eventually shocked myself by smiling.

I was right.

I clapped a hand over my mouth.

I was right!

The physical was completely separate. What happened to me in one life no longer affected the other.

Too exhausted to process any further, too confused to know if I wanted to laugh or cry, I cleaned up the mess I'd made on the floor, then collapsed back onto my bed and, surprisingly, fell into a deep sleep.

"Sabine! Are you up?" Mom called out.

I rolled over and groaned. I could have done with more sleep, like a week's worth.

"Yes!" I called back so she wouldn't come in.

I sat up and rubbed my eyes. My stomach was aching— from muscle strain but also hunger. I was throwing up more than I was eating of late.

"Hurry up, or you'll be late for school," she yelled from down the hall.

School. I hadn't thought about it for days. As a result of my admission to the hospital, I'd missed Monday at school in my other life. I wondered if they'd let me go back at all before graduation. Unlikely, given how insane they thought I was— and what I'd just done to confirm their theories. I groaned again and headed for the bathroom, hoping a hot shower would help wash away the other me and let me be exactly who I needed to be in this world.

When I was wrapped in a towel, hair and makeup done, I came out of my bathroom to find Mom waiting, an excited smile lighting up her face. It didn't take long to see why. Lying on top of my bed was a gorgeous sunflower-yellow pleated skirt and a short-sleeved cream cashmere top.

"Oh, Mom, they're beautiful," I said, fingering the edge of the soft cashmere.

Her smile widened. "I wanted you to have something nice to start your last week of school with."

She waited while I dressed and then nodded, tugging on the hem of the skirt until it was just right.

"There. Perfect."

I slipped into a pair of heels and assessed myself in the mirror. Mom was right. With my new blond hair, the outfit suited me perfectly; I looked like a new me. "Thanks, Mom. This is exactly what I needed," I said, smiling as I spun around.

"You're welcome. Actually I was thinking maybe we

could meet up after school. Grab a coffee, like old times," she said, looking hopeful.

"Oh, sure. Sounds good." My phone beeped with a message.

Mom gave a relieved smile and kissed me quickly on the cheek before heading out of my room.

I checked my messages. Miriam.

I'm coming up the driveway!

Sure enough, when I peeked through the curtains to my balcony, I could see her white SUV coast to a stop.

I grabbed my cherry-red Alexander Wang bag and headed for the front door, stopping only to grab two of Mom's muffins and an apple on the way. I desperately needed to recharge.

Slipping into Miriam's car, I handed her a muffin.

"Ooh, cinnamon?" she guessed, grabbing the muffin and taking a quick bite. "Low fat?"

"Naturally." Mom was devout when it came to her muffins and fat content.

Then Miriam looked up and her full mouth dropped open. "Oh. My. God. Your *hair*!" She dropped the muffin and started clapping and jumping in her seat.

I laughed, but kept my cool.

Once she'd settled down, her eyes narrowed playfully. "You know you owe this all to me. You finally came to your senses and took my beauty advice."

"Yes, it was all you, Miriam," I replied drily.

She gave a self-satisfied nod and we both laughed.

Lucy was waiting for us at the front entrance of our school. Once she'd stopped hyperventilating about my new hair, we entered the halls together for the start of our last week.

"You know, I think I'm actually going to miss this place," Lucy said.

"Well, we do rule the school. It isn't going to be fun starting at the bottom again. At least we're naturally talented at moving up the ranks. It won't be long," Miriam said confidently.

I nodded. "And even though we're going to different colleges, we'll still talk every day and see each other every second weekend. Remember the schedule."

We had drafted a calendar that showed when each of us would visit the others at their new schools. If nothing else, the three of us were determined to stay friends. Drifting apart was not an option.

Lucy and Miriam nodded and we all linked arms—until Brett sneaked up from behind and tossed a very unhappy Miriam over his shoulder. Lucy and I laughed as Miriam hit Brett on the back, demanding to be put down. Everything was just as it should be, and when Lucy and I parted ways to go to our first class of the day, I did my best to concentrate on the day ahead of me rather than the one I'd just left behind.

But some things are easier said than done.

It wasn't until I was sitting down at lunch and Dex clicked his fingers in front of me, saying, "Earth to Sabine? What's with you today?" that I even realized half the day had passed.

I covered up as best I could. I sent him a sly smile and flicked a pasta shell in his direction, which led to him dragging me onto his lap. I laughed and we all joked around as we signed each other's yearbooks. But I felt increasingly distant; something was nagging at me that I couldn't put my finger on.

When Dex walked me to my final class, he leaned in to kiss me in the corridor. I think we made it to around seven seconds before the kiss even registered. When it did, the intimacy suddenly felt unbearable.

The strangest part was, for the first time I wondered if the problem wasn't me, so much as *us*—Dex and me—as a couple. Then there was the image of someone with messy dark hair that had surfaced during the kiss, causing a shiver to run through my body before I managed to shut it down.

This was crazy. I was just confused with everything that was going on. Dex and I were perfect together. Everyone said so. As a couple, we were golden.

"Do you want to do something this afternoon?" Dex asked, his voice low and intimate.

"Oh, I can't. Mom wants to take me out after school." I rolled my eyes for effect. "She's getting all nostalgic."

Dex smiled, his hand moving up and down my back. I forced myself to stay there and relax, while mentally chastising my runaway mind.

"You know, everyone is looking at you," he said.

I raised my eyebrows.

"That new hair has earned you quite a few admirers."

I smiled sweetly. "Jealous?" I teased.

He pulled me closer—a fast, possessive move. "Not at all," he growled and kissed me again quickly before stepping back. "You're mine and everyone knows it." He planted another kiss on my forehead. "You better get to class."

I nodded, a little thrown by his behavior.

Final class of the day was French. Mademoiselle Moreau seemed to accept no one was really concentrating on classes this week. Essentially school was finished. This last week was more a matter of saying our good-byes to teachers, getting our yearbooks signed, and preparing for the graduation ceremony. She told us to put away our books, and simply asked each of us to take turns explaining in French what we'd be doing during our break and what our plans were for the year ahead. If only she knew what a complicated question that was for me.

Luckily, she started from the opposite side of the room, and I knew it was unlikely we would get through everyone before it was my turn. Just in case, I jotted down a few points. As I did, I flashed back to the night before—to Ethan, smiling, joking about my coming back and speaking in German. Suddenly, instead of summarizing a future I wasn't even sure I would have, I was scribbling something else entirely.

My name is Sabine. I live in two worlds. I want Ethan to believe me.

I hoped I'd remembered it right. I was sure it was the general gist of what he'd said. When the bell rang and everyone filed out singing, *"Au revoir, Mademoiselle Moreau!"* I approached the front desk.

"Excuse me, mademoiselle, I was wondering if you might be able to point me in the right direction to get a German translation?"

Mademoiselle Moreau glanced up from her papers. *"Parler en français, Sabine."*

"Je suis désolée," I apologized, then repeated my request, this time in French.

She shook her head. *"Je ne sais comment me présenter en allemand,"* she said, explaining that she only knew how to introduce herself in German.

I took out my pen and wrote down her translation for "My name is Sabine." *Mein Name ist Sabine.*

"Merci beaucoup, mademoiselle," I said, and headed for the door.

"Sabine!" she called out.

I turned to face her.

"There are lots of translation sites online, but they are not so reliable. The library will have a good German translation dictionary."

"*Oui, merci,*" I said, not daring to reply in English.

I rushed through the halls, keen to collect my bag and get straight to the library. Miriam and Brett were waiting by the lockers.

"Hey, we're going to the mall. Want to come?" Miriam asked, while Brett snuggled her from behind. For some reason, their easy togetherness grated on me today.

"Ah, no," I said, feigning disappointment. "I have to go meet Mom for a coffee." And then, in case they decided to hound me, I smiled and added, "But maybe after."

"And let me guess, you'd like to be chauffeured to your coffee date?" she offered.

I did a quick calculation. I was sure I could have coffee with Mom and still make it to the library in town before it closed.

I threw Miriam a sheepish look and she rolled her eyes. "Come on."

Sala's Patisserie was the best coffee shop in Wellesley—famous for their afternoon teas. By the time I walked in, Mom was already seated, a tiered cake stand of finger sandwiches and delicate pastries in front of her. My stomach rumbled, still hungry despite my pasta-salad lunch.

I sat down, ordered a mocha, and let Mom do all the talking—which was exactly the way she wanted it, pausing just long enough to enjoy dainty mouthfuls of the miniature éclairs and tarts, which she dissected and critiqued from every angle. For my part, I devoured the too-small sandwiches and what was left of the pastries and tried to marshal my scrambled thoughts.

For the first time in forever, I was going to try to actually prove it—that I lived in two worlds. There had always been reasons, good ones, to keep it a secret, but those didn't apply anymore. Not in the same way.

As each minute passed, I grew more determined. Ethan didn't believe me. He didn't *want* to believe me. But what would he do if I managed to deliver what he'd so easily joked about? For the first time in my life, I wanted someone to believe me. And not just anyone . . .

Ethan.

The thought of seeing his face when I spoke those lines in German ignited a hope in me I'd never dared entertain.

Of course, when I remembered the way I'd left things in Roxbury, my confidence faltered. All of this would rely on me being . . . Well, I'd need to be . . . alive.

When I shifted tonight, knowing how much digoxin had been in my system, I couldn't be sure what would be waiting for me. Had I played it too close to the line? Taken too high a dose? Would I even get my chance to show Ethan the truth and make him believe me?

"Sabine? What's wrong with you? You look like you're about to explode out of your seat," Mom said, her eyes going to my bouncing legs.

"I . . . er . . . I just need to get to the library before it closes!" I blurted. "There's a book I need before graduation." I shrugged and pushed back my chair, knowing I couldn't wait any longer. "You don't mind if I catch up with you at home, do you?"

I had to try. I had to find a way to make him believe me. At least one person in my worlds was going to damn well know me, know the truth. Someone *had* to.

Mom's shoulders dropped. Clearly she'd been hoping for more than just coffee. She'd probably had visions of a shopping trip afterward. I felt a pang of guilt, but there was no way I was going to give up this opportunity. When Mom gave a sigh and nodded, I leaned down and gave her a tight hug. I'd make it up to her later.

"Thanks, Mom," I said, and then I was out of there, headed straight for the library in the center of town—straight toward proof of my crazy existence.

It wasn't a perfect translation, but the words were there and in order and that night I sat in bed, a piece of paper resting on my lap. A small, crumpled square of paper that suddenly meant so much.

I was glad I'd set my alarm. I'd never imagined I'd be able to fall asleep, but after enduring a gossip-filled dinner, where Mom and Lyndal ran through the checklist of every scandal in Wellesley, I'd slipped away to my room, and shortly thereafter, exhaustion had struck. Thanks to my alarm, I woke up fifteen minutes before the Shift. Just enough time to do a final run-through of my lines.

My pronunciation wasn't brilliant, but it would have to do.

CHAPTER SIXTEEN

Roxbury, Tuesday

My eyes flickered open. I was shaking uncontrollably, the tension and confusion from the Shift only adding to my body's free fall.

I was back in Roxbury.

The room looked yellow; the halo around the ceiling light pulsed above my head.

Oh God. I couldn't breathe. My chest was pumping so hard, but slow. It hurt. There was yelling, someone called out for a crash cart. Not encouraging.

I squeezed my hand. Someone was still holding it, thankfully, acting as my anchor. Ethan?

I had mere seconds before my mind would slip away.

"Ethan," I croaked.

People all over me.

Messing with tubes.

Sticking in needles.

"E-than!" I choked out.

Suddenly he was there, close beside my face.

"I'm here." His voice was breathy. Scared.

It was now or never. *"Mein Name . . . ist Sabine."* I had to pause, each breath shorter than the last. *"Ich habe zwei Lebensunterhalt . . . und ich mochte . . . Ethan mussen mir glauben. Bitte, bitte glauben . . . Sie mir."*

Someone called out, "She's talking. Is she coming around?"

But I wasn't. I was going under.

Someone else: "Why is she speaking German?"

More urgently, another voice: "Where's the Digibind?"

Footsteps came running into the room. "We've got it. Here, we have it!"

Something cold pressed down on my chest. A needle in my arm.

"Jesus, her bradycardia is at twenty-six. I don't know how she's still conscious, but she won't be for long. Someone get that IV in."

More jabbing. I was fading. Could feel my body taking over, pulling at my mind. It felt like I was drowning.

Then . . . "What did she say? In German, what did she say?"

Someone cleared his throat. "She said her name, that she has two livelihoods and that Ethan must believe. Then she pleaded for him to believe. Or something like that; it was broken German."

"What time is it?" Ethan's voice. It sounded near and distant all at once.

"Just past midnight. Why?"

Disorientation and pain reached their peak as the last of me started experiencing the full extent of the damage I'd done to myself. Even so, I heard him. His voice close to my ear, his hand squeezing mine tighter than ever before.

"Stay with me, Sabine. I heard you. Stay with me!"

But I couldn't.

Everything went black.

What happens when we die? Do we go somewhere?

I can't say I believe in pearly gates. Coming from the world, *worlds*, that I do, I'm more inclined to believe in some form of reincarnation—a sick flick of a switch and we start over. That's much more believable. Much less appealing as well—to be stuck on a constant setting of repeat.

I was pretty sure of one thing, though. Death didn't come with the monotonous sound of beeping machines. Or a raw, scorched throat. Or, for that matter, a body that felt as though someone had taken a meat-tenderizing mallet to every inch.

My hand fumbled with the oxygen mask. I hated the

feeling of something being over my face, even if it was there to help. As my eyes started to blink open, my struggling became more urgent.

A set of warm hands settled over mine. I relaxed instantly.

It took a moment for my eyes to adjust and recognize the owner of those soothing hands.

I think I expected Mom. Even Dad.

As if he knew, he spoke. "Your dad was here. Your mom couldn't leave your sister alone and they didn't want to bring her in. He stayed until you stabilized, but he . . . he had to go."

Ethan gently removed the oxygen mask.

I was so groggy I could barely keep my eyes open and I missed some of what he said, his voice dropping in and out of my consciousness. But just hearing it helped.

". . . should sleep . . . body's been through a lot . . . if we hadn't known what you'd taken . . . was so scared . . ."

I opened my eyes again. One of his hands covered his face and his shoulders were slumped.

I swallowed a few times before I could speak.

"Do you . . ." I rasped, "believe?"

He sighed. "I . . . I asked your father if you could speak French. He said you'd never spoken a word of French in your life."

I felt a wave of fury toward my father. *Mon père peut être un idiot*," I whispered.

Ethan smiled grimly. "I'm gathering those aren't words of love."

"*Non*."

Without thinking, I lifted my arm toward him, my hand cupping his face. His eyes widened, but he didn't move away.

"Need someone to know me," I murmured. Begged. Because we both knew he still hadn't answered my question.

"Why?" he asked, his voice breaking.

"'Cause no one ever has." My hand dropped.

Ethan looked down, cleared his throat, and looked back at me. "They're moving you back down to your room after your labs come through. Was it only the digoxin you took?"

He watched me carefully as I nodded.

"And you just figured it might be handy to write the name of the antidote on your cast?" His eyebrows lifted gently.

"Don't want to die," I said, and tried to shrug.

He half-laughed, but then sadness clouded over his expression. "Could've fooled me—and everyone else."

My eyelids were too heavy. I was sliding back under. "Want a chance . . . to really live," I murmured.

Ethan said something but I'd lost focus. I missed it.

The next time I opened my eyes I was back in my room. The first thing I noticed was that my closet had been mostly cleared out. Just a few articles of clothing remained, folded on one shelf.

I felt under the sheets. I was back in a hospital gown. I knew without looking that my butterfly necklace was long gone. At least I wasn't restrained.

I turned my head toward the other side of the room. Macie was sitting in the armchair, watching me, an open magazine in her lap.

I swallowed painfully a few times, and she waited for me to settle.

"You were vomiting a lot and they had to intubate you at one point. Did you really write the name of the antidote on your hand?" she asked, her tone incredulous.

I didn't answer and instead asked, "What time is it?"

She rolled her eyes. "That's all you ever want to know."

"Yeah, well, if you were me, it'd be on the top of your need-to-know list too."

She stared at me like I was a puzzle she didn't want to have to solve. Eventually she looked at her watch.

"Congratulations," she said mockingly. "You've been out of it all day. It's five p.m." She stood up. "I'll let Dr. Levi know you're awake."

Oh yeah, she had the hates, bad. I had a feeling it was more to do with me kicking Mitch in the face than anything else. If I had to guess from the looks they gave each other,

Mitch and Macie were sneaking visits to the supply room on a regular basis.

I must've drifted off again because when I opened my eyes Dr. Levi was standing over me, writing something on his clipboard.

"Hello, Sabine. An eventful evening, I hear."

He started to take my vitals.

"You seem to be mending well. How do you feel about that?" he asked, his tone no different than if we were talking about the weather.

I couldn't think of an appropriate answer, so I turned my attention to the open door. A nurse I hadn't seen before was standing in the hallway, observing.

Dr. Levi put down his clipboard. "Sabine, the attending physician mentioned you spoke some German while you were semiconscious last night, and your father said that you told Ethan you can speak French. Is it true you can speak other languages?"

It was no major surprise. I knew I would have to deal with the fallout from my experiments.

I sighed. "*Je ne parle pas allemand, mais je peux dire ce que vous voulez en français. Je le parle couramment depuis que j'ai cinq ans. Et vous avez quelque chose de vert entre les dents,*" I said, explaining that I couldn't really speak German, but that I'd been speaking French fluently since I was five years old and . . . that he had something green stuck between his front teeth. I couldn't resist the add-on.

Dr. Levi watched me carefully and when I finished he turned to the nurse in the hallway.

She was smiling and seemed on the verge of laughter. But when she looked at Dr. Levi, she sobered and nodded.

I suddenly realized why.

She was there to confirm what I'd said. She spoke French—or at least enough to know if it was genuine and not gibberish.

Dr. Levi took a moment, dismissing the nurse and then turning back to me. "That's very impressive, Sabine. How did you teach yourself to speak French?"

"I learned at school." I shrugged. "Had a tutor at home."

"She did not!" came a holler from the hall. A moment later my father appeared in the doorway. I flinched. I should've guessed he'd been hiding out there, waiting to pounce.

"Where did you learn French, Sabine? What game is this to you?" He was livid. Clearly the time for concern and compassion had passed—assuming he'd had such feelings in the first place.

"*Dad.*" I said the word sarcastically, since it was a name I no longer felt he was entitled to. "Nice of you to visit." Before he could answer I rolled away from them onto my side, wishing the locked window looked out to something more pleasant than a concrete parking lot.

"Dr. Levi," my father ordered, and I could hear him stomp back out to the hallway.

After a considerable sigh, Dr. Levi followed, but he paused at the door. "I'll be back shortly, Sabine. Perhaps we could chat further."

"Not likely," I replied, not bothering to turn and look at him.

My father's words could be heard easily.

"Her mother has been put on Valium for Christ's sake! She can't have this . . . unrest. What's wrong with Sabine? How can she suddenly speak *French*?"

Good question, *Dad*.

Dr. Levi's tone was several decibels lower than my father's, but his voice still carried in the otherwise quiet hospital.

"She appears to have created an alternate world where she, in her mind at least, exists for part of the time. It also seems that this has been going on for many years. From what Ethan has written in his reports, she's extremely convincing. There's no doubt she has carefully constructed every element of this new life so that, despite any evidence we provide to the contrary, she has a way of explaining away our logic. It is . . . Well, it's obsessive but also quite brilliant. To have created such a complex world as she has, her mind would have to be borderline genius, as well as—"

"Insane!" my father snapped. "But that still doesn't explain the other languages."

"Actually, it does. If she's submerged herself so completely in this fantasy existence, it would also be believable that she could've given herself the tools to justify it. It's possible Sabine has been teaching herself French in private for many years—and with her level of intelligence, it's doable."

Shit.

I tuned out from the conversation and wiped away a few tears. No matter what I did, I was going to be pegged as crazy. I'd been wrong to think I could make someone believe me. Ethan had written his reports, said I was *convincing*, but that was it. The worst thing was, there'd been a moment, I was sure, when I'd seen a small glimmer of curiosity—a suggestion that he was willing to know more. Had I just been seeing things because I wanted to? Things that hadn't been there at all?

When Dr. Levi returned, I kept my attention on the window. He asked question after question. Stupid, pointless stuff mostly. Every now and then I would answer in the hope that it would make him go away, but I offered no new information. It would only be manipulated to incriminate me further.

"Sabine, I need to know if you have any further intentions of harming yourself. Can you tell me that?" he asked, starting to sound fed up.

I didn't answer. He wouldn't believe me if I said no, and I'd be back in restraints if I told him the truth.

He sighed. "Then I'm going to have to keep a day nurse with you."

I didn't react, even though I wanted to argue.

"Okay, Sabine. Get some rest." As I heard him gather his things, I rolled over.

"Can I . . . Can I use a phone?" I knew I hadn't done anything to deserve it in his eyes, but I had to try.

At first I thought he would say no, but after a moment he gave a short nod. "Ethan will be here shortly. I'll tell him you can make one call, but he will have to be present for the conversation, I'm afraid."

I nodded, relieved to at least have this.

Dr. Levi stopped by the door. "I can help you, Sabine, but you have to want the help. It's a two-way street, this talking stuff."

"So is listening," I replied.

He half-smiled. "Then I will try to listen more if you try to talk a little more, starting tomorrow."

I turned back toward the window.

Talking was really not the answer. Talking had landed me in this mess. Talking—and the tests. But I'd *needed* to do the tests. And they'd worked. The physical didn't cross over anymore. I knew that now. The rules had definitely changed.

When I'd started all of this, I hadn't allowed myself to contemplate this moment. To actually let my mind go there— to that final step. The choice. But there were no more tests. Now I needed to make the final decision.

And do it.

CHAPTER SEVENTEEN

Roxbury, Tuesday

Ethan brought in a tray of dinner, placing it on one of those wheelie tables before taking up position in the armchair.

I struggled with the bread—almost as much as with the silence. The broth, however, was good, and soothed my raw throat.

After I'd done what I could with the meal, Ethan stood, collected the tray, and left. He returned a moment later, phone in hand.

"I'm sorry, but I have to stay in the room. I'll try not to intrude," he said awkwardly, and handed me the phone.

I took it and punched in Capri's number as Ethan moved to the window, his back to me.

"Yep," Capri answered. Her standard greeting.

"Capri, it's me."

"Sabine?"

"Yeah."

"You sound awful. Where have you been?" Her voice dropped. "If you were at some all-night party on Sunday and are just coming back to the world of the living now, I'm gonna be so pissed!"

My smile was grim. Capri was so wrong, but so right at the same time. "No. Nothing like that. I, um . . . I'm not well."

"Where are you? I went over to your place. Your dad flipped out and wouldn't let me in. So Davis and I climbed that big-ass tree outside your room and broke in. You weren't there, obviously."

"Wait, how'd you get the window open?"

"Oh, that." I could almost see Capri's face scrunching up into her guilty expression. "Well, Davis had a crowbar in his car and we figured it came down to a safety issue. That window's been stuck for, like, ever. I mean, what if there was a fire and you really needed to get out of there one day? It was a public service more than anything."

I dropped my face into my hand. "You don't know how right you are," I mumbled, wishing Davis and his crowbar had been around when Team-Insane-Recruiters had turned up to haul me out of there.

"What?" Capri replied, sounding hopeful she was off the hook.

"Nothing. And you're right, the window doesn't matter."

I heard her blow out a breath. "So, are you home now?"

"No, I, um . . . I'm . . . I'm in the hospital," I said, my voice still hoarse.

"Oh my God! Why?"

"It's just . . . some bug or something. They don't know, so they're testing me for a bunch of stuff," I fumbled, realizing I hadn't fully prepared for this conversation.

"Oh, you poor thing. Angus and I will come visit you in the morning before school. Davis too, he's been really worried, Sab." I knew where this was leading.

"Capri, would you please drop this Davis stuff. I don't like him like that. I never will." I don't know why, but at that moment my eyes darted to Ethan's motionless frame, his back still turned to me. I'm not sure what I expected. Nothing, I suppose.

"But—"

"Capri!"

"Okay, okay, got it. No Davis. So when can I come see you?"

"Oh. They, um . . . don't want me to have visitors at the moment. You know," I said, trying to keep my voice lighthearted, "in case I'm contagious."

"I don't mind. If I get it, they can just give me the bed next to yours. Ooh, we can both blow off the last week of school!"

My chest tightened with my next words. "You're a great friend, you know."

"Save the pickup lines." She snorted.

"Ha-ha. I just wanted to let you know where I was.
Mom and Dad are really overprotective right now. I'll let
you know what's going on in a couple of days. I just . . . I
need to ask a favor."

"Name it," Capri said without hesitation.

"Can you find a way to get to Maddie and check on her?
She'll be worried. Don't tell her where I am. Mom and Dad
have probably told her I'm in Disney World for all I know."
I couldn't hide the sting in my voice, but Capri let it slide.
Her mom was no picnic either and she hadn't seen her dad in
three years. "Can you just make sure she's okay? That she . . .
she knows I'm thinking of her and that . . . I love her?"

"Jeez, Sab, this is heavy. Are you sure you're okay?"

"Yeah, it's just important that she knows. And that I'm
going to be fine. Tell her that, please."

"Okay," she said hesitantly. "I'll play babysitter."

I blew out a grateful breath. "Thanks, Capri. I, um . . . I
better go. Take care, okay."

"Sure thing. Call me soon," she said before hanging up.

I put the phone down. Ethan was still standing by the
window. He didn't turn around.

"I'm . . . I'm finished," I said.

"So I hear," he said, his voice low.

His hand went to his face, and for a brief moment I
wondered if he was wiping away a tear. Before I could say
anything he suddenly spun around, his dark eyes fixing on

me, causing my breath to lodge in my throat. I braced for him to say something, but after a second he just snatched the phone off the edge of the bed and left the room while I stared openmouthed after him.

Ethan didn't come back until 11:40 p.m. I know this because he brought a clock with him. Battery powered—no cable I could hang myself with. I held back the sardonic laugh; I didn't want to risk being without a watch or clock again.

"Thank you," I said shakily.

Ethan shrugged. "Here," he said, holding out a piece of paper.

"What is it?" I asked, puzzled by the list of questions.

"Do you know the answers to any of these?"

I studied the questions briefly before turning to him in confusion. Maybe he was the one who was insane.

He sat down in the chair, watching me.

"You said your memory goes with you, and that there were some things that are the same in both worlds. General constants." He pointed to the piece of paper in my hand. "That's a list of things I want you to tell me straight after midnight."

I glanced down at the list again.

- *Two numbers whose sum is 26 and product is 165*
- *Cardiovascular benefits of chocolate*
- *Translate:* Thesaurum omnis vitae

"Look, this isn't some game. I can't . . . I can't take this list with me; it won't travel."

Ethan crossed his arms and swung his feet up on the edge of the bed. "Well, start memorizing." He gestured to the clock, looking irritatingly smug. "You only have fifteen minutes left."

I started to scoff, but he was looking right at me, into my eyes like no one had before. I tried to ignore the unwelcome tingle it set off in my body. Was . . . was he *daring* me? Challenging me? Or even . . . willing me to prove it to him? Suddenly a steely determination settled over me. My eyes darted from the list to Ethan and back.

"Sabine?"

This was a chance. *My chance.* I looked at the clock, swallowed back the midnight nerves and nodded.

"What language is the last one?" I asked.

Ethan just looked at me.

I rolled my eyes, but didn't waste much time before getting back to memorizing the list.

The minutes flew by as I read and reread each question. But when there were only two minutes to go, I couldn't take it anymore and I dropped the list, my hands and body shaking all over.

I really didn't want to throw up in front of him. Again.

"Is this normal?" Ethan asked, sitting up, watching me too intently for comfort.

I took a deep breath to stop from being sick. "When I'm awake for the Shift," I tried to explain.

"Is it involuntary?"

"It's fear, okay!" I snapped, embarrassed.

He got quiet and moved back in his seat.

I closed my eyes and tried to recite the questions to myself, using them to distract me. After a few rounds I realized I should have shifted by now and opened my eyes. I was still in the hospital. Ethan was still sitting in front of me, watching as closely as ever.

Shit.

I looked at the clock. 12:04 a.m. *How can . . . ?*

I looked at Ethan again. His expression was intrigued and . . . nervous.

I glanced at the clock again. 12:05 a.m.

"So," he said casually. "Do you have my answers?"

I was so confused. This had never happened before. Oh my God, what did this mean? What in the hell was happening to me?

I glanced at the clock again. The clock Ethan had just brought me. Suddenly it clicked and I turned to glare at him.

"You son of a bitch!"

"Sorry?" he responded, playing dumb.

"Oh, you heard me. You changed the time! It's not midnight yet! You tricked me."

His eyes widened, but he tried to cover it up by acting suspicious. "How do you know that?"

"Because I didn't freaking shift! How long?" I shrieked, because right then, I didn't care if he believed me or not, didn't care one bit. What I cared about was the damn time! "Do you think this is a game? My *life*? Do you have any idea how awful it is, getting ready to shift? Shit! What's the time?" I was losing my breath, grabbing at my hair, trying and failing to hold myself together.

Ethan looked horrified at my outburst. "Okay, okay. I'm sorry. It was a lousy trick. I just . . . I thought it might help."

I stilled myself and turned a cold stare on him, speaking low and level. "Ethan. What. Time. Is. It?"

He pulled a watch out of his pocket. His face was stark as he looked back in my direction.

"Sabine, I—"

But it was too late. It was midnight.

CHAPTER EIGHTEEN

Wellesley, Tuesday

Tears streamed down my face the instant I shifted to Wellesley. The nausea that usually struck me when I was awake for a Shift took a backseat to the overwhelming sadness.

The betrayal.

I pulled my pillow to my chest and buried my face in it to smother the gulping sobs.

How could Ethan trick me like that?

My body trembled as I considered my cruel reality. I couldn't take it anymore. The freakishness of my existence was bad enough, but the loneliness that constantly tortured me was far worse. I had thought there might be hope. That maybe I could make Ethan believe me.

But that wasn't going to happen.

He didn't want to believe me. He *wanted* to disprove me. I wouldn't be so stupidly trusting again.

I finally managed to calm myself down, knowing that if I broke into all-out hysterics, I'd risk waking Mom. But the emptiness stayed with me even after the tears went away. I slid further down into my silk sheets, curled around my pillow, and tried to go to sleep. But it was futile. Even after what he'd done to me, I couldn't stop thinking about Ethan.

Why had it suddenly become so damn important that he believe me? Especially since my future in that world was becoming increasingly less likely.

The thought made me gasp.

There. I'd admitted it.

And it was true.

The only thing holding me to my Roxbury world now was Maddie. My parents had pretty much disowned me. They'd probably even be relieved. And Capri would be okay; I had to believe that. But Maddie . . .

Should I try to see her? Explain somehow? I shook my head at myself. I couldn't do that. There was nothing I could say that would make it okay for her. I was no good to her there anyway, locked up in a mental ward. Eventually she'd find out. She'd hate me then. But I couldn't just abandon her.

I opened my teary eyes, a new thought stirring.

Ethan could tell her.

He was the only one who knew about my worlds from my point of view. After I was gone, one day when she was older, he could visit her and tell her the truth so she'd understand that I wasn't dead. Just the opposite.

But to do that . . . it brought me full circle. First, I still had to make Ethan believe me.

In a panic I fumbled for my lamp switch and a notebook, scribbling down Ethan's questions while I could still remember them.

The thought of having to work at making Ethan *really* believe me was frightening. But making him understand was about Maddie now. I had to do it, despite how furious I was with him.

When I woke, my anger toward Ethan gave me a renewed determination to make my Wellesley world everything I wanted it to be. At breakfast I asked Mom if she could pick me up after school and take me to get my Audi from the garage. I needed to be able to get around on my own. Mom already had a spa treatment booked, but she was on the phone to Lucas before I could stop her. I actually heard his groan through the telephone. Mom, however, remained oblivious and was thrilled as she hung up, assuring me that Lucas would be there to pick me up at the end of the day.

Miriam showed up soon after.

"Cute dress; it matches the circles under your eyes," she said, motioning to my plum A-line dress.

I shrugged, pulling down the visor to reapply some concealer. "Do I look that bad?" I asked and looked into the mirror.

"Don't panic. You look fine, pretty as ever, and Dex can only see your fabulous hair at the moment anyway. What gives? Were you up all night partying? Will Dex look just as tired when I see him?" She raised her eyebrows playfully.

"No, I just didn't get much sleep," I answered, hoping the conversation would end there.

"Sure," she teased.

The problem was, Miriam was right—I did look exhausted. I was starting to fray at the edges in this world and I couldn't let that happen. As I continued adjusting my makeup, I wondered how long I could keep this up.

But I had to. Falling apart was not an option. I needed to be the person people expected me to be here.

So when Miriam suggested we swing by the fruit stand to get more supplies for our diet, I suppressed the irks and smiled in agreement. It was worth it if Miriam went on believing that apples were the key to my recent weight loss. I even paid for our selection, carefully avoiding fruit-stand guy's eyes the entire time. With everything else that was going on, he was the least of my concerns.

Dex found me as soon as we pulled into the parking lot; he took my bag and wrapped an arm around me as we walked into school.

"Nice dress," he commented, looking me up and down. I batted my eyelashes. Mom had followed yesterday's form and left a new outfit for me this morning. I had to agree with Dex: the perfect-shade-of-plum jersey dress was to die for and would assume prime position on my favorites rack.

"I still can't get over how amazing you look with that hair," he murmured in my ear, pulling me close.

I smiled, enjoying the attention. It might not always feel sparky and magical with Dex, but I knew one thing for sure— he adored me. He'd had his pick of all the girls at school and he'd chosen me, continuously, for the past two years. Not many guys do that. So what if he didn't make me feel that . . . *way* I'd always imagined the L-word would? Tons of people said that stuff came with time. And time was something Dex would give me.

I snuggled into his shoulder and blinked away the gnawing memory of Ethan—how just the way he looked at me sent shivers through my body.

"A bunch of the guys are going to Mixons tonight. You interested?"

I remembered Ethan's list. But maintaining appearances in Wellesley was important too, so I needed to show up at the senior hangout.

"Sure. I have to pick up my car this afternoon and run a couple of errands first. Meet you there?"

He stopped outside my math class, pulling me to one side

and kissing me quickly. "Sounds good. Tell Lucy and Miriam to come along too."

I nodded and he planted another quick kiss on my lips just as my math teacher walked past, clearing his throat.

"In class, Sabine."

"Sorry, Mr. Barlow." I blushed.

Dex, however, looked thrilled at being caught and lingered long enough to earn another reprimanding stare from Mr. Barlow.

In class, Lucy didn't even bother to pretend to pay attention.

"I can't cope with this. We have eight tables of seven and every other table has ten. Every way I try to rearrange it, the possibility for a complete breakdown of room harmony presents itself." Lucy flapped her table plan at me, looking desperate.

Lucy was head of the graduation committee, which meant she was in charge of the seating plan for graduation dinner. It wasn't like our prom—we'd had that a month ago—but it was just as important a tradition at our school. Graduation was everyone's day. The smart students were acknowledged one last time, the socialites had their final opportunity to flaunt their connections, and everyone got the chance to reveal which colleges they would be attending. And last but not least, we got to parade around with our boyfriends and girlfriends for the last time—all while looking fabulous.

I glanced over Lucy's shoulder at her table plan as Mr. Barlow made a last-ditch effort to get control of the class. He suggested we call out random mathematical problems and jointly solve them for a bit of fun.

"Here." I pointed to her plan. "Can't you put this table together with this one and break that one into two, like this?" I pointed out the people to keep together and who to separate. "Then you'll just have Sahara left, and she could sit at table sixteen, which would bring that up to eight."

Mr. Barlow cleared his throat behind us.

"Sorry, sir," I said.

"Oh my God, that's totally perfect!" Lucy shrieked, oblivious to the fact that her outburst earned *me* yet another stern look.

"Perhaps you have a suggestion for what the class could work on, Sabine?" Mr. Barlow asked.

I swallowed, looking at the whiteboard. There was an advanced trigonometry equation already up there. Math was not my strong suit.

"Oh." My mind was racing. When I opened my mouth I didn't seem to be able to control what flew out. "Er . . . two numbers where the sum is twenty-six and the product is one hundred and sixty-five."

I expected Mr. Barlow to snap at me for wasting everyone's time, but instead he broke into a smile.

"Just the thing we need in our final week—a little bit

of lateral thinking. Well done, Sabine. Okay, class, how about it?"

I walked out of math with Lucy singing my praises and the first answer on Ethan's to-do list.

I had planned to sneak away with my laptop at lunch, hoping to find out what language was on Ethan's list, but Lucy intercepted me in the hall.

"Where are you going?"

"To the sports field," I said vaguely.

"Absolutely not. You can't! I need you. If I don't get this table plan finished during lunch and the order of the service finalized by the end of today, I won't be able to go to Mixons tonight." She pouted. "You have to help me, Sabine! Noah is going to be there! And I heard he still hasn't invited anyone to the graduation dinner." She threw me a plaintive look.

I smiled and sighed. Despite my dire need to be elsewhere, there was a girl code of conduct when it came to these things, and Lucy deserved to turn up at graduation on the arm of the hottie she'd been drooling over for the past two years. Mixons was the perfect opportunity to make something happen.

"On one condition," I said, hoping I'd still have enough time to get my final answers as well as get my car back and go to Mixons.

"Anything!" she chirped.

"If I help you get everything done and Noah is there tonight, you have to *promise* me you're actually going to ask him to go to the graduation dinner with you."

"But—"

I cut her off with a hand in the air. "Those are my conditions, take them or leave them."

She glanced down the hall to where Noah was looking hot, leaning against his locker and joking around with Dex and Brett. They really would be a beautiful couple, and I was sure I'd caught him checking her out when he thought no one was looking. She took a deep breath and scrunched up her face.

"Okay, okay!"

I smiled triumphantly. "Okay then. Let's get to work."

It took all of lunchtime plus our study period to finalize the seating plans. When we finally emerged from the seniors' lounge, Lucy looked positively delirious knowing she could now delegate the remaining tasks to the other committee members.

"Now it's just down to decorating the hall on the day. Any chance you might be interested in helping?" she asked sheepishly.

To her surprise I nodded. By then, I was hoping I'd be a lot closer to having my own life sorted out. And maybe having things to keep me busy in this world would be just what I needed.

"No problem," I said. "I'm a fantastic supervisor."

Lucy slapped me on the arm playfully. "Of course, if you're too busy getting a bikini wax during the day . . ." She elbowed me jokingly. "I could always make an exception."

"You are *so* funny," I quipped, ignoring the twist in my stomach.

"Oh, come on, Sabine. Since when did you get all secretive about the big night? I thought you'd be planning out the entire thing. I'm surprised you haven't worked out a script."

I gave her a teasing smile. "*Well*, Lucy, I don't need a script. Not much talking involved."

She burst into a fit of giggles. But when she sobered, her next words threw me.

"You're happy though, right?"

"I . . . ah . . . Why do you ask?" I stammered.

"You've just seemed a bit distracted lately. I was thinking about it the other day, and I totally get why you've waited this long to . . . you know. It's a big thing. But you guys have been together for a couple of years. I guess I just wondered if there was any other reason that you hadn't . . . before."

I stopped walking, stunned by the insightfulness of Lucy's comments. It was true. I *had* made Dex wait a long time. I'd excused it as best I could, given all the right reasons, hidden behind parental expectations, self-respect, age, timing, blah-blah-blah. But it had stopped being about those things awhile back. In many ways, I'd been hoping to find that missing ingredient in our otherwise perfect relationship.

"Well, I . . . um." I sighed. "Luce, I'm . . ."

On the verge of spilling my concerns to her, I froze. This was my Wellesley life. If this life fell apart, right before graduation, what would I have then? No. I couldn't let that happen. Couldn't risk having both of my worlds in disarray.

I waved a dismissive hand through the air. "I'm absolutely happy, *more* than happy. Dex and I are going to be together for, like, ever. Waiting until the right time to take this step was key. If we'd jumped into bed too soon, we wouldn't be able to look back on this time and know how much we'd wanted it."

Lucy swooned. "Aw, you guys are so adorable. I hadn't thought of that, but it's so true." She nodded. "I hope Noah and I are like you two one day."

I blinked, surprised it had been that easy. But I gladly latched onto the change of subject. "Well, you'll never find out if you don't do something about it. Tonight."

"At least if he rejects me, I won't have to see him at school for much longer," she moaned as we made our way down the hall to our last class of the day.

CHAPTER NINETEEN

Wellesley, Tuesday

To my surprise, Lucas was waiting for me after school and drove me, as promised, straight to the garage to pick up my car. It was one of my favorite possessions. One thing Ryan, Lucas, and I shared was a love of cars. Ryan loved how cool he thought he was in his vintage Porsche, Lucas loved the mechanics, and I loved the freedom that my new-model silver A1 gave me.

When we arrived at the garage, I couldn't hide my excitement. I planned to inspect the car carefully, eager to see the new rims we'd ordered. But as soon as Frank, the mechanic, came out of the garage door to greet us, I knew the news wasn't good.

Frank was short and thin, his wiry hair now completely gray, along with the forest of hair on his chest and arms. He'd been the family mechanic since before I was born, and

I imagined he would keep going until he literally couldn't work anymore.

"Sorry, darlin'. If I'd known you were comin', I woulda called and told ya not to waste ya time. Those rims ain't come in yet and next delivery's not till Thursday." He pulled out a rag and started wiping his oil-smeared hands.

I opened my mouth to complain, but Lucas cut me off.

"That's okay, Frank," he said from behind me. "I'll give you a call in a couple of days, see how it's going."

"Best do that, Lucas. Sorry for wastin' your time."

Frank held out his hand to me. I shook it and tried to smile, but I felt deflated. And now dirty.

Lucas and I hadn't spoken on the drive to the garage and the drive back was almost as silent. We both tried a few times, but our attempts were lame. What little I did say—like our thirty-word conversation about graduation, or our-less-than-twenty-word chat about how Miriam had invited me to go to Cape Cod over the summer—only seemed to infuriate him. For some reason, Lucas had decided that I was an inconsiderate brat and he wasn't—as he chauffeured me around in his BMW, the car he used when he wasn't riding his Ducati.

I didn't know what his problem was, but he'd been like this for as long as I could remember. I'd always thought it had something to do with Mom and Dad's divorce. The process had been relatively smooth from our point of view.

Mom and Dad had followed "protect the children" protocol and had most of their arguments behind closed doors. I'm not sure what the final straw was, why Dad eventually packed up and left—though I suspected it had something to do with the waitress at the restaurant he'd made us eat at three times a week in the months leading up to his moving out.

When he left, Lucas decided to go with him. I think he just figured someone had to, and since Dad, a highly regarded criminal-defense lawyer, was always in New York for work, Lucas basically had the apartment to himself.

As we pulled up at the house I couldn't stop checking my watch. The trip had taken longer than I'd planned. Everyone would already be at Mixons, and I still didn't have my answers for Ethan.

"What's wrong with you?" Lucas asked, noticing my agitation.

"I'm supposed to be at Mixons already."

"Let me guess: Dex?" His tone dripped with judgment.

I wasn't up for defending myself to Lucas. "Yep," I replied, not bothering to look at him.

He turned off the engine and settled back in his seat. "Go get changed, or whatever you need to do. I'll drop you at Mixons."

I looked at him, wide-eyed.

He just raised his eyebrows as if to say, *Hurry up before I change my mind.*

I raced up to my room and quickly changed into a little white dress that was perfect for the warm evening and pulled my hair into a high ponytail to accentuate my cheekbones. After a quick touch-up of mascara and lip gloss, I transferred a few things from my bag to a small caramel clutch and was back in Lucas's car within ten minutes. Even he seemed impressed.

"Thanks," I said, when we arrived at Mixons after another almost-silent trip.

"No problem. I'll let you know when your car's ready."

I smiled. "Sure, thanks again."

He shrugged.

Inside, everyone was crowded around our usual booths at the back of the diner. I paused to check my reflection in the window, making sure everything was where it should be, before making my entrance.

"Sabine!" Miriam yelled from the far side of the diner, causing all eyes to turn to me.

I put my shoulders back, smiled coyly, and strutted over to the booths.

Miriam and Lucy had changed outfits too. But tonight it was Lucy who had gone all out, sporting a daringly short bright-red dress. She looked amazing.

I saw her anxiously waiting for my approval as I made

my way through our group of friends, saying hi and kissing cheeks.

"Lucy, if that doesn't get you on the ark, nothing will, babe," I whispered with a wink. "Where is the handsome Noah?"

Lucy blushed as red as her dress while pointing discreetly to her left and mouthing, "*Shhh!*" Noah was a few feet away and looking in our direction, his trademark golden curls flopping over his face. He lifted a hand to wave at me. I returned the gesture with a knowing smile that made him quirk an eyebrow.

"Have you spoken to him yet?" I asked, turning my attention back to Lucy.

She twisted her mouth.

"Sabine!" Dex called out from the next booth. He had considerately saved the seat beside him for me. Before heading over, I threw a parting comment to Lucy. "Remember, you promised. And I have every intention of holding you to it."

"I know, I know," she whispered frantically, shooing me away.

I put my clutch on the table and settled into place beside Dex, reminding myself this was where I was supposed to be. I fit into this world, I had a future in this world, I could make something of myself here. I could matter.

Everyone was hyped-up, excited that it was the final week of school. I went with the flow, letting Dex pull me onto his lap when Miriam squeezed in to sit beside me. As she did, she knocked my clutch off the table, sending its contents spilling onto her lap, which prompted Brett and Dex to give her a round of applause. Obviously Miriam had already had a few sneaky drinks, courtesy of the hip flasks I could see circulating. In fact, when I looked around, I noticed that most of the guys and a few of the girls were also glassy-eyed.

I glanced at Dex. He was staring right at me with a penetrating expression I hadn't seen on him before. I adjusted my position on his lap, embarrassed I'd caught him looking at me like that. But he didn't seem to mind. In fact, he kept watching me with the same intensity.

Dex wasn't the least bit glassy-eyed. He never drank. Not since the time he and some of the guys sneaked a bottle of vodka out of his parents' liquor cabinet in junior year. I'd never heard the full story; it was the one thing Dex didn't like talking about. All I knew was that some out-of-town kid ended up in the hospital that night. As far as I was aware, Dex hadn't touched alcohol since.

I leaned over to take a sip of the drink he'd brought for me and almost choked. Just because Dex didn't drink, didn't mean he wasn't willing to ply me with rocket fuel.

"God, what is that?"

"Rum and Coke," he said with a shrug, pulling me back against his chest.

"That is definitely not nice," I said, even as I took another sip.

"Sabine, what's this?" Miriam asked.

"What?" I spun around to her and froze. She was holding Ethan's list. "Oh, um . . ." I licked my lips.

Shit.

But then I remembered where I was—*who* I was. I sat up a little straighter. "They're just some stupid questions from a quiz my brother was doing today," I said, keeping my tone nonchalant. "I wrote them down and said I'd try to find the answers on the net tonight." My long history of deception ensured the lie came easily.

"Ooh, cool," Miriam said, now studying the list. "Ha! I know this one!" She jumped up. "I read an article about it the other day. The compound in chocolate that lowers the risk of cardiovascular disease is called . . ." She looked to the ceiling, bouncing up and down. "What is it? What is it?" Then a lightbulb obviously went off. "Flavonoids! That's it. Also found in such great things as berries and red wine." She curtsied.

"Flavonoids?" I repeated, unable to hide my excitement. Miriam nodded.

"Does anyone have a pen?" I asked urgently. As I looked around, I caught Dex staring at me strangely.

"Here you go," Miriam said.

I turned back to her and wrote down my answer.

"Hey, Dex, is that Latin?" Miriam asked, grabbing the paper from under me and passing it to him.

I went pale. "No, it's okay. Everyone doesn't need to help me. It's just a stupid quiz."

I don't know why, but all of a sudden I was terrified about the group trying to decipher whatever Ethan had written in another language. What if it was something that would give me away? Or, I don't know . . . something else . . . private.

Pulse racing, I reached for the list, but Dex got there first. "I know some Latin."

"It's probably not even Latin," I suggested, holding out my hand for the sheet of paper and trying to ignore my rising blush.

He took no notice and studied the list intently. When he paused and looked up at me, I was sure he knew what it said and that it was something terrible.

Shit.

Eventually he cleared his throat. I stopped breathing.

"Well, you're in luck," he said. "It's Latin, for sure. *Thesaurum* is 'treasure,' *omnis* means 'every' or 'all,' and *vitae* is 'life.' Pretty basic really." He held out the list and I had to force myself not to snatch it. "So what's the quiz for?"

I took another sip of my drink and shook my head. Ethan must've thought his message was hilarious. My anger flared. Who was *he* to start spouting that kind of crap to me? At least it hadn't given me away to Dex.

"Sabine?" Dex prompted, beginning to look annoyed.

"Oh, sorry. I, um . . . I don't know. Lucas didn't say. Are you sure that's the translation?"

"Yes."

I started to write it down.

"If it's just a quiz, why are you so upset?"

Only then did I realize I was still shaking my head. I stopped. "It's just stupid. My brother can be such a weirdo," I said, trying to recover.

Dex knew how fragile my relationship was with Lucas. I hoped he'd buy my excuse as I pulled myself together. To my relief, he nodded. "It's nice that you're trying to do something for him. He's not so bad, just the quiet type."

I smiled and stroked his face. "Thanks." I gave him a brief kiss and we relaxed back into the night, sharing a plate of nachos and then disappearing into a corner to share a number of sub-ten-second kisses. I guessed if you added them all together, I was improving.

It was Lucy who interrupted us, pulling me away from a somewhat frustrated Dex.

"So, I haven't asked Noah to the graduation dinner yet," she told me and Miriam as we perched by the jukebox.

"Why are you grinning from ear to ear then?" I asked.

She squealed. "Because he asked *me*!"

If ever there was a moment for a group hug, this was it.

Miriam settled us down. "Look how perfect everything is.

Me and Brett, Sabine and Dex, and now you and Noah. What were the chances of us all turning up to graduation dinner with our dream guys?"

"Totally! I can't believe it!" Lucy exclaimed.

I couldn't quite muster the same enthusiasm, but I put on a good show for Lucy's sake until I noticed the wall clock.

"Oh, guys, I've got to go. I didn't realize how late it was."

My stomach turned over. How could I not have seen the time? It was already 11:00 p.m. and it was at least fifteen minutes home by car.

"Is anyone driving?" I asked, panicking when I remembered I didn't have a ride home.

"Sorry, Sabine. I came with Brett and we gave Lucy, Josh, and Ollie a lift. It's a full car. What about Dex?"

An arm snaked around my belly from behind. "What about Dex?" he whispered in my ear.

"She needs a lift home," Miriam said brightly. "You wouldn't mind, would you?"

"Of course not." He squeezed me a little tighter and I forced myself not to squirm.

"Okay, well, that's all decided then." Miriam threw me a coy look. "No all-night partying again tonight, Sabine. You need your beauty sleep." She winked suggestively before spinning on her heel with Lucy in tow.

Dex's grip around my waist tightened to uncomfortable as we walked to his car.

211

"What was Miriam talking about?" His voice was rough. "Did you go out last night?"

"No, no!" I said quickly. "She was just teasing me because I looked so tired this morning. I didn't go out, Dex."

His grip loosened and I stepped away from him.

"Are you sure nothing else is going on? You seem . . . different lately."

Shit.

I needed to fix this. Now.

I smiled sweetly. "Different good, or different bad?" And before he had a chance to answer, I stepped into his arms and kissed him like I'd never kissed him before. For the first time ever, Dex was the one to pull away, breathing heavily.

"Promise me you aren't seeing someone else," he demanded.

My hesitation only lasted a split second. "I'm not."

Dex cupped the side of my face in his hand. "Kiss me again, Sabine. Like you did just then." Something about his tone made it seem as if he was daring me to refuse.

I didn't.

I did everything necessary to assure both of us that Dex *was* the guy for me. The seconds went by; I tried not to count until he finally pulled back, satisfied with my response. As I opened my eyes, I was shocked by my feeling of disappointment—I'd been wishing to see someone else's face.

Was it possible? Was that irritating, game-playing,

cynical guy getting under my skin? Was that why it was so important that he know the truth?

"Oh God, Sabine. I can't wait for Monday night." Dex traced a line from my brow down to my bottom lip.

I forced thoughts of Ethan aside and fixed a sultry smile on my face.

"Me either."

CHAPTER TWENTY

Wellesley, Tuesday/
Roxbury, Wednesday

I was as ready as I'd ever been. Midnight was minutes away and I was sitting cross-legged and calm on my bedroom floor, surrounded by pillows. For some reason I didn't want to be in my bed. Usually any deviation in routine upset me, but tonight I felt strangely empowered by the change.

When I shifted, my composure came with me; it only took a few seconds to adjust to being in my Roxbury body. As the adrenalin faded, I just caught the end of the sentence Ethan had started before my last Shift.

". . . so sorry."

I kept my eyes closed until I was ready, then I lifted my head and opened my eyes, taking slow, steadying breaths. The only way to manage this situation was to stay in control.

Everything was exactly as it had been when I left. I was in

the hospital. It was midnight. The clock lying on the bed now read 12:10 a.m. And Ethan sat wide-eyed and frozen.

I felt a stab of annoyance and narrowed my eyes, taking him in. His eyes were more shadowed than I remembered. He looked exhausted. His front teeth were firmly embedded in his bottom lip, moments from drawing blood. I glanced down at his hand, still holding his watch in midair. Was it trembling? He looked tired and worried, but it was more than that. He looked . . . sorry.

And he was beautiful.

I stared at him, his dark hair a messy bird's nest, his full lips teasing me, his eyes showing a depth of soul I'd never seen in another person. Like he knew something the rest of us didn't. A part of me began to ache.

As I watched, he glanced down at his hand, which was still shaking slightly. He lowered it to his lap. "Sabine," he whispered.

I felt an overwhelming urge to be closer to him. I cleared my throat. "It's okay. I know it's after midnight."

"Does that mean you . . . ?"

I ran my hands through my shaggy dark hair, pushing it off my face. "Just listen before I forget. I'm tired, Ethan, and what you did to me . . . it . . ." But I couldn't even explain. I shook my head and went on, "Fifteen plus eleven equals twenty-six, and fifteen times eleven equals one hundred and sixty-five. The compound in chocolate that helps protect against cardiovascular disease is called flavonoids. It's also in berries and red wine. The language was Latin and the words translate to 'Treasure all life' or something like that. Nice touch."

Before Ethan could say anything, I threw back the sheets and stood up. "Stay in your seat, take it all in. I'll see myself to the bathroom. I promise I'm not hiding anything sharp or dangerous, but I need to go throw up. And if you ever try to control me at midnight again, you and I are not going to get along at all."

I held it together until I was just out of the room, then I slapped a hand over my mouth and bolted for the bathroom.

I threw up only once, but I stayed in the bathroom for a while, giving Ethan time to absorb. The odd thing was, I thought I'd be feeling smug, but instead I was just nervous. Would he be waiting with a syringe and restraints when I got back? Would he even be there?

When I couldn't put it off any longer, I padded back to my prison cell. Ethan was standing by the window. I stayed by the door.

He glanced at me over his shoulder. "I'm sorry I betrayed your trust, Sabine."

I sighed. "Call it even for the digoxin."

He rolled his eyes. "Not exactly a fair trade."

I shrugged and waited for him to say more.

Eventually he turned to me and gestured with his hand helplessly. "This is a lot to . . ."

"Look, if this is the part where you tell me you need some time to . . . think or whatever, save it. My father already gave that speech. Sharp needles followed."

He tilted his head. "Actually I was thinking I could do with a drink." He half-laughed.

I couldn't help the small smile. "Yeah, well, I second that. We should hit the local bar—you know, dance up a storm while we're at it."

He looked at me oddly, like I was an abstract painting he was trying to decide if he liked or not. Finally he moved past me toward the door, a look of playful mischief in his eyes.

"Ethan?"

"Get dressed. I'll be back in two minutes." He left the room, closing the door behind him.

I didn't hesitate, shimmying out of my hospital gown. If there was any chance of ditching this joint, I was in. I didn't think Ethan would actually take me dancing, but getting dressed at least meant going somewhere—even if it was just around the block.

I threw on the best of my limited supply of minis and the shortest of my T-shirts—it covered my bandage while still flashing a little belly skin—but then changed into a different one, chastising myself. Oh God, I was seriously crushing on this guy. I mean, he was my nurse and had done nothing to make me think he cared for me more than . . . nurse–patient stuff.

I groaned internally. What was I doing? As far as he was concerned, the night before I'd attempted suicide.

But true to his word, Ethan came back in a few minutes, pausing with his hand on the door when he saw me. He coughed lightly, looking down. "You might be cold outside."

I shrugged, enjoying the little swing in power. "I'm good. Don't have a coat."

His Adam's apple bobbed.

"You okay?" I asked, smirking.

He nodded and stepped inside, pulling the door closed behind him.

"I thought we were going out?"

He smiled. "We are. That is, if you feel up to it?"

I flashed him a wide smile. "Definitely."

With that, he dangled a set of keys from his hand and made his way to the window, first unlocking the security grilles and then the window, sliding it open fully.

"After you," he gestured.

I raised an eyebrow. "Don't you have to work or something?"

"They have someone else covering my other duties while I'm monitoring you. No one will notice."

"Is this meant to be some kind of bonding thing? You pretend to sneak me out, but really three doctors and a couple of security guys are tailing us the entire time."

He gestured to the window again. *"This* is me trusting you."

I climbed out the window quickly so he wouldn't see the tears in my eyes.

It felt strange walking the city streets after midnight. Unlike most teenagers, I was routinely asleep at that time.

We must have walked for nearly twenty minutes in silence. The strange thing was, it was comfortable. Calming. But Ethan was right: it was cold. When he offered me his jacket, as much as I wanted to, I didn't refuse. And when I put my hands in the pockets and felt his set of keys there, I was very glad I hadn't.

We passed a twenty-four-hour convenience store and a few late-night cafés, but Ethan didn't stop. When we came across a bar, to my surprise he headed straight toward it. I was even more surprised when no one stopped me for ID at the door.

Inside, things were in full swing. Ethan pointed to an empty table in the back corner and we made a beeline for it.

I sat down, but he stayed standing. "I'll get drinks. What do you want?"

"Rum and Coke," I said, wondering if it would taste different in this life. Things often did.

He raised his eyebrows. I raised mine back.

"You're underage, Sabine."

"I think I've proven that may well be debatable, Ethan." I held his gaze. I didn't want to be treated like a kid tonight. At least for tonight, I wanted to make my own choices.

When I saw the tug at his lips I knew I'd won. He didn't say anything more, just disappeared into the swarming crowd. I hoped I wasn't going to get a virgin drink and a lecture on his return.

I relaxed into my chair. The music was loud and I let myself sink into it, my body starting to sway to the beat. I liked this place. I wished I could get out more at night. The city really changed at witching hour, in a good way.

"Sabine?"

I flinched, spinning in my seat.

Oh, mother of all things that wreck my lives.

Shit.

"Davis! Hi!" I said, completely freaked out. I hadn't even considered running into somebody. I was such an idiot. I should've at least looked around before sitting down—and *Davis*, of all people. "What are . . . what are you doing here?" I blurted.

His eyes darted beyond me briefly. "Just hanging out with Finn while he's in town," he said, gesturing to where a guy was bent over the pool table, lining up a shot. I nodded awkwardly. We'd never met, but I knew Finn was his brother and that he was in the Navy.

I plastered a cheesy grin on my face. "How are you?" I yelled over the music.

"Shouldn't I be asking you that? Capri called me after she spoke to you. Said you were in the hospital and she has to go visit your little sister tomorrow." Davis was tall and, unlike Angus, clean-cut. He was a nice guy, but every time I saw him I thought of my father. The way he was always so neatly presented and careful with his words threw me. It was like he was crying out for approval. Some girls may look for a version of their father in a potential boyfriend—I am not one of them.

I stood up, trying to gain a little composure . . . and a plan.

"I, um . . . Davis, it's complicated."

He took a step closer to me, taking in my outfit, then glancing at my broken wrist. "How? Are you sick or not?"

"Well, they thought I was, but . . . ," I stammered.

Right then, an arm slipped around my waist from behind. Warm tender hands splayed territorially across my belly and Ethan pulled me back against his chest, planting a solitary, knee-weakening kiss on my neck before resting his chin on my shoulder to look right at Davis's stunned face. Heat poured through my body, every nerve ending suddenly alive.

When Ethan spoke, he made sure it was loud enough

JESSICA SHIRVINGTON

for Davis to hear. "I told you everyone would find out eventually, Sabine."

His words flowed so easily, his voice taking on a liquid quality that made the hairs on my arms stand up. His own arms stayed wrapped around me and I couldn't help but notice how different they felt compared to Dex's. No, how different they made *me* feel.

The place where Ethan had kissed me fleetingly on the neck burned, and before I knew what I was doing, my body took over and I was leaning back into his arms.

Shit!

"Sabine, what's going on? Are you with this guy?" Davis asked, staring daggers at the hands on my stomach.

This isn't happening, I told myself. Maybe I really have gone insane and I'm imagining things?

As if on cue, Ethan started to play with the bottom of my T-shirt, finding a small line of flesh. It was all I could do to stay upright. How could such a small touch do so much?

"Sabine?" Davis prompted impatiently.

Ethan took over. "Look man, I snuck her out of the hospital for a few hours—she's going straight back, no harm. Her parents won't approve of us and we just wanted to have a bit of time together. You know how it is."

Some part of my brain finally clicked into gear and I realized what Ethan was doing.

"Davis, um . . . this is a friend of mine," I said, avoiding using his name in case it got back to the hospital—or my parents. I wasn't going to let Ethan get into trouble for me.

"Boyfriend," Ethan clarified, somehow managing to move us even closer together so that I could feel the full length of his body against mine.

Davis wasn't happy. I knew that Capri had been trying to set us up, but until now I hadn't realized that Davis had clearly been in favor of the idea too. "I didn't know you were seeing anyone."

"Oh, it's new. *Really* new." Me? Breathless?

"But when you know, you know, right?" Ethan added unnecessarily.

I craned my head to give him a look, but the way he was positioned my lips were basically on his before I quickly spun back toward Davis. Pulled tight against Ethan's chest, I could feel every breath he was taking and I was sure he could feel my heart hammering.

"Why all the lies?" Davis said curtly.

"It's not lies. I was in the hospital. I mean, I am. I just . . . I snuck out. You won't tell anyone, will you?" I asked nervously.

"Like Capri? Your best friend."

"Davis, please don't be mad at me. I'm sorry that you and I . . ." I swallowed. Ethan stayed silent, still holding me. "But if my parents find out, they'll go nuts."

Out of nowhere Ethan planted another, more lingering

kiss on the base of my neck, his nose trailing a path up to my hairline. Was he smelling me?

My legs almost gave way, but I kept my eyes on Davis, hoping he wouldn't lose it.

After a tense pause, he sighed. "Sure, Sabine."

I smiled in relief.

Davis looked at me questioningly. "So, you're *definitely* with *him*, then?"

Ethan chose this moment to become impatient. "Yeah, man. She's with me, *then*."

I elbowed Ethan, but he didn't let me go.

"Davis, I—"

"It's okay," he said, cutting off my apology. "I won't tell anyone I saw you."

"Thanks, Davis. I'm . . . you know," I said, still fumbling with my words.

"It's all good." Davis looked over to his brother—who had abandoned his cue stick and was watching us curiously—and lifted his chin in the direction of the exit. He then looked back at us, nodding once. "I was just on my way out." And with that he turned and headed straight for the door.

I spun around. Ethan dropped his arms and stepped back, retrieving the drinks he'd left on a nearby table. I sat down again and took a sip—rum and Coke.

I couldn't look at him.

"What was that all about?" I asked, staring at my drink.

"You were freaking out. This way you can tell your friends you snuck out of the hospital with a secret boyfriend and they'll leave you be. At least about *why* you're in and out of the hospital."

"And when they expect to see you and me walking hand in hand afterward? What then?" I blushed, thinking of how nice that would be.

When I glanced up he was looking at me, his expression tinged with sadness. "It won't be a problem."

"What does that mean?"

He shrugged. "It means you'll think of something." After a pause he smirked. "You can tell them I turned out to be a loser."

"That won't be hard, I suppose." I returned the smirk.

He sat back in his chair. "Anyway, we're here to talk about you, Sabine."

Now was the time to take my chance, while I still had it. I couldn't get sucked in again. Ethan had proven he was full of tricks, and despite his help with Davis I couldn't trust him. I leaned in innocently. "Ethan, I'm . . . I just need a moment. I'm going to go to the ladies' room, okay?"

He looked at me suspiciously, but what was he really going to say? He nodded. "I trust you."

If words could hurt, they did.

I started to weave my way through the groups of people. When I was sure Ethan could no longer see me, I quickly slipped out the front door and ran toward the convenience store we'd passed a few blocks away. When I stumbled in, physically exhausted, the old man and his wife sitting behind the counter stood up. "Are you all right, girl?" he asked, looking beyond me to see if someone was following me.

I took in a few breaths. My heart was racing. Running right after my recent medical adventures might not have been the best idea. "Yeah. Fine. Just in a rush. You don't happen to offer a key copying service?"

The man smiled, and pointed to a sign above him: KEY COPYING $1.99 AND UP. "Do you have the key?"

I dipped my hand into Ethan's jacket pocket and pulled out the set of keys. I removed the one Ethan had used to open the window and passed it to the man.

"Just that one?" he asked.

The truth was, I would have liked them all. For all I knew, one of them was a key to the front door. But I couldn't risk the extra time. I nodded. At least a key to the window meant I could get out.

When I got back to the table, Ethan looked relieved to see me. I shrugged off his jacket and sat in my chair. "The ladies' bathroom is much more interesting here than at the hospital," I said conversationally.

Ethan smiled, watching as I took a sip of my drink. "Go easy on that; it's the only one you're getting."

I rolled my eyes, settling back and trying hard not to look out of breath. I'd run most of the return trip.

"Do you think it's a parallel world? Or another place, like another planet or something?" he asked, getting down to business.

"I don't know. It's just like here, only different. I'm different. The world is generally the same, but . . . I don't know how to explain it."

"Would this place exist there?" he asked, looking around the bar.

"Maybe, maybe not. But even if it did, it'd be different. Maybe run by different owners. Sometimes it's like the worlds have the same general plan, like they've been mapped out or something, but then because the people are all different, everything has been interpreted differently. You know, buildings, houses, schools . . . It's like everything is similar, but just not quite the same." I tried not to look as nervous as I felt. I'd thought about this stuff for so long now, but I'd never tried to explain it to anyone.

"So you have different people around you?"

I nodded. "Every now and then I'll see someone in both worlds. It's weird. I call it a glitch. But I've never met anyone like me—anyone who knows they're living two lives."

He let this sink in. "So maybe we all live two lives, but

we have no memories of the days between midnight. Maybe some of us have several lives, but we don't know it—like a form of reincarnation, but we live all of our lives at once, until they all run out."

"Like a cat has nine lives, you mean?"

"You tell me?"

I twirled my straw. "It's possible. I've wondered the same thing. Both of my lives are in Massachusetts, but it's a big world, so people could be doubling up all over the place."

He smiled and leaned forward. "So maybe my other life is in California." He looked as if he liked the idea.

"Yeah, or Scotland. You'd look interesting in a kilt."

He laughed loudly. Which made me laugh too.

"Why are you so happy about that?"

His eyes lit up. "I like the idea that there's more to life. You know, that we go on. Have you ever considered that what's happening to you is a version of the afterlife—even a kind of heaven?"

My smile faded. "No, Ethan. I live this. It's not heaven. If anything, it's hell."

"I'm sorry, Sabine. I didn't mean to imply it was easy. But I can't help but think, if this *is* happening to you, maybe it's for a reason. And maybe it could be amazing if you just . . . I don't know, accepted it."

When he saw the look on my face, he quickly changed his tune. "Do you have a boyfriend in Wellesley?" he blurted, and judging by his expression, I wasn't the only one surprised by the question.

"I . . . I . . . Why?" I asked. And why hadn't I just answered?

He bit down on his bottom lip and started toying with the condensation on his glass. "Just wondering."

I stared into my near-empty drink. "Yes."

"And I'm assuming, since Davis obviously thought he had a chance with you, you aren't seeing anyone in this world at the moment?"

"Um . . . no, I'm not. I don't think that would exactly be right."

I could feel his eyes on me, studying me intently, before he nodded. "Do you love him?"

"Who? Dex?" I asked, startled by the question.

"If that's his name, *Dex*." He said the word like he already knew him and didn't like him. For some twisted reason, I liked that.

When I didn't answer he raised his eyebrows, prompting me.

"Ethan, I . . . It's different there." I looked down at myself, at my miniskirt and tight T-shirt. "*I'm* different. Dex is . . . he's good to me and we're a good match."

Ethan's voice moved down a gear, his eyes narrowing. "You didn't answer the question, Sabine. Do you love him?"

I suddenly felt defensive of my Wellesley life. "Why are you asking, anyway?"

He was still, his chin now resting in his hand, his gaze piercing its way into me. When he answered, it felt like his eyes were saying something completely at odds with his words. "Just curious."

Caught in his gaze, it took me a moment to remember myself. "I'll answer you if you answer two of my questions first." I couldn't let this guy get the upper hand, beautiful lips or not. I had to remember that I needed to protect myself.

He leaned back and crossed his arms over his chest. "Shoot."

"Do you believe me?"

He took a sip of his drink and put it down, his eyes never leaving mine. "God help me, I think I might be starting to. But I'm still going to ask you to do things for me, keep proving it to me, if that's okay. Thing is . . . I think I like the idea too much *not* to believe you."

I felt a sudden rush of tears. It wasn't a declaration of belief, but it was a start.

"And two?"

I swallowed, my nerves returning. "Are you my nurse, Ethan? Or is this something else—are we friends? Are we . . . ? Or is this just nurse–patient stuff?"

Ethan studied his hands. When he looked up, his eyes were pensive. "Technically I do some night nursing at the hospital, like a night supervisor, I suppose. As for whether this is nurse–patient stuff . . . It should be. But nothing about this is normal." He gestured to the drink he'd bought me and then to the bar. "Look around—does this look like a nurse–patient environment?"

"No."

He nodded as if that answered everything. Which of course it didn't.

"So now answer *my* question," he said.

The words were out of my mouth before I knew it. "I count when he kisses me. Every time, except once . . . I've never been able to get past ten seconds very successfully." I glanced up. He was looking right at me.

"Why are you with him if he makes you feel like that?"

"Because he's . . . Dex. And in that world, all I ever wanted was to be his girlfriend. He's perfect for me."

"Sounds ideal," he said drily.

My eyes narrowed. "He is."

Ethan wasn't deterred. "What happened that one time?"

"Sorry?" I asked.

"When you stopped counting?"

"Oh, I was thinking of someone . . . something else."

Ethan's teeth played with his bottom lip again and my insides flipped. I knew what he was about to ask, the next obvious question. What would he say if I told him I'd been thinking about him? Could there be a chance . . . ? But then I remembered the plan. Everything I'd been working toward:

Dex, graduation night, my future in Wellesley. I spoke quickly before Ethan could.

"Dex is good to me. He . . . he's my future. After graduation night everything will be easier with him—and for me."

"What do you mean?" he asked, sitting back.

I shrugged. "We . . . we've made plans," I said uncomfortably.

Ethan's jaw clenched tightly and I cursed my rambling mouth. He knew exactly what I meant.

"Oh. Right. Sounds magical. Hope you can count that high." He looked at his watch. "We should get you back."

Deflated, I nodded and followed him out of the bar. We walked in silence until Ethan stopped a block away from the hospital and leaned against a wall, folding over at his waist to brace his hands on his knees.

"Are you okay?" I asked.

"Just a headache." He pushed off the wall. "Let's go."

We continued the walk silently, but I noticed the pace was considerably slower.

When we reached the open window Ethan helped me in and then followed, locking the security grille behind him.

"Night, Sabine," he said quickly. He walked toward the door without looking back.

"Good night, Ethan," I replied, but he was already gone.

CHAPTER TWENTY-ONE

Roxbury, Wednesday–Saturday

Whatever Ethan had written in his report, I figured I owed him one. I was still escorted everywhere by Macie, but it seemed the reins had been loosened. Bathroom visits now included locked-door privacy, though time restricted, and I was allowed to eat my meals with the "general community."

Unfortunately my hopes of finding a kindred soul— someone who would give me the inside gossip, show me the secret tunnels, and sneak me into Dr. Levi's office to search through and destroy my files—were short-lived.

My table of lunch companions included an elderly woman, Daisy, with lollipop-pink lipstick—which wasn't just on her lips. Her lunch was entirely liquid and her only words were to tell me there was a butterfly hatching out of my ear. I assumed she was from the top floor. Next to her was an overweight guy, Gus, who was probably about my age and didn't even look up from his PSP long enough to say hello. We'd passed each other in the halls, so I knew he was from my floor. I watched him for a while, interested in his ability to shovel food into his mouth without ever looking away from his game.

My final lunch buddy was a slender girl, Abigail, who was younger than I am, fifteen at most. I found it hardest to look at her. Something or someone had yanked out all the hair from one side of her scalp, leaving weeping flesh exposed. When she took a few, very measured mouthfuls of food, I could see other exposed wounds up and down her arms, as if the skin had literally been scraped off. I had an awful feeling Abigail's injuries were self-inflicted. No wonder Ethan had been so angry to see my cuts.

Dr. Levi had sent a message that morning asking to reschedule our daily appointment to 2:00 p.m., so after lunch I headed to his office. When I knocked and opened the door, he was on the phone. He gestured for me to take a seat in one of the cane chairs. I moved across the room awkwardly and then made the decision to go ahead and drag the chair to the same spot by the window.

"You should be resting," Dr. Levi said into the phone. Then, "You do know you have nothing to prove to anyone . . ." He glanced at me. "Okay, fine . . . If that's what you want, but I'll be back up soon and I'm arranging for Dr. Milton to stop by." He hung up, a worried expression shadowing his features before he seemed to snap out of it.

"Hello, Sabine. How are you today?"

"Fine," I said, settling into my position and closing my eyes toward the sun.

He sighed. "I thought we were going to try to do some of that talking and listening today."

I hiked my legs up onto the windowsill. "I talked to Ethan."

"He mentioned that. But he's not the only one you can talk to."

"Don't see any point in explaining myself again. It's a waste of time."

"Well, judging from his report you didn't say a great deal."

I felt my heart skip a beat. Had Ethan kept our conversation last night private? It was hard to suppress the smile. I shrugged for Levi's benefit.

His next words weren't what I was expecting. "Want to play darts?"

I opened my eyes and looked at him. "Are you sure I can be trusted with sharp objects?"

"Not entirely," he answered, even as he held the darts out to me.

I couldn't stop the grin. I knew it was probably some therapy technique, but I'd always wanted to try playing darts. Levi stood in the middle of the room, his dated suit and glasses making him look older than he probably was—I guessed he was around forty-five. I could see why people liked him and would want to talk to him when they had problems. In some ways, I wished it were that simple for me. But I also knew Levi was a man of logic—it was how he brought people around. He needed that logic as the foundation of everything he did, and I wasn't going to be the one to take that away from him. But darts . . . ?

I stood up and took them from his outstretched hand. "What the hell."

"Indeed."

I was edgy with anticipation. I'd always associated this level of anxiety with the Shift, but this wasn't the same kind of fear. And yet, counting down the minutes to Ethan's arrival seemed just as nerve-racking. It was hard to make sense of everything that had happened in the early-morning hours with him. I didn't know if he would be happy to see me tonight or not. Mostly I just wanted to see his face.

When he finally opened my door, I'd been waiting so long I'd almost accepted he wasn't coming. But then my eyes met his and something inside me relaxed. I couldn't be sure, but I thought maybe something in him did too.

He held out a coat draped over his arm. "So you don't get cold."

I beamed. "Where are we going?"

"To the park."

"At night?" I took the coat and slipped it on. I could tell it was his. It had his wintergreen scent, and I had to stop myself from nestling my face into the fabric.

"It's my favorite place, day or night."

My heart leaped at the thought of Ethan taking me somewhere that was special to him. As if he wanted to share it with me.

Just like he had in the early hours of that morning, Ethan unlocked the window and we slipped outside. I was now grateful for my ground-floor room—and the easy access to the parking lot. Ethan walked straight up to a car, an old-model silver Jeep covered in dry leaves, and opened the passenger door.

"Don't drive much?" I asked, looking at the state of the Jeep.

He shrugged. "I live nearby, so I hardly use it. Levi lets me park it here."

I jumped in and before I knew it we were driving through Boston. The relief was so immense, I actually groaned.

"What is it?" he asked, glancing between the road and me.

"Oh, nothing. I just love driving—the freedom. I like the idea that you could put all of your stuff in a car one day and drive until you wanted to stop."

He nodded, like he totally understood.

I wasn't sure where we were going until he parked on Arlington Street. "The Public Garden?"

He smiled, jumped out of the car, and came around to open my door. The garden was part of the central city parklands in Boston. I'd never been there; it was visited mostly by tourists or inner-city workers during their lunch break. But I followed Ethan as he led the way over the waist-high gate and into the park. He stopped near a large weeping willow by the lagoon and started to shake out a blanket.

"Aren't we prepared?" I teased, noticing he had a whole bag of supplies.

"I come here a lot."

I looked around. "Is it safe here this late?"

He kept unloading things, creating a small picnic for us. "There are some homeless people around, but I give them some money or food now and then and they never bother me. We're safe."

It certainly seemed as if we had the park to ourselves. It was amazing—the lights of the city bouncing off the lagoon and highlighting the vibrant green foliage of the willow, its leaves just grazing the water's edge. The famous swan boats that drew in all the tourists were tied up for the night, their craning white necks turned toward us, while the glowing white lamps above the suspended footbridge completed the fairy-tale effect. And there I was, in the middle of Boston. With Ethan. I felt the oddest sensation then; this scene didn't belong in either one of my lives. And yet, it felt right.

He motioned for me to sit, and when I did he draped another blanket over my shoulders. "Just in case."

But then he sat down and I noticed that he was the one who looked as if he needed a blanket. His eyes were dark and he looked tired.

"Are you sick?" I asked.

"I'm fine. I just get bad migraines. It's annoying; everyone's always telling me to rest." He looked out over the lagoon as a family of ducks paddled by.

"Maybe this wasn't such a good idea."

He smiled and my breath caught as the light hit the perfect angle on his face. It was getting harder to ignore that he was utterly gorgeous.

"You think I'd be better off staring into the hospital's fluorescent lights with a headache?" he asked, looking amused as he noticed the way I was staring at him.

"I guess not." I averted my eyes and leaned back on my elbows. "Aren't you going to get into trouble if someone catches us?"

"Probably."

"Doesn't that worry you?"

"I guess I think some things are more important than just following the rules." He glanced at me with a raised eyebrow. "And you don't seem to fit into any guidelines anyway."

I blushed, pleased he didn't just view me as one of the patients. "What do you do in the daytime?" I continued as I wriggled to make myself more comfortable.

He lay back beside me, putting his arms under his head. "This and that."

"That's kind of vague. Family? Friends?" I prompted, eager to know more about him.

"No brothers or sisters, and I spend all my time at the hospital, so I guess most of my friends are there. I keep in touch with some college friends, but not as much as I'd like to."

I was surprised he seemed so isolated, but somehow it only made me feel closer to him. Still, I couldn't help thinking Ethan had his own fair share of secrets. "Parents?" I asked.

I saw the pain cloud his eyes before he quickly turned his attention back to the lagoon. "House fire three years ago. I was away on a camping trip with my girlfriend at the time." He cleared his throat. "No one could even contact me. I didn't find out they were gone until four days after."

My heart sank for him. It also explained a lot. I wanted to tell him how sorry I was, but it seemed such a hollow sentiment. "That's why you're so . . . Why you care about . . ."

He raised an eyebrow again. "Whether you live or die?"

I grimaced, but nodded.

"Partly," he responded, pulling out a piece of paper from his pocket. "Before I forget."

He was changing the subject. I looked at the list and held back the sigh. More of the same. Languages and chemical questions mostly, for which I was grateful. At least I didn't have to work out any long mathematical equations. I memorized the list, and when I tucked it away I grabbed hold of Ethan's wrist, turning it to see the time. Eleven p.m. I bit the inside of my cheek nervously.

"It's to the second, I promise," he said.

Despite the deception of the previous night, I believed him.

"Will you stay out here, with me? While you . . . At midnight, I mean." He still couldn't say the word "shift"— it would mean he believed me, when clearly he was still making up his mind.

Normally I hated being around people when I shifted. Hated being somewhere unfamiliar. But tonight . . . tonight I found myself nodding, which seemed to please Ethan greatly.

"What happened to your girlfriend?" I asked at one point.

I saw his smirk from the corner of my eye. "She wasn't for me."

"So you have a type then?" I asked, teasing despite my racing heart.

He tilted his head toward me, amusement playing in his eyes. "No, I've always been more interested in finding a one of a kind."

I bit back a smile, but he still caught it, and I heard his soft chuckle.

We stared up at the sky, talking every now and then. Ethan asked questions but didn't bombard me or push his views or judgments on me . . . too much. For the first time in my life—*either* of them—I felt like I could talk about my lives honestly. And each time I touched his wrist he raised his arm to show me the time, as if we'd always done this.

I tried to keep my cool, but a few minutes before midnight I couldn't hold back the trembling. Ethan didn't say anything, he just reached over and took my hand in his. And as I shifted, I found myself hoping he might never let go.

For the next few days I did everything Ethan asked, sneaking off during my lunch breaks in Wellesley to find the answers to his questions on the Internet. I even managed to find a semi-reliable translation program for the languages. I went back and forth between my worlds, maintaining appearances in Wellesley and giving Ethan all the evidence he'd requested.

Each time I shifted back to Roxbury, he was there, holding my hand, anchoring me. Each time he watched me intently, looking for something. I don't know what. The night after the park, we went to a late-night café, but I suggested we go back to the garden the following night. He seemed happiest there.

Ethan asked me lots of questions. Some I could answer and some I couldn't, and for some . . . there wasn't an answer he wanted to hear. He just couldn't accept that I didn't believe there was a way to live in both worlds happily.

We were lying under our weeping willow on Friday night and I'd just shifted back from Wellesley and recited my answers—once again, all flawless—when I finally snapped.

"What would you have me do, Ethan? What's supposed to happen if I get married one day? Have *kids*! Am I supposed to do that in both worlds? Leave my children behind every day and go to a new family? Never tell anyone who I really am? *Love* two different people?"

Ethan rolled onto his side and looked into my eyes, gently wiping away the tear sliding down my cheek.

"I don't know. No. Probably not. If you love one person, you love them fully, or there's no point. Then again . . ." he trailed off.

"Then again, *what*?" I sniped.

"You're the one who seems to think that when you're with someone you can't kiss for longer than ten seconds, the thing to do is stay and, how did you put it, *make plans*."

I shook my head at him, but couldn't manage a response. Why did he care so much anyway?

"Maybe you could find the same person in both worlds," he suggested, but he seemed to be sharing in my sadness now.

"It's unlikely, Ethan. And anyway, even if I did, there's

no guarantee they would be the same or . . . argh!" It was impossible to explain.

He bit his lip, thinking, and I couldn't help staring while it slowly slipped out from under his teeth.

"Sabine, have you ever seen me there?" he asked hesitantly.

"No."

"Didn't think so."

"Why do you say that?"

He shrugged, still looking at me closely. "I think I'd know if I'd met you before. I mean on some level, even if I didn't remember exactly, part of me, I guess my soul, would know deep down."

"Maybe." But I wasn't sure I agreed with that. I'd seen people in both worlds before, like fruit-stand guy—people who would surely recognize me if they knew on "some level."

"You *are* pretty annoying. That kind of sticks with someone," he said with a smirk.

"Then I definitely haven't met you in my other life."

He laughed before settling back down beside me, both of us watching the willow branches sway in the predawn breeze.

"Sabine?" he said softly.

"Hmm?"

"The choice you've been considering . . . Have you made up your mind?"

The question threw me. I'd thought I had. But saying so to Ethan felt wrong. I couldn't explain to him how this was my one chance to have the life I'd always wanted. This could be my one chance to actually live.

I sighed. "Ethan, don't."

"Yes, then." It was his turn to sigh. "Won't it be hard to leave everyone? Your family, Maddie, Capri? Don't you want to be here for them—be a part of their futures?"

I sat up, not looking at him. "You didn't put yourself on that list."

He sat up quickly, grabbed me by the shoulders, and spun me toward him. "Listen to me. This is not about me! This is a choice you have to make for you. It doesn't matter how much I . . . It has to be about other things. Not me, Sabine. *Not me*."

I recoiled, pulling myself out of his grasp. I was so shocked, I just sat there, frozen. So hurt. Utterly embarrassed.

Finally, when neither one of us said anything, I stood up. "Sun will be up soon. You should take me back." I started walking toward the car so he wouldn't see my face.

When we got back to my room I went straight to the bathroom to change for bed. I couldn't believe I'd made such a fool of myself. There I was, sneaking out with Ethan every night, thinking maybe there was something between us, something more than I'd dared to even hope for . . . But there wasn't. He didn't want to be part of my world. *Not me*, he'd said. He didn't even want to be a consideration.

I'd let myself get carried away.

I stared at my reflection in the bathroom mirror, angry that I'd allowed myself to be derailed so badly. If I'd been more focused on what I should've been doing, maybe everything would have been sorted out by now. Instead of focusing on Ethan, I should've been concentrating on my plan. I still had no idea how I was going to make everything work.

"Especially since I'm stuck in this shit hole!" I cried to myself, leaning against the sink.

When I got back to my room, I was surprised to see Ethan still there, sitting in the chair, head in his hands.

I climbed silently into bed and rolled over, turning my back to him. "I'm tired, Ethan."

"Your graduation is coming up, isn't it?"

I didn't answer.

"You said the other day that after graduation everything would be better. You didn't just mean you and Dex, did you? It's *all* gearing up toward then, isn't it? So how does it work—does this life end before or after graduation day in your other life?"

I took a deep breath, trying not to give away the fact that I was crying. "After," I admitted.

"You've got it all worked out. You and Dex will be together, you'll tie up any loose ends in this world and get your one life. All your dreams will come true." His words were heavy with accusation.

I couldn't stand it anymore. "It's the only dream I have!

But thanks for understanding. I get it now, Ethan. I can see how little you think of me. How pathetic I must seem. I should've realized sooner and then I wouldn't have . . ."

He was on his feet and by my bed. "Wouldn't have what?"

I shook my head and buried my tear-streaked face in the pillow. "Just go, Ethan."

I heard the door close behind him.

CHAPTER TWENTY-TWO

Roxbury, Saturday–Sunday/
Wellesley, Saturday–Sunday

The rest of the weekend passed by, each day dragging as I tried to develop the plan that would end all of this torment. But even in Wellesley I struggled to pull myself together, Ethan's words playing over and over in my mind.

Not me.

To make matters worse, Ethan didn't turn up to work on Saturday night—which felt like a slap in the face. And in Wellesley, things weren't much better. I slept most of Saturday. After shifting and hobbling to the bathroom, I'd caught a glimpse of myself in the mirror and decided that, for today at least, sleep came first. I was shockingly gaunt, with dark circles under my eyes. It had become impossible to keep track of the waking-versus-sleeping hours of my lives. Staying awake for the Shift every night and, more often than not, ending up with my head over the toilet was taking a visible toll. No wonder Miriam was so convinced the fruit diet was working.

The good thing was, my school days had officially ended on Friday, and if ever anyone deserved to have finished their school education, it was me. Now the only thing left was Monday's graduation.

When I finally made my way downstairs, wearing a white maxiskirt and simple black camisole, the house was empty. There was a note from Mom on the kitchen counter saying she'd left me to sleep in and enjoy my first official day of freedom—with a P.S. telling me she'd deposited some money into my account so I could go and buy the dress I'd been eyeing for graduation dinner.

I checked my watch. It was after lunchtime and I could think of nothing I'd rather do than be my normal Wellesley self and take part in some serious retail therapy. I texted Miriam and arranged to meet her at the mall.

"Are you going to buy the black or the silver?" Miriam asked, as we walked toward the formal-wear shop.

"The black." There had never been any doubt from the moment I'd tried it on. When I imagined myself in that dress, I felt sexy. Mature. It was the perfect choice. And Dex would love it.

"Did you confirm your hotel reservation?"

"Yes."

"Transportation?"

"Dex is driving."

"And what about your mom?"

I shrugged. "I told her a while back that I was going to be staying in the city on graduation night. It was weird; she didn't even ask me anything about it, just said okay. I'm pretty sure she knows who I'll be staying with and figures it was inevitable."

"You're eighteen, what can she really say?" Miriam gave an excited clap. "That's everything organized!"

I nodded.

Later, as we waited for my dress to be bagged, Miriam turned to me. "Is everything okay, Sabine? You look a little . . . freaked out."

I concentrated on rearranging my wallet. "Yeah. Just . . . I don't know, nervous maybe."

She studied me for a moment. I expected her to make a joke, but instead she flicked her perfectly styled hair and looked at me seriously. "If you aren't ready, you don't have to do anything. Once you go down that road, things change." She sighed. "Don't get me wrong; I love Brett and I'm glad that we are . . . you know, but I think if I could go back in time, I would've waited a little longer. The first time can be a bit . . . uncomfortable."

"Wow. I never thought I'd hear you say that."

She nudged my shoulder. "And I'll never admit it again,

but if you aren't a hundred percent sure, maybe you should just talk it through with Dex."

I bit my lip. "I don't think I can do that."

She gave me another long look while the cashier handed me my dress and then we were back out on the street.

"Sabine, is there someone else?" Miriam asked eventually.

I blushed. "No. Why? Why would you think that?"

She raised her eyebrows at me. "I don't know. It's just . . . you seemed so ready and now you look so unsure, and Dex asked me the other day if I'd seen you hanging out with anyone else. I can't help but wonder if you might've met someone who's changed your mind."

I thought of Ethan. Absent Ethan. His words: *Not me.*

"No, there's no one else." Except in my overactive imagination. And Dex's. I couldn't believe he'd been asking around about me. "Like I said, I'm just nervous. Dex and I have waited long enough." I glanced down at my dress bag. When I looked back up at Miriam, I was smiling. "Earrings?"

She returned my smile. "Definitely."

Preparing to shift back to Roxbury on Saturday night was terrible. For the first time since being admitted to the hospital, I'd be shifting back to an empty room. And the reality of where that room was—in a mood-disorders ward, which was just the PC way of saying "psycho ward"—felt harsher than ever.

When I shifted, the sense of loneliness stayed with me. After my usual run to the bathroom, I settled myself in my bed and tried to sleep straight through to Sunday afternoon. Sheer exhaustion helped stop my churning mind, and I think I could have slept even longer if a visitor hadn't arrived.

Dad sat in the chair usually filled by Ethan and fidgeted awkwardly with the armrests.

"How have your sessions with Dr. Levi been going?"

I sat on the end of my bed, feeling exposed and vulnerable. I was no longer his daughter. I was now in the category of "patient." My entire relationship with my parents had changed forever. The strange thing was, staring at my father I realized he looked almost as weary as I felt. I wondered if his visits to the local bar had become more frequent.

I decided to offer an olive branch. "They're okay. I had one today. He seems to think I might need some medication. That part of this could be a chemical imbalance or something." Which was a complete lie.

My father let out a quivering sigh. "That's good, that's good, Sabine. I think Dr. Levi really knows what he's doing."

I didn't correct him—didn't explain that Levi had no idea what he was doing, that I wasn't the average patient.

"I know you hate me right now. I know you think we let you down, but we just want you back." He ran a hand through his hair, struggling for words. "I'm sorry about how things went at home; we handled it badly. But, Sabine, please understand that we didn't know what to do. We just want our daughter back."

Their daughter—the one who had to lie every day, I thought bitterly. But looking at his face, I could see that he'd meant it as his own kind of olive branch.

"How's Mom?" I asked, pulling my knees to my chest and wrapping my arms around them.

He shook his head. "You know your mom. She likes things to be a certain way. This whole thing has really blindsided her. She feels responsible, like she should've prevented this before it got so . . ."

"Will you tell her that's not true? No one could have prevented this."

He smiled weakly, looking relieved.

"Maddie misses you terribly."

My heart twisted. I hated not seeing her and dreaded finding out what Mom and Dad had told her. "I miss her too. What does she . . . ? Does she know that I'm . . . ?"

He knew what I meant. "We told her you've gone away on a future careers camp. That you got a last-minute placement and had to leave right away."

I nodded. As desperate as I was to see her, I agreed with that decision. "Do you think . . . ?" I swallowed. "Dad . . ." I choked on the word. Calling him Dad was a big concession on my part. "Do you think we could keep this from her? Like, never tell her? I don't want her to ever know I was in here. Ever."

He nodded. "It would be better if she didn't. Let's just see how things pan out."

The trouble was, I *knew* how things were going to pan out. I looked down. "Okay. Tell her I love her. And Mom too."

He stood, looking more himself. "I will. Your mom will visit soon." He leaned over to give me an awkward hug before leaving.

I dedicated the rest of the day to developing an indifference to all things Ethan—especially the ache in my heart.

Macie popped her head around my door in the afternoon to let me know I had phone privileges, so I called Capri. Luckily I was no longer on day watch, so Macie didn't have to hang around for the call.

Despite Davis's promise, he'd gone ahead and spilled to Capri, telling her he'd seen me out on the town. She was barely talking to me. After half an hour of groveling she forgave me enough to demand every detail about the mysterious guy Davis had also, accidentally on purpose, mentioned.

I guess he figured he owed me no favors.

I guess he was right.

I told Capri it was just a brief thing that lasted a couple of days, and that it turned out the mystery guy didn't actually care about me at all.

True enough.

"So are you in the hospital or not?" she asked with a huff, possibly feeling a little sorry for me now that she'd heard the state of my pathetic love life.

"Yeah, I am." And then I made a decision. "Mom and Dad had me committed."

"Huh?"

"They think I'm crazy."

"What? How the hell . . . Sabine, what is going on with you?"

"It's complicated. But I'm basically locked away in a hospital. Did you go see Maddie?"

"I saw her yesterday. She's fine—thinks you're away at some camp or something. I told her that I'd spoken to you and that I might be seeing you soon. She asked me to give you a really big rabbit hug or something."

I smiled, looking at my cast, running my fingers over Maddie's bunnies.

"Sabine, I'm seriously starting to freak out and that goes totally against my beliefs. Even Angus thinks this is weird, and you know he doesn't like to think. We need some answers here."

"I know. Can you come meet me tonight? I promise I'll have answers."

"Sure. What time and where? Do I have to break into the hospital?" She sounded almost hopeful. Capri did like to live on the edge. If breaking glass was involved, all the better.

"No."

And then I put the first part of my plan into action.

As I'd expected, Ethan didn't turn up to work on Sunday night either; I'd heard a nurse talking earlier that day in the corridor, saying he wasn't well. Still, it felt like a blow to my increasingly fragile heart, and it further weakened my hopes that he might be the one to explain things to Maddie after I was gone.

After dinner, I did everything I was supposed to do. Showered, fake-socialized with the other tenants of Crazyville, acknowledged nurses, tried to be cooperative. I even hung out in the patients' lounge, pretending to watch a pointless game of Ping-Pong before heading back to my room, only to endure another random room search by Macie and Mitch. I passed with flying colors.

Once the lights were out, I was ready to move. Final room check always came fifteen minutes after lights out, and Ethan had somehow gotten me exempted from the other nightly spot checks to facilitate our outings. I was taking a chance those relaxed rules still applied.

I got dressed quickly, jumped back into bed until the final room check was done, and then I was up and digging around in my underwear. Disgusting, I know, but if there's one place no man or woman will ever check it's the crotch of your panties. Luckily most of my panties had a double-layer lining, providing an awkward yet effective hiding place—perfect for a key.

I stood in front of the window grilles and used the key I'd copied from Ethan's set to let myself out. Once on the other side I relocked the security grille and closed the window, hoping that in the event I was caught they wouldn't know how I'd escaped and I might be able to keep the key hidden for another day.

Capri was waiting in her mom's beat-up van, which looked as though it had more rust than paint. It was truly a wonder she got that thing moving without having to push it.

I ran across the parking lot and jumped into the passenger side.

"Hey."

"Hey, yourself," Capri said, pushing her almost dreadlocks back from her face. "Nice escape. Was the ass-out-first part for my benefit?" She'd had full view of my window.

I laughed. "Yes, the ass in the air was all for you."

"Figures," she quipped, and then looked ahead. "Where to?"

"Home first and then I need to make another stop."

"Not exactly what I had in mind." Capri looked out the window. She was hesitating. I didn't blame her. She had just helped spring me from the loony bin.

"I'm so grateful you're helping me, Capri. I know I've said it like a million times, but I'm sorry I lied. Being here . . . it wasn't exactly something I wanted to publicize. Things have been pretty screwed up of late." I held my breath and waited. The worst part was, I *was* truly sorry—even if my apology had been wrapped up in more deception. I was about to make her my unwitting accomplice.

"Just tell me you aren't really crazy or whatever?" she asked clumsily.

"I swear to you, I'm not insane." I smiled, trying to help her relax. "Well, unless you count the part where I'm friends with you."

It took a moment, but she cracked up, leaning across and nudging me before turning the key in the ignition. It took half a dozen tries before the engine fired up, but finally we were on our way.

Standing outside my house, it struck me that until now I hadn't known if I'd ever come home again. The way things had been going, not to mention the way I felt about Mom and Dad, I'd stopped thinking of it as home. But seeing Dad today had changed that a bit.

Actually a lot.

Maybe it was knowing that the end was near. I'd wanted it so much, my chance to be normal. But all Ethan's talk about the price I'd have to pay to get it . . . it wasn't all crap. At the very least, I wanted to make some kind of peace with this life before I said good-bye to it.

The house was silent. Lights off. I looked at my watch—just before 11:00 p.m. I didn't have time to waste if I was going to get everything done and be back by midnight.

We scaled the tree, and, balancing precariously, Capri helped me jimmy open my bedroom window. Yet again I was thankful she and Davis had taken it upon themselves to fix that little problem. Since Mom and Dad didn't know about their break-and-enter, they also hadn't known to relock the bolt.

We both slid into my room, clanking into things and being too loud. Thankfully no one seemed to stir.

"Stay here," I whispered to Capri. "I'll be back in a minute. If anyone comes in, make a run for it."

She nodded. Capri was a pro at these things. She wouldn't hesitate to split if need be.

I crept down the stairs and into the kitchen, avoiding the creaky spots in the flooring. The house seemed so foreign to me now. It was weird—such a short time away to feel like I didn't belong here anymore. Had I ever? I bit my lip and squashed the smoldering thought.

It took me awhile, but after carefully looking through a few drawers I eventually hit the jackpot when I spied Dad's coat hanging over one of the kitchen chairs. I grabbed the keys to the store, palming them to stop the jingle, and headed back to my bedroom.

Running into Maddie had not been part of the plan. But as I passed her room, her bedroom door swung open and she looked up at me, half-asleep. "Binie, you're home! I missed you so much." She rubbed her eyes. "Can you take me to the bathroom?"

My insides melted just seeing her, and before I knew what I was doing I'd picked her up to hug her tight and was carrying her to the bathroom. On the way back, she rested her head on my shoulder. "Are you going away, Binie?" she asked.

I took her into her room and gently placed her on the bed. "What makes you say that, kiddo?"

She shrugged sleepily. "I had a dream that you had to go somewhere else. You were so sad. You didn't want to say good-bye to me, but you had to."

Oh God. Was this happening?

"Hey, you know how much I love you. It doesn't matter what happens; I'll always be with you, even if . . . even if I can't really be here. Do you know what I mean?"

"I think so." She yawned.

I brushed the hair off her face and she snuggled into her blankets. "Life is precious, Maddie. Always remember that." The irony of choosing Ethan's sentiment in that moment wasn't lost on me. I hated him a little for that.

"You're not the same as everyone else, Binie. I love you always. Do you still have my rabbits?"

I bit back my tears and nodded. "Of course I have your rabbits." I pointed to my cast. "They will always be with me, just like you. I love you too, Mads. Don't tell anyone you saw me, okay?"

She nodded, already falling back to sleep. In the morning, she'd probably think it was all a dream. Maybe it was for the best. I kissed her on her forehead.

Capri had waited for me, even though she'd heard Maddie moving around. She wasn't happy about being kept in the dark, but she nevertheless drove me to my next destination and waited outside while I let myself into Mom and Dad's store and collected the items I needed. It would be a terrible cocktail—one that had no chance of failing. Given Macie had launched a random room search on me today, I figured I'd have just enough time to keep the drugs hidden before . . .

Capri drove me back to my house. I sneaked in alone, returned the keys, and wrote a quick note, which I slipped under my mattress. They would find it one day. When we pulled into the hospital parking lot, Capri didn't hold back. She demanded some answers.

"It's complicated," I said, which didn't seem to help. But I'd given it some thought since we'd talked on the phone and decided it wouldn't help her to know everything—she'd only feel worse at the end, or try to stop me. I knew deep down that I was telling myself what I wanted to hear, but I couldn't stop now. The best thing I could do for Capri was to let her stay ignorant.

"Look." I sighed, knowing I needed to give her something. "Mom and Dad found out I was seeing that guy and thought he was a bad influence. Dad just flipped." I leaned back into the headrest, convincingly spinning my web. "He used his medical contacts and fed them this whole story about me being insane to get me locked up in here, just to keep me away from him." Capri's mouth was hanging open and I knew she was buying it. "The worst thing is . . ."—I swallowed, my emotions turning uncomfortably real—". . . they were right about him, but since I've refused to speak to the doctor, they're making me stay. The whole thing is screwed up. I . . . I'm considering getting out of Boston, you know, making a new start somewhere else." I bit my lip. So many lies.

"Where would you go?" Capri asked, shocked. "You can't leave me!"

I stared down at my hands. "If it meant getting away from all this craziness and being able to start again, you'd forgive me, wouldn't you?" It was terrible. A terrible, awful thing I was doing to her—but in my own way, I had to do something that might help her understand.

"I guess," she conceded, though she still looked unhappy.

I reached over and gave her a tight hug. "I promise I won't do anything unless I'm sure it's my only choice. If I do go, just remember it's because I was absolutely sure it was the right thing for me, okay?"

She nodded. "I'll just miss you. I don't have any other girlfriends."

I wiped away a tear. "Me too. You're a great friend, Capri. Whatever happens, you know I love you."

There. My best good-bye.

She was teary herself even as she shrugged off my words and pushed me out of the van. "Whatever you just lifted from your parents' store, I'm sure it'll fetch a fierce profit in there."

I smiled, knowing that when all was said and done she would remember this conversation and hopefully realize I was telling her that everything was for the best. I hoped she'd be okay.

"Be happy, promise?" It was something we used to say to each other when we were bullied at school by the cool kids.

"Promise," Capri said.

Sunday in Wellesley gave me a chance to spend a lazy morning with Mom by the pool. Around midday Dex called to say he was on his way over to hang out, and no amount of fake smiles could get rid of the churning in my gut. I tried to rope in Miriam and Lucy, suggesting a spur-of-the-moment pool party, but they were no help. Miriam seemed to be in a permanent hip-lock with Brett these days, and Lucy was in a pre-graduation spiral.

I was so desperate I actually called Ryan, wondering if it was his weekend to visit Mom. He just laughed and said no, teasing me that now that school had ended, I was staring straight into a friendless existence. His planned visit was still three weeks away, and he wouldn't be home before then. When I heard someone call out to him in the background, he hung up without even saying good-bye. Bastard.

When Dex arrived, daisies in hand, I blushed and put them in a vase before moving into action mode—keeping us as busy as possible, offering to get the graduation programs printed for Lucy, and collecting the dry cleaning for Mom. Basically anything that left us little time for what Dex had in mind. For once, he didn't seem to care. I guess he figured our night together wasn't far away.

And he was right.

If you didn't count my other life, G day was tomorrow.

CHAPTER TWENTY-THREE

Roxbury, Monday

On Monday night Ethan was back, quietly opening my door, checking to see if I was awake.

I was sitting in the armchair. My days of trying to sleep through the Shift were over; my routine was so out of whack there was no point trying to change things now. Not when I didn't plan on juggling it for much longer.

When I saw him, I put down my notebook and the pen I'd finally been entrusted with. The pen privilege was no small feat on my part. Lately, Levi's efforts had doubled; he insisted I start talking openly, and that if he couldn't be sure we were making progress certain privileges would be revoked. Bottom line, to avoid going back to peeing with an audience I'd spent an hour talking to him about absolute crap, making sure to focus on my "feelings" and avoid explaining much about my two worlds. It was obvious Levi thought I'd fabricated my Wellesley life to give me some sense of control

I was supposedly lacking in my Roxbury world. He even hinted that I made elements of Wellesley challenging just so I could reward myself by overcoming them. It took a lot of effort not to scream at him.

After the session, I'd spent the afternoon writing letters to Maddie. I'd given it a lot of thought since seeing her and decided I didn't want her to be exposed to things she shouldn't be; didn't want her to think I'd condone something that in other circumstances would be terrible.

The ironic thing was—I really didn't condone it.

I still had trouble admitting to myself that what I was considering, what I was now *planning*, was technically . . . suicide.

But how could I go on this way?

I honestly didn't believe I could survive if I had to go on living two lives. They may have me in a mental ward for the wrong reasons, but if I didn't make this change—give myself the chance to live a normal life—I might end up in a place like this in *both* of my lives. I couldn't risk that.

I'd written one letter to be given to Maddie straight after I was gone, and others that I wanted to have set aside for her birthdays until she was eighteen. It was the best I could do to try to help her understand that I was okay, how much I loved her, and how much I valued life. I hoped they'd get to her.

"Hi," Ethan said, his voice raspy. He looked exhausted.

"Hey," I said, and glanced at him briefly.

"I'm sorry I wasn't in the last couple of days."

I shrugged, trying to hide how much his absence had affected me. "Everyone deserves a day off now and then."

He bit his lip but didn't say anything else. Instead, since I was sitting in the chair, he perched on the edge of the bed.

I stared at my cast. The bouncing bunnies were starting to fade.

Finally, since it was clear I wasn't going to, he spoke. "Levi is talking about putting you on some meds."

I grimaced. He'd said as much, but I'd hoped that all my talking in our last session might have changed his mind. I guess I hadn't been that convincing.

"I don't care what he does."

Ethan shook his head at me. "You think you have it so bad. Did you ever stop to think that maybe you're lucky? Maybe you have a chance to do something amazing with your lives? You could . . . I don't know, you could change the world, maybe more than just this one. You could make a difference. Do you know how incredible that is? Have you ever considered that you could use your knowledge in one world to benefit the other? Have you ever even investigated?"

"You want me to make a difference? Be important?"

"Yes!"

I looked up at him. "Do you know what I want, Ethan?"

He spoke quietly. "What, Sabine? What do you want?"

His eyes bored into me and my heart fluttered. I hated the

involuntary reaction I had to him. Especially now—knowing I meant nothing to him. I ignored the feelings welling up inside and held his gaze.

"I want to be able to breathe. I want to know I'm with people who care about me—about *all* of me. And I want to be free to care about them too. To be able to tell them everything about me, not lie and pretend all the time. I want to know that if I drift off to sleep by accident one day, I'll wake up in the same place. I want to live each day once, the best that I can live it. Who are you to deny me that? I told you I don't want to die, Ethan, I *want* to live. Is that so wrong?"

"But how do you know you're choosing the right life?" he pleaded. "What if you're giving up something you don't even have yet, a future in this world that would give you more happiness than you could have ever imagined?"

"It's a risk I have to be willing to take. There are a lot of what-ifs in life. I can't live my lives hedging my bets. Trust me, that's no life."

"But that's exactly my point, Sabine. It's like that song says: life is what happens when you're busy making other plans. You keep thinking one life will be better, but how can you give up half of who you are and think it will make you happier? And while we're on the subject of what-ifs—*what if* you're wrong? You can't be sure that if you die in one world, you'll go on living in the other. What if you lose both worlds? What if you die?"

I rubbed my bare arms. "I did the tests, everything backs up the theory." I glanced nervously at the clock and then stood, pacing a couple of times. "Not long till the Shift. Do you have anything for me tonight?"

He pulled a piece of paper out of his pocket. "Why do you care about convincing me if you're just going to do it anyway?"

It was a complicated question, with an even more complicated answer. I stalled by reading the list. "*Uskon sinua.* Don't suppose you want to give me a heads-up on what language that is?"

"It's Finnish," he answered, surprising me with the clue. "You haven't answered my question."

I folded the list and shrugged vaguely.

He didn't let it drop. "I think it's because you aren't sure at all. I think there's a part of you that wishes you could find a way to have both lives and make them work together."

I started to get onto the bed, wanting my second-to-last Shift to be as smooth as possible. Ethan moved down to the end, giving me room.

"And I think you think too much," I mumbled.

At 11:45, I could feel the panic building, the blood draining from my face. Ethan's words played on my mind, eroding my confidence. I needed to get him away from me. I didn't want to be vulnerable tonight.

"You want to know why? I just want to convince you so

you'll agree to give Maddie the letters I've written for her, since I know my parents won't."

I heard his gulp. I expected him to take the comment as the slap it was intended to be and storm out of the room, leaving me to shift pathetically on my own.

The silence was broken when he finally started to move, the bedsprings squeaking. To my surprise, instead of getting off the bed, he lay down behind me and put his arm around me, steadying my trembling body.

"I can see right through you, Sabine," he murmured in my ear, pulling me closer, his wintergreen scent enveloping me. My shivers remained, but the reason for them changed entirely.

No one had ever come this close to knowing me. If anyone could see through the layers, down to the real version of myself that even I didn't know, it was Ethan.

"I'm here. I won't let go. As long as I'm here, I promise you, I won't let go."

My heart raced at both his words and his nearness, my body's reaction conflicting with my still-angry and confused mind.

"Ethan? What's going on?" I whispered.

He sighed and I felt his warm breath move around my exposed neck, as if it were claiming me. "There are things I want to tell you, things you *need* to know. But not yet. Please, Sabine, try to trust me when I say you need to make your decision thinking only of yourself. It didn't come out right the other night. I didn't mean it the way it sounded."

"It was pretty clear."

"Then why am I here?"

I had absolutely no idea.

"Just think about it. Keep thinking about this decision you're making. Keep thinking about all the conversations we've had, all the things you've told me—how extraordinary your life is. In this world, Sabine. Don't just think about how much better everything would be if you only had your other world; think about what you would miss if you didn't have *this* world."

"Why, Ethan? Why is it so important to you?"

"You said you wanted someone to know you. Maybe I just want to have someone know me too. Without you in this world, the memories of every moment we've shared together will be gone. We only exist because others see us. Part of my existence . . ." he said with a swallow, ". . . an important part, only exists because you are here to see it."

What he said was . . . beautiful. Earth-shatteringly, profoundly beautiful. And frightening. Totally and utterly terrifying.

I found myself half-laughing to stop from crying. "You know everyone thinks I'm crazy. They think Wellesley is my imaginary world. I was thinking about it today, thinking that maybe they were right—maybe I am insane. But the thing is, who says it's my Wellesley world that isn't real? Maybe it's this life that doesn't exist."

"Is that your way of telling me I'm just a figment of your imagination?"

"Maybe."

"That's impossible, Sabine." His arm tightened around me. "If I were a creation of your mind, you'd never have made me this way, believe me." I opened my mouth to question him, but before I could speak he went on. "And anyway, some things are so real you can feel them to your core. It doesn't matter where you go, they go with you. Anywhere."

I didn't know what to believe anymore. I was so tired of it all. Literally exhausted and bone weary. And Ethan was turning out to be a complication I seemed to understand less and less every day.

"It's your graduation day in your other world, isn't it?"

The lump in my throat stopped me from answering, but I managed a small nod.

"Don't . . ." He paused. "Don't forget to bring me my words," he murmured, reminding me that I still needed to gather his proof.

The Shift was coming. My stomach sank and I rolled over to face him, not bothering to hide my tears. For a moment I thought he was going to say something else, but he was quiet. "You may as well just say you still don't believe me."

His hand clasped the side of my face, tilting it back, his fingers biting into the back of my neck. "That's not what I'm saying. I just want you to get the translation."

His eyes softened and I couldn't seem to tear my own away. We stayed locked like that, his hand on my face, and before I knew what I was doing my own arms went out, wrapping around him. If only this once, I needed to hold him.

I barely managed to whisper, "Ethan, it's almost midnight. What is it you couldn't tell me?"

He shook his head. "I refuse to believe you've made your final decision, and you need to do that first. I don't want this to influence it." He took a deep breath. "And I wish I wasn't so selfish, I do . . . but Sabine?"

I shot a look at the clock. So did he. One minute till midnight.

"What?"

"Don't."

"Don't what?"

"Don't do it tonight . . . with Dex. Don't. Come back to me, Sabine." His hand slipped all the way around my neck. "Please forgive me, but . . . I love you." He pulled me to him, his lips going to mine hungrily as he gripped me so tight I could feel his arms trembling. He kissed me in a way I'd never imagined possible. *I* kissed *him* in a way I'd never thought possible.

How had I never known a kiss could shatter everything?

I matched his need with my own until I thought I might explode with the sheer intensity of my desire.

Instead, lost in the moment, I shifted.

CHAPTER TWENTY-FOUR

Wellesley, Monday—Graduation Day

I rolled right off the bed, searching for Ethan's arms, before realizing he wasn't here. And I wasn't *there*. My hard thud on the floor helped punctuate the point.

I flopped onto my back and lay there, staring at the dark ceiling, trying to remember how to breathe, how to exist. But how could I? Life as I knew it had changed in every way. I didn't know if simply breathing the way I always had would be enough; I didn't know if anything operated on the same playing field anymore. I mean, Ethan had said . . . and then he had . . . and I had . . . and it was . . . and now . . .

What?

Reality came crashing down in the form of one more quick thought.

Was it possible?

Was Ethan playing me still?

Treating me for some illness he thought I had?

I didn't want to believe it, but despite what he'd said, insinuated, done—he still hadn't told me the one thing he knew would change everything, the thing I needed and wanted to hear more than anything else in the world.

"I love you" are admittedly the words most girls want—but what did they really say? I want to spend time with you, I want to get close to you, I care about you. But the weight of those words still didn't give me what I needed from him. Nothing about what he'd said told me that he, Ethan, *believed* me.

Time was ticking.

He knew it as well as I did. He'd made his thoughts clear on the matter. He thought I was wrong and was making a mistake. Was this his way of forcing my hand? And, if so, would I let him walk me down that road?

I stared at the ceiling, wishing that I understood what was happening to me. Wishing I could go back and see his eyes on me after that kiss. I think I would have known then.

But I couldn't, and it was graduation day.

And I still couldn't forget his words. *Not me.*

Tears started to slip from my eyes. Ever since the day I'd met Ethan, my worlds had been spiraling out of control. Maybe he was the problem—the part that didn't fit. Maybe getting away from him was the key.

I wiped away the tears and forced myself to stop crying. Today was not the day for puffy eyes. But of course sleep was out of the question, so I slipped downstairs, microwaved a pot of wax, sliced up a cucumber and carried it all back to my room. After a thorough leg waxing, I placed the cucumbers on my eyes and did everything I possibly could, including singing my school anthem, to stop thinking about Ethan.

I had a plan. A good plan. He didn't know what my lives had been like. He didn't know what it was like when I was seven and woke up after wetting the bed, going into a fit of terrified shock at what my father would say when he discovered the mess. What it was like to feel that kind of intense childish fear only to be pulled from it and thrust into another reality for the next twenty-four hours, knowing all the time that you would be thrown back into that same state of terror at the end. He didn't know what it was like to be constantly thinking about what I was saying, double-checking I wasn't giving anything away, living in fear that eventually someone would find me out, call me insane. And he didn't know what it was like to never truly belong—to have two lives that were so taxing they left you with no idea of who you really were. The truth was, I was no one at all. You can't explain that to someone.

When the sun came up, Mom wasted no time floating into my room, cradling a gorgeous emerald-green knee-length wrap dress.

"I saved this one for last," she said, holding it out to me proudly. "I ordered it online ages ago, and when it arrived

I knew it would look stunning!" Mom had a slight online-shopping addiction. So far, it had been working out pretty well for me.

I smiled brightly, admiring the dress.

"You look different, you know," Mom said.

I looked up at her self-consciously. "What do you mean?"

She gave me her proud mom smile. "Grown up, ready to take on the world. I don't know really. It's almost as if you've just woken up with it this morning. You look . . . beautiful." She swept a hand down my hair and I threw myself at her, hugging her tight.

"Love you, Mom."

"I love you too, Sabine. Are you okay?"

"Yeah, just . . . all this growing-up stuff is hard sometimes."

Mom sighed. "This wouldn't have anything to do with Dex and tonight, would it?"

I gulped. "No. I . . . Mom, can we not talk about that?"

She laughed lightly. "We don't have to talk about it. You're a sensible girl. I trust you'll be responsible in your judgment. If things feel right for you, then they probably are. But if they don't, I know you'll listen to that too." She pushed me gently away from her, staring at me proudly. "Get dressed. Remember, you promised to help Lucy set up. We'll see you there, in the front row. Your father, Lucas, and Aunt Lyndal will be there too." She eyed the dress. "I can't wait to see how it looks." She headed out, but I stayed where I was. I knew she wouldn't be able to resist.

Sure enough, she paused at the door. "Ah, honey. Hair up with that one I think."

At least some things would always remain the same.

The day flew. When I arrived at the hall, Lucy was already in full melt-down mode. After calming her down we ran around for the next few hours, setting out chairs, placing programs, and arranging the lecterns, photo area, and the tea and coffee stand. By the time we actually lifted our heads from the work, the seats were all filled and the ceremony was about to start.

I couldn't have been happier. Distraction was the best medicine for me.

We received our diplomas and endured the long, drawn-out speeches from the principal and valedictorians—there were two this year, double fun. But it was incredibly satisfying. I'd waited twice as long for this day, and since I was going to miss it in my other life, I soaked up every moment, laughing with friends, getting my graduation handshake, tossing my hat into the air. Miriam received a special mention for her history grades, I received a special mention for my achievements in French, and Dex got an award for athletics.

I could hear Mom clapping loudly and gave her and Dad a wave. Dad looked great in a charcoal suit. He was sporting a new haircut, working the salt-and-pepper look for all it was worth. He probably had a new love interest. But he was there, applauding me along with Mom, Lucas, and Aunt Lyndal—who was wearing a shocking shade of bright orange. Mom kept sending her horrified looks. I was willing to bet Aunt Lyndal had done it just for the kick she got out of irritating Mom. No surprise Ryan hadn't bothered to show— something about a pressing assignment. Yeah, right.

After the ceremony, everyone hung around drinking coffee and tea and taking photos. Dex's parents insisted on having me in their family shots, which should have made me beam, but instead made me feel queasy. All too quickly the day was over and everyone started heading off to prepare for the dinner.

"We're so proud of you, sweetheart," Dad said, walking me to the front of the school grounds, where Miriam was waiting. Miriam, Lucy, and I had long planned to get ready for the evening together.

"Thanks, Dad."

"I can't believe my youngest child has finished school," he said, shaking his head proudly.

"Yeah. You're getting pretty old," I quipped.

He looked to the sky as if having a private word with God and smiled.

"Your mom and I will see you at the party. We are still invited, aren't we?"

"Yes, but remember—"

"Just for two drinks," he said, cutting me off. "After which we have to leave."

I nodded, satisfied it wouldn't be my parents who would linger annoyingly. Including them in the cocktail portion of the night was a nice gesture and all, but some parents could be reluctant to leave.

I spotted Dex as I slipped into Miriam's car. He was heading out with Noah—probably to go hang out at Brett's before the evening. He winked and threw me a look that suggested he couldn't wait for the night ahead. There was a time I would've killed for that look. Instead, my fingers went to my lips and my thoughts traveled to another world. To another person altogether.

"Come on!" Miriam yelled. "We only have, like, two hours to get ready and get to the Pavilion!"

She was right. I closed the car door. "Let's go."

"I've got first dibs on the shower," Lucy snapped.

"Three bathrooms, brainiac!" Miriam replied.

"Oh yeah." Lucy laughed. But then her eyes narrowed. "I've got the first turn with the hair straightener."

Silence. Then both Miriam and I erupted. "No way!"

The bantering and laughing didn't stop until we were dressed and ready.

Lucy wore a shimmering golden gown with tiny spaghetti straps. It looked amazing against her olive skin and perfectly styled dark-brown curls. She kept her makeup simple and looked all the better for it, applying her trademark strawberry lip gloss at the very end.

Miriam had gone with a cherry-red color and the dress floated effortlessly around her perfect figure, highlighting everything it should. Her hair fell loose and wavy around her shoulders and she wore a thick gold retro necklace low around her neck. On anyone else it might've looked weird, but Miriam owned the look.

Beside them, staring into the full-length mirror, I was wearing the black dress I'd coveted since first laying eyes on it. It was simple but elegant. A slim column all the way to the ground with a small kick in the fabric at the base. The top of the dress cut a straight line across my chest, and the straps draping my shoulders were made of intricate lace that was also featured in a corset at my waist. I had my hair down and styled around my face, thanks to Miriam, and black strappy shoes to finish the look.

"We look perfect," Miriam said, clapping her hands.

Lucy and I couldn't help our small nods.

"Tonight is going to be amazing," Lucy agreed. "And just think, come tomorrow, everything will be different."

Lucy didn't realize just how right she was.

"Sabine, what is it with you? You've been doing that all day," Miriam said, starting to laugh.

I looked into the mirror again and saw I had my fingers pressed to my lips. "Oh, nothing. I . . . I . . ."

"Am just thinking about Dex?" Lucy offered.

I nodded even as I swallowed hard.

"Brett says that Dex is totally making all these plans for you guys in the future. He said he wouldn't be surprised if he asked you to move in with him after your first year at Harvard," Miriam said.

"Oh. We'll see," I said in a daze, my fingers unconsciously going back to my lips. Because the thing was, despite my efforts, despite keeping myself busy all day . . . I hadn't been able to get Ethan out of my mind.

"You two are so cute," Lucy continued. "You know, love like yours only comes around once in a lifetime, if that."

I bit my lip. What if . . . What if a love like the one I *wanted* only came around once in any of my lifetimes? What if . . . ?

Shit.

"Girls! The boys and cars are here!" Miriam's mom called out. And suddenly I was rescued from my thoughts and caught up in the buzz of the night—the photos, cars, guys turning up, and our all-important entrance to the Pavilion. Any time I had a second to myself, someone interrupted it, expecting me to smile. And I did. Wanting to be who I was supposed to be in this world. And I was.

Mom and Dad performed perfectly, playing the happily divorced couple, leaving not first but in the first third of departing parents. I would thank them tomorrow. Dex's parents were not so compliant and it took him a while to finally load them into a car and get them out of there, which gave me a little breathing space to get my head right.

By the time we settled into each other's arms on the dance floor and I had sipped on a glass or two of the boys' "special punch" that was covertly making the rounds, I was confident that this was the right thing. I was doing the right thing. Ethan was . . . It didn't matter. Dex was my constant. He cared about me and wanted a future with me. That's what I needed to concentrate on.

"Can you believe school is over?" he said, as we danced.

"No. It's surreal. But good surreal. I'm looking forward to starting college."

He nodded, pulling me closer to him. "I'm looking forward to being able to spend the next couple of months alone, with you."

The lump in my throat wouldn't go away. So I smiled and hugged him so he wouldn't see my face.

"Are you ready to get out of here?" he asked.

This was it.

I could be sure about this—about my place in this world. I couldn't base my choices on someone else, just because I couldn't stop thinking about what it was like to be wrapped in his arms. No. I was the master of maintenance. I couldn't have changed so much in such a short space of time.

My Wellesley life was a great life. I couldn't live in a reality based only on, "What if?"

I slid my hand down and took hold of his. "Absolutely."

CHAPTER TWENTY-FIVE

Wellesley, Monday—Graduation Night

Dex drove, since he didn't drink, and I gave him directions to the hotel I'd arranged in the city. We only got lost twice, which for me was pretty good.

When we pulled into the Liberty Hotel, Dex's face was pure delight. "Nice. I've always wanted to check out this place. You know it used to be an old prison before they turned it into a hotel," he said, pulling into the valet area.

I hadn't known that. And now that I did, it really wasn't helping my state of mind.

We walked to the front desk hand in hand. While we checked in, I couldn't stop my mind spinning with all the things Ethan had said to me.

Out of nowhere, I gasped.

Dex looked at me quizzically and I forced a smile. He went back to talking to the hotel receptionist, who was speaking with a strong and lilting foreign accent.

My thoughts continued to spiral. Ethan had said he *loved* me. Even by simply admitting that, he had risked everything. He was supposed to be part of the medical staff. He was *supposed* to be counseling me, *not* loving me. Surely there was no method of therapy that would condone or encourage that. But something *was* off—I was sure of it. Ethan was keeping something big from me, and it made me doubt everything more than I already did.

Dex carried on his conversation with the receptionist while still holding my hand. Eventually he squeezed it, drawing my attention. "Oh, wow, that's great. Hey Sabine, Annika here has upgraded our room to a king suite."

Hooray.

The fair-haired woman bobbed her head. "*Kylla.*" She nodded again. "I mean, yes," she corrected.

Kylla? Where had I heard that before? What language was that?

"Babe, do you want to wait here? I've just got to get our stuff from the car," Dex said.

I nodded, still looking at the receptionist.

"Um, what language was that?" I blurted as soon as Dex had left.

She smiled politely. "I'm Finnish."

Finnish. Oh my god. The words. I'd completely forgotten Ethan's request. Now, what were the chances of coming across someone, at this very moment, who could help me?

I could just imagine Ethan smiling and saying something about everything happening for a reason.

And suddenly . . . I had to know.

Shit.

"I . . . I . . . Could you translate something for me?" My hands were now flat on the desk as I leaned toward her anxiously. What were they? I couldn't remember the stupid words!

Shit.

"Of course." She smiled. "What is it?"

Shit, shit, shit.

Think. Think, Sabine. What were they?

"Um . . . um . . . *Ukso*, no *uskon*! *Uskon* is the first word and there's one more. Argh, I can't remember, something like *sins*, or . . ." I fisted my hand.

The receptionist smiled. "*Uskon sinua?*" she suggested.

"Yes! That's it. What does it mean?" I was close to bursting. I saw Dex approaching the glass doors with our bags. I turned back to the woman urgently. "Please!"

She started to laugh at me. "It means, 'I believe you.'"

Dex had me by the hand. We were walking down a hallway. Stopping at a door. How did we get there?

Had I lost time?

I couldn't think of anything but *uskon sinua, uskon sinua, uskon sinua, uskon sinua.*

Ethan.

Believed.

Me.

Crazy, locked-up, self-harming, digoxin-swallowing, two lives *me.*

We were inside a room. Crisp white linen, flowers, fruit bowl. Views over the city lights.

Ethan believed me.

A glass of champagne was suddenly in my hand. I was sipping it and must have looked confused.

"I brought it with me," Dex said, standing right in front of me. "I wanted tonight to be perfect." He was holding a glass too, a sip's worth in the bottom.

How could tonight get any more perfect?

Ethan believed me.

"This is amazing, you should check out the bathroom. There's a hot tub," he said, coming back from his inspection of the room and sliding his arm around my waist.

My hand holding the champagne flute was shaking. What was going on? Why couldn't I get a grip?

I swallowed nervously and took a few deep breaths, trying to calm myself down.

Dex ran his hands down my back, settling them low. *Too*

low, a voice buried deep inside me screamed. I downed my glass of champagne and held still.

"I've been waiting so long to see you, Sabine. Please tell me I can take that dress off?"

Shit.

I struggled for some kind of sanity. I had to regain control of the life Ethan had just detonated with the three most explosive words ever. He'd done the one thing he'd always tried to convince me could happen. He'd made my worlds cross over. And now . . . I was here, he was there, and everything had changed.

Forever.

Dex, however, wasn't waiting for permission and had already begun to unzip my dress, moving me toward the massive bed. I was on my back before I knew it and his hands . . . were everywhere.

I had to clear my mind. Find words. I should have been thinking only of Dex, but I couldn't. It didn't matter what I thought I should do, something in my mind—no, in my heart—wasn't going to let me.

"Dex," I said nervously.

"Hmm," he replied, not stopping.

"Dex, I . . . I can't."

He just moaned.

Shit.

"Dex, stop," I said, lifting the volume.

He pulled his head up from my neck and looked at me, confused.

"What?"

"I'm sorry. I'm so sorry, but I . . . I just can't."

His eyes narrowed, but he recovered quickly. "Sabine, we've been planning this for ages. I've never put pressure on you, because I knew we would get here eventually, but . . ."

I spoke quickly. "I know, Dex. You're amazing and kind and good and I'm so lucky to have been your girlfriend, but you deserve more than I can give you. You deserve someone who will make you really happy—"

He cut me off, sitting up. "Oh, whoa! Wait! This isn't just about tonight, is it? You're breaking up with me?"

I scrambled to sit up against the headboard. "Dex . . . I'm so sorry," I whimpered.

He jumped off the bed, glaring at me. "You're seeing someone else, aren't you?" he yelled, jabbing his finger at me.

I didn't respond. I honestly didn't know what the right answer to that question was.

He scoffed, "Oh, you bitch! You've been stringing me along. Teasing me!"

I shook my head urgently. "No, it's not like that at all. I thought . . . I really wanted this to work with us. I swear. It's complicated."

Dex ran his hands through his hair desperately. "Fuck." And then, frenzied, he grabbed his bag and the bottle of champagne and stormed out of the room.

Once the trembling settled down I checked the time.

11:30 p.m.

I hoped Dex was okay. I considered going after him, but I figured he wouldn't want to see me for a while—if ever. But as awful as I felt, now that it was done I was sure it was the right decision. Dex *did* deserve to be with someone who could make him happy. And perhaps . . . perhaps I deserved to be with someone who was right for me too.

For the first time in my life, I couldn't wait to shift. And the irony was, it was Roxbury I wanted so desperately to get back to. I pulled myself together and decided on a course of action, picking up the hotel phone and calling the most unlikely of people.

"Hello?" Ryan was laughing and I could barely hear him over the noise in the background. His dorm was obviously having another party.

"Ryan, it's me."

I heard the groan. "What do you want?"

"I, um, I'm not far from you and I was wondering if you might be able to come and get me. I . . . I haven't had a great night."

Maybe brothers just know what that means, maybe they have this built-in radar that goes off when their sisters are stranded in hotel rooms, I don't know, but Ryan's tone changed instantly. "Where are you? Are you okay?"

"Yeah." I gave him the hotel details.

"Is Dex with you?"

"He was, but . . . he's gone now."

I let him draw his own conclusions as to what that meant. He was quick to respond. "I'm on my way."

"Thanks, but . . . can you give me a few minutes? Maybe come just after midnight, like quarter past or something." I wanted to give myself enough time to shift in private.

"Okay," he said cautiously. "What room?"

I looked at the door Dex had left open when he stormed out. The numbers were displayed in gold. "Room eight sixteen."

After we hung up I walked out to the balcony. I wanted a few quiet moments to finally consider my feelings for Ethan.

Who was I kidding? It took about three seconds for me to come to the obvious conclusion. I was totally in love with him. The simple fact that I knew he was kissing me, at this very moment, in my other world and that the knowledge did *not* freak me out was evidence enough. But on top of that, he knew me.

I opened my arms to the night sky and flung my head back to the world of possibilities—the world of what-ifs. To the knowledge that in a few minutes I would shift right into the arms of the guy I loved.

I don't know when I started twirling with giddiness. But I do know the moment I stopped . . .

And saw Dex standing in the open doorway, staring right at me.

I walked back into the room as he stumbled closer.

He was drunk.

"Dex . . . ," I started, wondering how to explain. But his look stopped me in my tracks.

I don't know if it was the alcohol or the fact he'd seen me smiling that did it. I don't know if he'd come back with this particular plan or a different one altogether. All I know is that as soon as he took that last stumbling step toward me, he lost it.

The first punch to my face sent me straight to my hands and knees.

I screamed. But I was quickly silenced by a sharp kick to my stomach that catapulted me onto my back like I was no more than a rag doll. He dropped on top of me, straddling me as he hit me again.

I was defenseless under his weight. I couldn't focus. Couldn't work out what to do. I looked into his eyes between hits. This was not the Dex I knew. He was drunk and completely out of control.

After the fourth heavy hit to my face, an unwavering certainty came over me: Dex was not going to stop. My feeble attempts to cry for help were smothered by his fists.

My head swung to the side with the impact of a closed-fist punch that made it feel like it might explode. Blood poured into my eyes from a cut on my forehead. I spotted the digital clock on the bedside table.

Oh, please, please, please.

11:59 p.m.

Dex's hand went back again, relentless in his intentions. I closed my eyes, waiting for the impact, and . . . shifted.

CHAPTER TWENTY-SIX

Roxbury, Tuesday

From nightmare to dream. I was in his arms, his lips on mine. But my nightmare was still with me and I flinched, gasping, as my body anticipated the final blow from Dex's fist.

Ethan scrambled to his feet as I fought to catch my breath. He looked at the clock and grimaced.

I tried to calm myself down. *I'm okay. I'm back. With Ethan.* I closed my eyes for a moment. I was safe.

But when I opened them, Ethan was backing up toward the door, the sadness in his eyes making my heart twist. His brow furrowed and he bit down on his beautiful lower lip before looking away. "I'll leave. I . . ." He hung his head. "I'll leave you alone."

My eyes filled with tears. He thought I'd flinched from him. Thought that it meant . . .

"Ethan," I breathed, barely able to find the oxygen. "Please don't go."

He looked at me again. He must have seen my changed expression because he took a few tentative steps toward me. "Sabine, you're shaking . . . more than usual. Are you . . . ? Is everything . . . ? Did . . . ? Jesus, Sabine, just tell me!"

I took a deep breath. It was an impossible situation. The world I'd thought had crumbled was now resuscitating me— just as the world in which I'd put all my hopes and dreams for a future was tearing me apart. But right then, looking into Ethan's eyes, there were more important things to say.

"I love you too. And not just because you believe me."

In two strides he was back, sitting on my narrow bed, pulling me to him as if our lives depended on it. When he leaned back, his eyes searching mine, I could see what still haunted him.

"Sabine . . . ?"

I cupped his face with my hand. "No, Ethan. I didn't sleep with Dex. I couldn't. How *could* I?" And then he was kissing me while somewhere else Dex was killing me. But right in that moment, heaven was mine.

Would this be how it worked?

Would I die in Wellesley, after all of this?

Suddenly, despite all my theories, all the tests, I wasn't so confident that if I did die in Wellesley, my life—the life I'd been so willing to throw away—would go on in Roxbury.

A strange thing.

Ethan's hand stroked my face. "I love you," he murmured.

Before I knew what I was doing I had taken Ethan's keys from his pocket and was at the door, locking it silently. When I turned back to him and saw him staring at me, intense love in his eyes, I was sure there was nothing I wanted more than to be with him. I walked toward him, taking off my top as I did. Right now, there was nothing to stop us.

"Sabine—" he started, but I shook my head, joining him on the bed, laying a light kiss at the base of his neck.

"Don't say no, Ethan."

"I'm not really at my best tonight," he said, sounding nervous and breathless at the same time.

"Don't say no," I repeated. "Not unless you really want to."

He squirmed even as his arms went back around me. "There are things I need to tell you. I have no right to do this, no right to have you. When I . . . you might not want to."

I kissed him again. "Then don't tell me. Not now. Tell me later. Right now, I love you and you love me, and I don't know how, but I *know* this is right. I want it to be you, Ethan. I want my first time to be with you."

He ran his hands through my hair and pulled me close.

"A first and a last then," he mumbled, turning his face toward mine and returning my kisses.

He was everything I'd wanted him to be and so much more. Loving, gentle, considerate. He made the tiny bed seem like a good thing, and he slowed down when needed, caressing me, talking sweetly to me, and guiding gently. He seemed to savor every moment as if he were imprinting it on his mind, taking his time to search out every curve and freckle on my body, tracing my face over and over with his fingertips. He even found the birthmark behind the back of my knee. And after he explored me, he watched, fascinated, as I used my lips and my good hand to explore him in return.

When I found the bruises on his lower belly and what looked like needle marks in his arm, I started to question him, but he stopped me with the kinds of kisses that blew my mind.

Eventually—when there was no part of either one of us that had gone untouched, no place he hadn't made me tingle and sear and want for a lifetime of the same—he wrapped me in his arms.

"I was sure I'd never have this," he said softly, stroking my hair.

"What?"

"Love."

I half-laughed. "Do not even try to tell me you haven't done that before."

He chuckled too. "Not like that. Not with the love part."

I looked up at him. He was still out of breath. "Are you okay? You look . . ."

He raised his eyebrows. "Exhausted?"

I smiled, rather happy with myself. "Well, at least no one will ever accuse us of not being thorough." I didn't expand on it, tell him that a big part of it had been from my own desperation—to hang on to this for as long as I could before going back to face what I must. I couldn't bear to ruin the moment yet.

Ethan decided to get serious anyway. "I meant what I said, Sabine. You need to choose life, not death. You can't strip away half of what you are and expect to be okay."

I sighed, still not ready for this conversation. "It's just so hard. I'm two completely different people. I hate it."

"I get why you've had to do that in the past, but you're eighteen now. You've finished school—"

"Twice," I cut him off.

He grinned. "Twice. I know that if you put your mind to it, you can find a way to be you—the *same* you—in both worlds. You won't be like everyone else, but who has the same life as anyone else anyway?" He went back to stroking my hair and I relished every touch. "If you weren't here, I wouldn't have ever found you. You never know what could be just around the corner in either one of your lives."

Unfortunately I had a terrible feeling I knew what was around the corner in my Wellesley life. But as I lay in Ethan's arms, everything in that world seemed to matter so much less. "I like where I am right now," I said, my hand tracing the contours of his arms. He looked down and I saw how dark the circles beneath his eyes were. "When was the last time you slept?"

He shrugged off the question, refocusing on me. "This choice has to be about you, Sabine. It's not fair to make it about me and I don't want you to. I want you to make it for you. You need to think about that before you make any final decisions. Will you promise me that?"

I wasn't entirely sure the decision belonged to me anymore. Even so, I nodded. "Promise."

"And promise me that you won't do anything rash. Today, for example."

I nodded again and he held me close, sighing with relief. I was on the verge of telling him about Dex, about everything that had happened in my other world, but when I looked up he was already asleep. He looked so tired. I brushed my fingers lightly down his face. There was a cool sweat on his neck and his breathing seemed oddly shallow.

I watched him for as long as I could—strangely determined to guard over him—until finally I couldn't keep my eyes open. Before I fell asleep I swore to myself that by the time I shifted tonight I'd know what Ethan was hiding from me.

When I woke up he wasn't there. I was disappointed, but I also wasn't surprised. We *were* in a hospital; it wouldn't exactly be acceptable for him to be found waking up in a patient's bed. The thought actually made me laugh out loud—or maybe it was just the afterglow from having been with Ethan. Either way I brushed aside the feeling of unease and resolved to get through my day until I could see him that night. Then I'd tell him about Dex and we'd work out what to do, together.

My parents chose that day to visit—which didn't go too badly. Mom had clearly had a lot of time to think about everything, and after our awkward greeting and obligatory small talk she said, "Your dad and I were thinking that, well, if it's okay with you, we would like to consider some family counseling."

I nodded, appreciating her efforts. But more counseling was the last thing I wanted.

"Dr. Levi told us you've been showing very promising signs. I can tell he's confident things will work out soon," Dad proudly informed me. Mom and Dad had clearly taken this one bit of good news and run with it. As far as they were concerned, recovery was imminent. I let them believe it, even though I had started to formulate my own opinion of Levi's use of the word "soon." I was glad my appointment with him that morning had been canceled because of some emergency.

My parents did most of the talking. Apparently Denise had asked them if she could visit me. I don't know why—maybe she felt bad about me landing in this place after her random stock check of the drugstore. The thought reminded me of the current drug stash I had hidden beneath my mattress.

I sighed. Was now the moment to make my choice? Hand back the pills I'd stolen? Was today the day? Here, with my parents? That was what Ethan wanted—for me to make this choice for myself. But looking at Mom's and Dad's faces, their eagerness for everything to be okay, for it to be the way it once was, I just couldn't do it to them.

I'd let them have today and ask Ethan to help me get rid of the pills later. Also . . . I couldn't deny there was a small part of me that still wasn't a hundred percent ready to hand them over.

I took a deep breath. "It's really good to see you, Mom. I'm sorry things have been so . . ."

She waved a hand in the air, dismissing my attempts at an apology. I found it frustrating.

"Do you think I could maybe talk to Maddie on the phone in a few days? I really miss her."

Mom and Dad looked at each other before Mom turned to me with a small nod. "That sounds like a good idea. She's been missing you."

For the rest of the visit we talked about general stuff. When we said good-bye, they told me they'd visit again in a couple of days and couldn't wait until I was home, before more awkward hugging. I told them Denise could drop by tomorrow if she wanted.

After they left, I found myself thinking better of them than I had in a while. I was going to shift into an all-bad situation tonight—when Dex was done with me I didn't know what would happen. I hoped I would have the opportunity to set things right with my Roxbury parents.

For the rest of the day, the minutes dragged and raced all at once, my desperation to see Ethan building until it was almost unbearable. I needed to tell him about Dex, about what was happening to me. I needed to prepare *myself* for what was happening. Even though there was nothing I could do, I needed Ethan with me, holding me, telling me not to be scared. Where was he?

Night fell and Ethan still hadn't come.

I sat in my chair, paced my room, and stuck my head into the hall when there was a crazy rush of phone calls and nurses running up and down the corridors. But no Ethan.

When Dr. Levi walked into my room at 10:00 p.m., I was bordering on hysterical. It took a moment to register who he was, since he was in regular clothes instead of his usual doctor's coat.

"Sabine." He took off his glasses and rubbed his eyes. "Sorry to disturb you, but I was in the hospital this evening and thought I'd pop my head in and apologize for missing our session today . . ."

I tried to keep my tone calm. "It's okay. I figure I can just chat with Ethan tonight anyway. Is he here yet?"

Levi seemed taken aback. "Oh. Sabine, I'm . . . I'm terribly sorry . . . Ethan . . ." He cleared his throat. "Ethan won't be in tonight. Ah, would you like me to arrange someone else to visit you?"

"No! Where's Ethan?" I snapped, pacing again. "Is there something going on?"

Levi rubbed his face again, like he'd just gotten out of bed. "He's . . . Sabine, I'm sorry, but I have to get going. I'll be in to see you in the morning."

I started panicking, shaking my head. "Wait, I can't . . . I need to speak to Ethan! Is he at work at all? Is he home? Where is he? Can I at least call him on the phone? Please. I promise he'd want to take my call."

He shook his head. "Not tonight, Sabine."

And he left me all alone, like he couldn't get out of there fast enough.

I was breathless.

Petrified.

The worst Shift of my entire life was ahead of me and I was alone. I hadn't anticipated, hadn't even *considered* that he wouldn't come back to me.

Because he wouldn't do that.

Where was he? Something had to be wrong.

Had they found out about us? Was he in trouble?

I contemplated using my key to get out, to search for him. But where would I go? I didn't even know where he lived.

And if I got caught and they found the key, I knew they'd blame him. I couldn't risk that.

I glanced around the room in a panic; my eyes fell on the battery-operated clock. The time!

Shit.

I sat on the bed as the minutes neared midnight.

I had chosen to live. Now I was going to die.

And the only person I wanted to be with had disappeared.

I closed my eyes and gritted my teeth. I did everything in those final minutes to find my anchor. But I knew without a doubt, it was Ethan.

Deep breaths. I can do this, I told myself. If I wasn't going to be the one making this decision, I was damned if I was going to let someone else make it for me.

No matter what happened, I *was* coming back. To my life here, my family, my friends, my future.

To Ethan.

CHAPTER TWENTY-SEVEN

Wellesley, Tuesday

I felt my body convulse first, then the searing pain in my cheekbone from the sheer force of Dex's strike. The rest of the scene quickly came into focus. Dex on top of me, his weight heavy and clumsy, the room, the white bed, the half-open door, the empty bottle of champagne a few feet away. It wouldn't be long before I lost consciousness. If I wanted to try to stop him, it had to be now.

"Dex, please! I'm . . . sorry I hurt you!"

He slapped me with the back of his hand. "Not me that's getting hurt here, babe."

He lifted his hand again. I used the last of my strength to push him back and set him off balance. His drunken state helped and he fell backward. I could barely see through my swollen eyes, but I tried to move, to get away from him.

It was useless.

My ribs screamed with pain and I could do little more

than roll onto my side and clutch my waist in agony. "Dex . . . please, this isn't you! You're . . . a good guy," I said pleadingly.

But he wasn't listening—he couldn't. He had jumped to his feet and now swayed over the top of me. He landed another kick to my gut so startling it left me limp and gave him the opportunity to roll me back over so he could straddle me again.

"You're mine! No one else gets to have you!" he yelled, leaning over me. I closed my eyes, each breath more difficult than the last as my consciousness began to waver. I waited for the next hit. I hoped it would be over soon.

But the impact never came. Instead his weight was yanked off me, and, after hearing a number of curses and thumping sounds that I knew had to be punches being thrown, I opened my eyes to see Ryan gripping Dex by his collar as he reared back to deliver a no-holds-barred fist to Dex's face before throwing him hard into the wall. Dex, with blood gushing from his nose, slid awkwardly to the ground.

Ryan took one look at me and had his phone against his ear. He crouched beside me. "Sabine? Can you hear me?"

I nodded, barely.

"Hi, yeah, I need an ambulance at the Liberty Hotel, room eight sixteen . . . Yeah, my sister, she's been badly beaten . . . I don't know . . . Just hurry up! And call the cops!" He dropped the phone and grabbed my hand, probably the only part of me that wasn't crying out in pain.

"Sabine? You have to stay awake, okay?"

All I wanted to do was close my eyes, but I tried. I'd made myself a promise.

"Where are you hurt?"

I struggled to speak. "Ribs, face."

He nodded, giving me permission to stop talking, and glanced at Dex, who was starting to roll onto all fours. Ryan didn't even hesitate, striding across the room and pulling him up by the collar. "You son of a bitch!" He punched Dex across the face. Dex was out instantly.

Ryan rushed back to my side. He was shaking. "I'm gonna kill him! Sabine, stay awake. Did . . . ? Oh Jesus, Sabine, did he . . . ?" He looked like he was about to pass out.

"No. He . . . was drunk. Angry 'cause . . . I ended it."

"Well, can I just say, that was a damn fine decision."

"Ry, don't . . . hurt him . . . please. Mistake."

He looked at me like I was crazy. I was getting used to people looking at me that way. "Sabine, this goes beyond a mistake. He could've killed you. Jesus, if I hadn't gotten here early . . ." He squeezed my hand.

It was frighteningly true. I swallowed, my body exploding with pain. "Thanks, Ry," I whispered.

As the sound of sirens neared, he kept his eyes on me, making sure I stayed awake. Medics ran into the room, followed by the police.

Ryan quickly handed me over to the paramedics and

dragged Dex over to the police. Dex was starting to come around, and I could just make out the police trying to stop Ryan from knocking him out again.

The medics gave me something, morphine probably, that made everything go blissfully numb. They ran through the tally of suspected injuries—broken ribs, internal bleeding, and the outside chance of spinal damage—then put me in a back-and-neck brace and loaded me onto a gurney and into an ambulance to take me to the hospital.

Once the police had carted Dex off, Ryan stayed right by my side, snapping at the medics intermittently for being too rough with me, even though they weren't. In the ambulance he called Mom and Dad, told them what had happened, and suddenly kicked into wise, mature big-brother mode—reassuring them that everything would be okay, trying to calm them down before they got into their cars and raced over to the hospital. Which of course they did right away anyway.

I couldn't help but think of Dex. What he'd done to me was messed up, but I suspected it had more to do with the alcohol than anything else. I wondered if he knew it could cause this type of severe reaction and that's why he never drank. I was sure Dad would find out—he was a lawyer after all. Dex had already been arrested but I was certain that before Dad even arrived at the hospital he would ensure that Dex was charged with every offense possible.

They wheeled me into the emergency room. For the next few hours the doctors looked me over and ran tests, confirming my broken ribs and a small fracture of my cheekbone that would heal on its own. Amazingly there was no internal bleeding. And when the doctor finally leaned over me and said with a smile, "You're black and blue, but you'll live," I was actually relieved.

My Wellesley parents did not share my parents in Roxbury's inclination to keep family matters private. I knew that by the time they arrived, half the town would know about what had happened.

Sure enough, soon after they walked in, the flowers started turning up. It was embarrassing. Mostly because I'd been found in a hotel room. It wasn't going to take anyone long to figure out a close-enough version of what had happened.

In spite of my anger and pain, I felt sorry for Dex.

"Oh, Sabine!" Mom shrieked when she saw me. She rushed to my side. Ryan, who had been with me the entire time, started to move away, but I grabbed his hand. Right now, I felt safest with him beside me. He seemed to understand and stayed where he was.

"She's okay, Mom," he said.

Mom put her hand on his head. "Thank the Lord you were there." She started to sob.

Dad came back in after speaking with the medical staff. "I'm sure your mom has covered the obvious, so I won't bore you with a rerun." He cleared his throat, his eyes full of tears. "The doctor says you're doing well."

I tried to smile. "I'm okay, Dad."

He nodded, looking away. "The boy, *man*—he is over eighteen—has been charged with assault among other things. He will most certainly serve prison time."

I grimaced. "Dad, I think . . . I think this had something to do with him drinking."

He nodded. "It certainly did. That bastard should've told you he was prone to severe psychotic reactions to alcohol. He wasn't even allowed to drink alcohol. There was an incident when he was younger—he and his friends got drunk and he beat a young boy to within an inch of his life. He was only released back into his parents' custody under strict guidelines that he have an alcohol test every week until he turned eighteen. This, combined with what he's done to you . . . the case against him is straightforward."

I tried to take it in, both the revelation about Dex's past and the fact that he'd kept it a secret the whole time we were together. But even knowing what he'd done, I still felt guilty.

"Dad, I . . . He isn't this person. He never drank. I . . . I hurt him . . ." As I said the words my stomach churned.

Had I driven Dex to this? My Roxbury father often turned to alcohol to deal with his daily disappointments. Was I the common link? And yet, even as I thought it, I knew deep down it was more. Dex had a problem.

"None of this is your fault, Sabine," Mom said, standing up. "I won't let you blame yourself."

"I'm not. What he did was terrible. And looking back now, I should've known. I just . . . I think he needs help instead of punishment."

Lucas was standing in the doorway. "Sounds like you grew up overnight," he said, approaching the bed, putting a hand on my blanketed foot. "Glad you're okay."

"Me too."

He gave me a nod, something that looked like respect, then lifted his chin in Ryan's direction.

"You did good, man." He gestured to Ryan's badly bruised knuckles. "You should get some ice on those."

Ryan swallowed and quickly cleared his throat. "Yeah, thanks. I'll take care of it in a bit."

Maybe I wasn't the only one building sibling relations today.

Dad studied the window and then the collection of flowers. I knew he couldn't cope with seeing me all beaten up. "Sabine, right now all you need to do is concentrate on getting better. Let the police deal with Dex. The main thing is, he'll never hurt you again. And if, when it comes to it, you want to have your say, no one will stand in your way."

I nodded. It was all I could do for now.

"I feel so stupid for not seeing this coming." But even as I said it, I knew that in some ways the signs had been there.

"Creeps like that are sly, Sabine," Ryan said. "They treat you like a princess as long as you're exactly what they want you to be, but when things go wrong, or if they think they're going to lose you, everything can change in a heartbeat."

A nurse popped her head around the door. "I'm sorry everyone, but the doctor says she needs to rest."

Mom and Dad kissed me gently on the forehead and headed for the door, with Lucas following.

"Ryan?" Mom called softly.

"Tell them to get lost. I'm not leaving her until she asks me to."

Mom straightened. "Well, I'll do that then."

I smiled, holding my big brother's hand, knowing we'd never go back to the way we were. Even as I dropped in and out of sleep and day morphed into night and the night lengthened, Ryan didn't leave my side and I didn't ask him to.

Finally he said, "This might sound really weird, Sabine, but you look as if you're happy."

I looked at the clock; it was almost midnight and I had some truly amazing things to say to Ethan when I saw him again—things I knew he would be so pleased to hear.

"And this might sound really weird to you, but I am." I shrugged. "I'm alive."

I shifted.

CHAPTER TWENTY-EIGHT

Roxbury, Wednesday

I'd known Ethan wouldn't be there when I shifted back, but I still felt an intense yearning for him. I settled into bed, listening as nurses moved up and down the corridor, and eventually fell asleep from sheer exhaustion.

I woke up mid-morning to a knock on my door. A moment later Macie came into the room. She looked like she'd been crying, and I wondered if she and Mitch had had a fight. "You have a visitor," she said, without her usual bite.

"Who?" I asked, sitting up, suddenly hoping it was Ethan.

"Denise. She said she's a friend of the family and you're expecting her."

My shoulders dropped. "Oh, yeah."

"She's in the patient lounge. I can tell her to come in here if you prefer," she said, staring at the ground.

"No, it's fine. I'll go there."

Macie nodded and left me to get changed.

I quickly dressed in a mini and T-shirt, and made a mental note to go shopping for some new clothes once I got out of here. I knew it would take a while to convince everyone that I'd suddenly recovered, but that's what I was going to do. Ethan knew the truth and that was all I needed. As for everyone else in my life . . . it was probably easiest for them to *not* have to go there. It would take time—and no doubt a lot of talking with Dr. Levi—to convince people that whatever delusions I'd been suffering from had passed. I wasn't sure if I'd be able to make it fly that I suddenly couldn't speak French again. As much as I hated it, I've considered it might be easiest to just let them all believe I had learned it in secret, like Dr. Levi had suggested. Either way, Ethan would help me work it all out.

And I planned to help him too.

Whatever it was he felt he couldn't tell me, he'd now be able to. I'd made my decision—the way he'd told me I needed to—and now there was no reason for him to keep his secret from me.

Denise was sitting on one of the half-sunken sofas. When I came in she stood up, then clutched me in a warm embrace.

"How are you?"

"Actually, I'm good," I confessed. "I didn't agree with Mom and Dad sending me here at first, but I think in the end, coming here was exactly what I needed." It *had* brought me to Ethan after all.

She nodded, encouraged. "That's great, honey. I felt terrible about having to tell your parents about the stock." She looked down and I grabbed her hands in mine.

"Denise, don't apologize for caring. It was a stupid thing to do and I should never have done it."

At this she breathed a sigh of relief. "So, tell me about the place?"

I settled into my own uncomfortable seat beside her and smiled. "Well, it's like being in prison, and a few of the nurses hate me."

"Let me guess, you weren't exactly cooperative to start?"

I laughed. "Kind of. But Levi is okay—"

She cut me off. "Levi?"

I rolled my eyes. "*Dr.* Levi. He does most of my sessions."

She nodded. "Dr. Levi is a very well-respected psychiatrist. I passed him on the way in—he's had a tough couple of days."

I was smiling now, wanting to move onto a better subject. "And then Ethan has been helping out in the evenings."

Her eyes dropped nervously.

"Denise, are you okay?"

"Yes, honey. I just . . . Have you spent a lot of time with Ethan?" she asked.

I swallowed, not wanting to get him into trouble. "Yeah. He, um . . . He's been a big help. I guess he's the reason I realized I needed to get better."

"Sabine, did Ethan tell you much about himself? I mean, did he tell you . . . ?" She seemed to be at a loss.

I looked at her blankly. "What? Did he tell me what?"

"He . . . I . . . Oh, Sabine. Maybe we should get Dr. Levi to explain this. Hang on." She stood up and quickly walked out of the room.

I sat there waiting, wondering what all the fuss was about. Did they know about Ethan and me? We'd never been caught sneaking out, never given anything away, no one had ever seen us together. I knew Ethan wouldn't have told anyone, as much for my protection as anything else.

When Levi came in with Denise, I noticed he was still in regular clothes and looked uncharacteristically disheveled and unshaved.

"Sabine, hello. How are you today?" Dr. Levi asked, sitting on the low coffee table opposite me.

"Fine. Good, actually. What's going on?" I asked quickly, looking from one to the other.

"I . . . I'm afraid we . . ."

Was he tearing up?

"Sabine, I know you grew close to Ethan in your first few days here, and I imagine you've been wondering why he hasn't been able to visit you over the past week, but—"

I cut him off, shaking my head. "What do you mean past week? I know he wasn't here yesterday, but I saw him Monday night and . . . ," I trailed off.

Levi gave me an odd look. "How often did you see Ethan, exactly?"

"I . . . I've seen him every night, except for the weekend. Why?" I had a horrible feeling and the look on Dr. Levi's face did nothing to alleviate my fears.

He dropped his head, leaning over his knees. "He obviously cared for you greatly."

"What are you . . . ? What do you mean *cared* for me?" I looked around urgently. "Where is he? Why wasn't he at work last night? Did someone fire him?"

Oh my God, if they'd fired him—how would I ever see him?

Levi sighed. "Of course no one fired him. Sabine, did Ethan ever mention to you that he lived here, at the hospital?"

I shook my head. "No. Why would he live here?"

"He stayed on one of the other floors so he could be monitored. Ethan was sick."

"What are you . . . ? He told me he gets headaches. Is that why?"

"It wasn't headaches, Sabine. Ethan was very unwell. To be honest, I thought he would've told you. He had Hodgkin's lymphoma, stage four. He tried everything: radiation, chemo. But when the bone marrow transplant failed, treatment became . . . impossible. He insisted that he keep working and we . . . *I* let him, thinking it would be good for him. In return he agreed to stay upstairs instead of at his apartment by himself so we could at least monitor him and try to make things more comfortable. Last week he . . . he took a turn and was ordered to rest. He was also told to stop all work-related activities. To be honest, he seemed so determined to keep fighting it that . . . I thought he still had more time, but it wasn't to be. No one knew he was sneaking down here to see you."

I wanted to argue, explain that he was *supposed* to be there, that he was working. But I couldn't think of one person who'd seen us together apart from in those first few days.

This was his secret.

I could see my hands shaking, but I couldn't feel them. I couldn't feel anything. I had to get to him.

"Where is he? I have to see him!" I choked on the words. Denise dropped to her knees beside me, clutching my hands.

"I'm sorry, Sabine. The cancer had spread into his bones and lungs. Ethan passed away on Monday. The doctors said it was remarkably peaceful, no sign of any pain. They said his body held on for longer than anyone had expected, longer than anyone believed possible, but in the end it just shut down." I watched the tears streaming down Levi's face. Denise was crying too.

I couldn't breathe.

All his words played back. All the things I'd been too blind to see. Too selfish.

Not me.

I like the idea that there's more to life. You know, we go on.

There are things I want to tell you, things you need to know.

I was sure I'd never have this.

Please, forgive me, but . . . I love you.

Not me.

I didn't realize I was the one making the awful wailing noise, thrashing about. I felt so removed from everything—as if I were watching it all unfold from some distant hell as my heart broke into pieces that would never be mended. But it *was* me and the needles came and went. Eventually the screaming stopped and my eyes were forced to close, two words repeating over and over in my tortured mind.

Not him.

Not him.

Not him.

CHAPTER TWENTY-NINE

After Ethan

I was in my hospital bed, suddenly awake, holding Ryan's hand. He was staring at me questioningly.

"Sabine? You okay? Your face . . . You looked so happy and now . . ." He glanced over his shoulder. "Are you okay? Did you see something?"

It came to me instantly—no blissful moments of reprieve that everyone always talks about, no split-second where he was still alive until I remembered. But the feelings came more slowly, taking what seemed like an excruciatingly long time to envelop my confused mind. Somehow I knew they'd always be with me, always be strangling me from the inside out.

"Sabine?" Ryan said again.

Everything meant nothing.

I let go of Ryan's hand. "I'm going to get some sleep, Ryan. It might be best if you go."

I didn't wait for his response, just rolled over, wishing that the drugs they were pumping into me could help with the most horrible pain imaginable.

In the morning people came and went, but I was numb. Mom and Dad visited. I didn't move from my curled-up position all day, and into the night. The doctors assumed it was a reaction to what Dex had done. I let them.

None of it mattered. Ethan was gone.

I drifted in and out of sleep. Eventually I must have shifted, because the next time I woke up, I was groggy and coming to, back in my room at the Roxbury Clinic.

Mom was sitting in the armchair. It must have been late in the day.

Tears were streaming down my face before I'd even opened my eyes. I wondered if I'd cried all through the sedation.

"Sabine? Denise called me. She . . . she told me about the young man who worked here and passed away. She said he'd helped you and that you'd become close. We used to see Ethan at the store; he was always very nice. I'm sorry, Sabine."

I was an empty shell. On some level I wanted to be angry with Mom, to blame her and Dad for doing this to me. I wanted to lash out and tell everyone that he didn't just help me. That he loved me, and I loved him. But it was useless. The thing I wanted most, I would never have.

Finally Mom left me, patting my hand like I was some lame animal, telling me she'd be back soon. Once I was sure I was alone, I pushed the armchair up against my door and dug underneath my mattress, pulling out the bag of supplies I'd taken from the drugstore. I emptied the contents onto my bed.

I was determined to get back at him. Just when I thought he hadn't been playing tricks on me, he'd proved me wrong. There I'd been in his arms, committing to a life I'd thought would be with him, and all the while he'd been saying good-bye to his own life.

Shit.

"Damn you, Ethan. How could you leave me? How could you make me want to stay and then . . . just leave me behind!"

My hands shook as I picked up the first box of pills and popped the contents onto the bed. It would be so easy to take them and then start screaming again. The doctors would come back in and put me under. With any luck I'd never wake up again. I wouldn't have to go through any more pain, wouldn't have to live in this world another moment without him, remember how much I wanted him.

I cupped the pills in my hand, letting them fall through my fingers before doing it again. Wherever he'd gone, maybe I could go with him?

But the minutes passed and still I couldn't take the pills. I kept thinking of Maddie. If I did this, I'd be leaving her just like he'd left me.

"What have you done to me?" I cried.

Because as much as I didn't want to, I could hear all the things Ethan had tried to tell me so clearly. The way he'd said that he only existed because I'd been there to see it. He'd been telling me then. I just wasn't listening. Telling me that my memories of him would make him go on. Was I his only witness?

Ethan had wanted to live. He'd done everything he could to try to stay here, and when that failed, he'd given all of his hope, all of his life, to me.

I hated him so much.

I loved him more.

I understood now, why he'd liked the idea of my two lives, the idea that we went on. I got it. He'd wanted more, and to him . . . I had it. I shook my head at myself, more tears beginning to stream. No wonder I'd frustrated him so much. I didn't know how he'd put up with me—and even more, fallen in love with me. I could almost picture him standing there, looking at the pills in my hand and telling me I was being a damn fool—and worse, making him an accessory.

Ethan had believed I could never know what future one life might offer at any time. He'd made me promise to think about this choice I was making—to consider not only what it would be like to have one life, but what I'd be missing out on if I left my Roxbury world behind. I picked up the pills and shoved them back in the box, half-cursing him, half-missing him more than ever. He was right.

"Ethan," I sobbed. "God, I want you back."

Leaving this world, this grief, would be easy—but it would stay with me in my other life and what would I have in its place? Would I eventually come to believe *this* life was a fabrication? That Ethan had never been real? I wouldn't be able to trust the truth of my memories, and I needed to be able to do that, always. To remember Ethan: his messy heap of hair, his kind, searching eyes, the garden where we'd lain together, the walks we took, the kisses we shared. If I left this world, who would remember everything that was amazing about him, and us?

I wrapped my arms around my waist, rocking in my ocean of sorrow. I had to hold a pillow to my face to stifle my sobs. Every breath made it worse.

I had thought death was the answer. I had believed it would be the thing that would give me the world I wanted and needed.

The worst of it was . . .

I was right.

It just wasn't *my* death.

Ethan loved that line in the John Lennon song that said that life is what happens when you're busy making other plans. It was true. I'd been so obsessed with fixing what was broken, I didn't see all the other things that were going on around me—his illness most of all. I'd known something wasn't right, but I'd been so caught up in the immediacy of my world, I'd made it too easy for him to keep his secret. I'd thought I was going through something terrible and was angry at him for leaving me alone. All the while it had been him facing his end, alone.

Dex was another failing. If I'd had my eyes open, I would've noticed that my pulling away was triggering his possessive tendencies or even questioned him more about why he never touched alcohol. And maybe I would've been honest about my feelings earlier and distanced myself from him. Maybe that night would never have happened . . .

I wrapped up all the pills and shoved them back under my mattress. Then I stood up only to collapse to the floor a minute later and burst into another bout of gut-wrenching tears.

Eventually I would have to stop, but not now. Eventually I would go on—for me, for him, for the brief memory of us that meant so much—but behind closed doors there would be a part of me that would cry for him forever.

The days passed. I tried my best to function, but not a second went by that I didn't think of him, yearn for just one last touch. Often I would be doing something, thinking I was okay, and then out of nowhere I'd just stop being able to breathe and break down.

For the first time in my life, the terror of night wasn't about the Shift. It was all about missing him.

I went to my sessions with Dr. Levi. He was as professional as always, but he'd changed—aged maybe. Macie seemed to like me a little more for some reason too, or maybe she was just being nice to me as some kind of homage to Ethan.

I did everything requested of me. Everyone still struggled to understand how I'd suddenly been able to speak in another language. But in the end, like some things must, it went into the can't-explain basket.

I saw them all looking at me strangely at times, wondering why I'd had such a horrific reaction to Ethan's death. They didn't know. I didn't tell.

My memories were for me to carry and hold in my heart.

"Are you still traveling between your two lives, Sabine?" Dr. Levi asked one morning while he waited for me to take my shot.

I threw the dart. I was focused. Bull's-eye.

"You *have* met my parents, haven't you? Sometimes I suppose it was just easier to pretend I belonged somewhere else."

"So you were able to influence your other world? Make things the way you wanted them?"

I refrained from rolling my eyes and shrugged noncommittally. "In the end, things just went too far. I see that now." I passed him the darts.

He eyed me suspiciously. "That's quite a change in viewpoint," he said, turning his attention to the dartboard, lining up his first shot.

I nodded. "I guess. The thing is, everything just got out of control. Once I started saying these things, it was hard to go back. One thing just led to another and I got all muddled up in it."

He took his shot. Outer rim. He glanced at me sheepishly while I grinned at his poor aim. "But now you're not? Muddled, that is."

"I don't think this is an overnight thing," I said, playing the game. "It's going to take some time to repair the damage I've done and gain back my family's trust. But I'm ready to try."

"Did Ethan's passing have anything to do with your change of heart?" His pretense of a casual approach faltered as he stopped what he was doing and turned to me.

I wanted to cry just hearing his name. Fold over and scream. But I stood tall and ignored the ache. "I think it might've. Life's too short. If Ethan taught me anything, that would be it. I want to get on with living mine."

"Just the one?"

"I'm just me, Dr. Levi. What you see here is what I am."

He seemed satisfied and took another poor shot. I suspected he was losing on purpose. "That's good to hear, Sabine."

"Good enough to get me out of here?" It was worth a try.

"Not just yet. But soon, Sabine. Soon."

I nodded, knowing what that meant. At the end of the session I pulled out a small bag from where I'd tucked it into the waistband of my miniskirt, and held it out to him.

He took it. "What's this?"

"A bad decision."

He looked in the bag and saw the pills. "Where did you . . . ?" He looked nervously from the pills to me.

"Can you give them to Mom and Dad? They'll be able to check their stock. Every last pill is there."

"How did you . . . ?"

I considered giving him the window key too, but I wasn't an idiot. Levi had been using that "not yet, but soon," line on me ever since I'd started cooperating, and I knew it was his way of stalling. A girl needs a backup plan.

I shrugged. "Do we really need to get into the technicalities? The point is, I don't want them anymore." Which was true.

"Why not just throw them out?"

"Clean slate," I reasoned.

He pursed his lips, confused. I knew the look. It almost made me smile. Yeah, I was a mystery. And as long as he continued to believe that, he wouldn't figure out I'd simply played the best hand I could with the cards I was holding. It was only a matter of time before inventory reared its ugly head again, and if I hadn't taken the proactive step to remedy it, then things would've blown up in my face for sure. At least this way, I'd controlled it and maybe even earned myself a little extra trust that I was hoping he might extend.

In Wellesley I grieved too, unable to pretend I wasn't completely broken. No one questioned me. After what Dex had done, they figured it was because of him. But Dex wasn't even a blip on the pain radar.

The police came to see me, a male and a female officer. I told them the truth—everything I could. It wasn't for me to decide whether what Dex did was excusable or not, so I told them how I'd planned the night, how I'd made him wait and promised him that we would be together. I told them how he'd always respected me previously, but that he'd also become increasingly possessive. I confessed that up until the moment I said no I hadn't actually realized I was going to break up with him—but that once I did, he grabbed the champagne and disappeared. Until he came back. I told them I thought he would've killed me.

They took notes, nodding as I spoke.

I expected them to say I got what I deserved. I half-wondered it myself. But when they stood up, it was the man who put out his hand to shake mine. "Thank you for your honesty. I'm sorry for what happened. No matter what led up to it, there is never, ever any excuse to justify what he did to you."

I shook his hand. "Thank you, Officer."

I wish I could say it made me feel better. At least it hadn't made me feel worse. I wasn't sure what would happen to Dex. But I'd done as much as I was willing to do. A better person may have done more, or less. I don't know.

Ethan's funeral came and went. Everyone at the hospital who'd known him was invited, but with no living family, the service felt incomplete. My heart ached for him. Capri came with me and we sat in the back. She didn't push for information, she was just there, withstanding my bruising grip on her hand. I had planned to be stoic.

I cried the whole time.

That night after midnight, I used my window key and walked all the way to the Public Garden. I sat under our willow tree until the sun began to rise. The funny thing about life is, even when you make the decision to live it, to be in it, that doesn't necessarily mean it will let you. But the days went by and I kept turning up. It was hard.

Having a goal helped and getting out of the hospital was mine. I needed to get my life back in this world. I didn't know exactly what that would mean or where it would take me, but I was determined to find out.

A few days after the funeral, Levi came to my room, looking confused.

"Do you mind if I come in?" he asked.

I put away my notebook—it had now become a journal in which I was attempting to document every moment, every conversation, every outing I'd shared with Ethan.

Levi sat in the chair and looked at me as I sat cross-legged on the bed. "Sabine . . . um, you might not have realized this, but Ethan had been quite thorough in his preparations. He'd regularly updated his will, and since his parents are no longer with us, he'd asked me to look after the proceedings. The will was read today."

"Oh." Had he left something for me? I didn't know if I could bear it, but at the same time I would've done anything for a photo. I didn't have a single photo.

"Sabine, it seems Ethan left some instructions for me, in regard to you."

He pulled an envelope out of his pocket and a folded piece of paper. He handed me the sealed envelope. "Sabine" was simply written on the front.

He opened the piece of paper. "Ethan left us both a note. Mine . . . Well, at the end of it, he said . . ." He cleared his throat. "'Please give my other letter to Sabine. I know that you have all formulated your opinions about her, but for what it's worth, it is my professional opinion that she is of sound mind and not in any way a threat to herself or any other person. Take your time, Levi. Be sure, as I know you will be, before you let her out. But I know your instincts will tell you the same thing, and I implore you to trust in them as you always taught me to do. Furthermore, I hereby bequeath, after the donations earlier stipulated, all of my holdings, my apartment, and most importantly my car, to Sabine in full.'"

He looked at me again as I stared back at him, hot tears rolling down my cheeks. He shook his head and cleared his throat once more. "I don't know what went on between you two. I'm sure I probably don't want to know either, but he also wrote one last thing." He smiled. "'P.S. Buy her a pair of jeans.'"

It was the P.S. that made me lose it. Him too.

Dr. Levi and I bawled like babies.

That night, I read Ethan's letter.

My Sabine,

I just left your room. You were so beautiful lying there sound asleep that I couldn't bear to wake you. But I'm not feeling so great and there are things I promised to tell you that I fear I may not get the chance to.

I know you had once hoped that I would be the one to pass on your letters to Maddie once you were gone. But, as it turns out, I think it is going to be me who ends up leaving the letters behind.

Be mad at me. You should. But after that, try to understand that I did what I thought was best. I wanted to tell you. So many times I snuck down to your room planning on telling you everything, but I just couldn't.

Partly it was for you—yes. You needed time and I didn't want to influence your choices, even once I realized what was happening between us, even more so then. Falling in love with you only made those choices more complicated and I feared that you might choose to stay for me and then, after I was gone, change your mind. I couldn't let that happen.

Partly the choice was selfish, and for that I am sorry. For so long now people have been trying to fix me, but where they failed, you succeeded. You've given me more life in the last couple of weeks than I've had in years. Being with you, loving you, making memories with you, fearing for you, wanting to show you the beauty of life instead of the terror—it was bittersweet, but more importantly, Sabine, it was real.

I know this is the part when I beg you to go on, live your life and be happy. But I don't need to say those things. I know you. Your lives will be extraordinary. You certainly made mine feel that way.

Please find it in your heart to forgive me one day. I wish we'd had more time, but I want to thank you—for giving me life in my time of death.

My love for you is eternal.
Ethan

P.S. I've left you my car, because I know you love the
freedom—and my apartment, because you need something
to come back to. We joked once that I was a figment of your
imagination—you'll see my whole life in that apartment, if
you want to, so you can always be sure I was there. I hope
it might be a place you can call home—a place where you
can be yourself.
    E.

CHAPTER THIRTY

Two and a half weeks after Dex's attack in Wellesley, I was starting to look more like myself again. Most of the bruising on my face had faded and, apart from still having to move about slowly because of my ribs, I was functioning. Physically anyway.

Miriam and Lucy had visited me often during the five days I spent in a hospital. They tried to ask me about what happened a few times, but I just told them I needed to move on. They seemed to accept that, but I also saw the change. The way they looked at me differently. And when I told Miriam I wouldn't be able to go away with her to Cape Cod, the small sigh of relief. I understood. What had happened had changed things for all of us, and it would take them time to accept that our bubble of perfection had burst.

On my second Saturday home from the hospital, Ryan called to let Mom and me know that he was on his way.

Mostly he was checking if it was still all right for him to bring his friend. I knew he was asking for my benefit, so I told him it was no problem. When I got off the phone, Mom was staring at me.

"What?" I asked.

She looked me up and down. "I just, I've never seen you in . . . *jeans*."

I looked down at my outfit of fitted dark-blue jeans and a white tank top. It was definitely not what she was used to. I shrugged. "I'm just trying out something new." The truth was, I was just trying, period.

"You look completely different," Mom went on.

"I'm still me. Just me, Mom."

With that she hugged me and headed off to play squash with Aunt Lyndal.

I hung out in my room, looking at my college material, trying to decide what I wanted to do—if Harvard was really where I wanted to go. I didn't know.

When I heard the familiar sound of Ryan's car horn, I dragged myself off my bed and went out to the balcony. He was opening up the trunk and waved at me. I waved back before heading down to greet him.

Ryan would never be my shitty brother again. In fact, we were becoming pretty close. And while Lucas and I didn't exactly talk on the phone every other night, things were better there too.

Walking downstairs, I saw a guy standing in the front doorway, his back to me. Ryan's friend, obviously.

"Hey," I said.

He spun around. I lost my footing and slid down the last few steps, landing ungracefully on my butt and bumping my ribs in the process.

"Hey, are you okay?" He raced over to me, crouching close.

I closed my eyes, my heart racing. Too frightened to look. That voice.

How? It couldn't be. It must be my mind playing tricks on me. I was seeing ghosts.

"Did you hurt yourself?" he asked, that voice again, so familiar and yet so foreign at the same time.

I felt the sting of tears behind my eyes and clenched my jaw, not sure if my emotion was dominated by fear or hope.

Slowly I opened my eyes and lifted my head.

Dark hair. Full, unmistakable lips. Deepwater-blue, beautiful eyes.

"Ethan?" I whispered.

He smiled, looking relieved. "Yeah, I'm your brother's friend." But then his smile faltered. He looked more closely at me, his eyes blinking. "I know you." His voice had dropped to a whisper.

He held out his hand and mine flew to his, fitting just as I remembered. Just as I'd dreamed every night and thought

I would never feel again. He helped me up, his hold firm, warm, alive.

I staggered, trying to make my legs work.

Ethan.

I couldn't stop the tear that slid down my cheek. "It's you," I whispered.

"Are you sure you're okay?" he asked, his other hand on my shoulder, supporting me. I could feel exactly where the pad of each finger pressed.

"No." I was trembling all over, but also amazed. "But maybe one day," I said, soaking up his touch and gazing into his gentle eyes. He was different. His hair was short and neat. He looked bigger, stronger. That made me smile. Healthier.

We stared into each other's eyes as if drawn together by some invisible magnet that was beyond our control. He half-laughed, baffled. "Why do I feel like I want to laugh, or cry, or hug you? Something," he said, brow furrowed. "Who are you?"

I smiled, remembering a conversation I'd once had with my Ethan. "That's a complicated question." I squeezed his hand. "But I will tell you. If you truly want to know. Another time."

"Why am I so sure I know you?" he asked, dazed.

Over the lump in my throat, I said the words that Ethan had once said to me. The words I now realized were the ones that made me fall in love with him. "Because some things are so real you can feel them to your core. It doesn't matter where you go, they go with you. Anywhere."

He chuckled, squeezing my hand back. "I have no idea what that means."

"You will."

He was still staring at me when Ryan came stumbling through the door with a couple of bags.

"Thanks, buddy, great help," he said, looking at Ethan. "I see you two have met." Then he noticed just how close we were standing and his expression changed to suspicion. "Ethan, back off. And Sabine, be nice. Ethan here just got out of the hospital himself last week."

My eyes went wide. "Why? Are you sick?" Oh God, please not again.

His gentle smile returned. "No, I just fainted. A bit of a medical mystery, really. They ran a bunch of tests and I'm fine. They figure I must have eaten something bad or caught an odd bug." He watched me, looking fascinated by my concern and then pleased with my relief.

"Come on, Ethan. I'll show you to the pool house." Ryan started walking toward the back doors. When he turned back and saw Ethan still staring at me, he let out an exasperated sigh. "Dude, you're macking on my sister." I thought Ryan might go into his newfound protective big-brother mode, so I looked at him pointedly and smiled.

Smiles had been so rare lately.

Ryan slumped against the wall, still holding the bags. "Down boy! She'll be here all weekend." He rolled his eyes.

Ethan smiled at me and followed Ryan to the pool house, looking back every few steps as if to check that I was real. I understood completely. I couldn't take my eyes off him.

It turns out *my* Ethan had been absolutely right. You never know what's just around the corner. Of course, Dr. Levi would have another explanation altogether. Not that I cared.

I walked out the front of the house and tilted my head to the clear blue sky, a small breeze finding its way to me. "I'm ready, Ethan. You were right. I *was* lost. But you found me, between the lives."

I didn't know if this Wellesley version was like my Ethan. Nothing would ever take away the memory of Roxbury's Ethan. I'd always love him and I had every other day to walk in my Roxbury life and honor that. I didn't know if this Ethan would love me like I'd once been loved, or if I could one day love him too. But I knew, unequivocally, I would do whatever it took to find out.

ACKNOWLEDGMENTS

It has been a privilege to work with the people who have helped bring *One Past Midnight* to readers. It takes a small army to produce the final product and I have been so lucky to work with such an enthusiastic, passionate, and talented team.

As always, I must start with my agent, Selwa Anthony, whose friendship, guidance, and upport are invaluable.

Thanks goes out to the entire team at Bloomsbury Children's Books, with special thanks to my editor, Emily Easton, for first selecting *One Past Midnight* to be represented on the Bloomsbury list, and whom I am thrilled to be working with. Sincere gratitude also goes to assistant editor Jenna Pocius, as well as Laura Whitaker, Ilana Worrell, Melissa Kavonic, Donna Mark, Bridget Hartzler, and Lizzie Mason.

Thank you to the team at HarperCollins Australia, where the journey of this story began. Many thanks to publisher Tegan Morrison, CEO James Kellow, Christina Cappelluto,

Matt Stanton, and Tim Miller. I'd also like to give a shout-out to Elizabeth O'Donnell, Amy Fox, Janelle Garside, and Gemma Fahy.

To my family, who endured early drafts and dared to be honest, I love you all, and your honesty! To my husband, Matt, who goes beyond constantly, I do not deserve you but I'm never giving you back! And to our girls, Sienna and Winter, whose hearts grow bigger and minds grow stronger every day.

Finally, to all the readers and bloggers out there who have supported my books: your enthusiasm and support are continually humbling. This story means so much to me, and I'm delighted to have this opportunity to share it with you.

CARMEL CLAY PUBLIC LIBRARY

3 1690 02150 1722

JESSICA SHIRVINGTON is the author of the Embrace
series. She lives in Sydney, Australia, with her husband, FOXTEL
presenter and former Olympic sprinter Matt Shirvington, and
their two daughters.

www.jessicashirvington.com